THE
AWAKENING

SECOND EDITION

THE EVARAN CHRONICLES
BOOK 1

ADAIR HART

Editing done by Laura Petrella
Cover done by Tom Edwards
Interior design done by Colleen Sheehan
Proofread done by Alexa
Published by Quantum Edge Publishing

www.AdairHart.com

To get updates on new books and other notifications, sign up for my mailing list at:

www.AdairHart.com/MailingList.aspx

THE
AWAKENING

PROLOGUE

Jerzan Graduul knew that as the leader of the Bloodbore mercenary group, when a large derelict alien ship appears out of nowhere, you loot it clean, take slaves, and kill those who get in the way. He had been napping in his living quarters when his command crew contacted him. After six months hiding away on a cramped ship, he was ready for a change of scenery.

Resources were low, and the crew's morale showed it. He had no doubt they would come across something, and one thing the Bloodbores were known for was getting what they wanted by any means necessary.

His crew was mostly Dalrun, like he was, and stood on average about six feet tall, with pale skin and humanoid bodies. There was no doubt in his mind that his crew could handle anything, and he had been hoping to come across a pleasure cruiser. Those were always the easiest to raid and much more enjoyable than a cargo transport.

After slapping on his formfitting under armor, he went to the command center. When he arrived, he took a quick look at the various screens that covered the circular room. A captain's chair stood in the back of the room, with six high-tech workstations arranged in front of it in a half arc, lining up against the curve of the wall. The lighting was bright, but that was typical of any Dalrun merc ship.

He saw his fellow Dalruns Galkett Karus, Jahl Kinobkin, and Hulldar Ricast working at their stations. Hosk was the lone Greer on the crew, and his humanoid assault robot, G-85, stood off to the side. The Greer were four-foot reptilian humanoids, and Hosk was typical of their species.

Galkett was a recent member, and Jerzan had his doubts, but up to this point, Galkett had been solid. Hulldar was wild and unpredictable, and his face was normally used when the viciousness of the Bloodbores was discussed. Even now he was just wearing boots and underwear. Jahl, Jerzan's second in command, was reliable and had been with Jerzan for as long as he could remember. Hosk always looked like he was ready for battle, and with his piloting skills, Jerzan knew the ship was in good hands.

"So we gonna check that alien ship out?" asked Hulldar, looking around.

"What do you think, shit for brains?" asked Jahl.

Hosk and Galkett laughed.

Hulldar smiled. "Fuck you."

"All right, all right," said Jerzan.

Everyone focused on him.

"What do we know about this ship?" asked Jerzan.

Galkett swayed his head. "Not much. Something's not right."

Jerzan sighed. "You say everything's not right. Is this that Evaran shit again?"

"Look at the facts. Tolkus Gare, Jalt, and Dolgus Kree were captured a while back. The top three most wanted by the Bilaxians. Rumor is that Evaran was involved."

Jerzan raised a finger. "*Allegedly* involved."

"Maybe so, but there were eyewitness accounts of seeing someone that matched the historical records, and there were sightings of his weird ship. He's been around for a long, long time, from what I studied, just messing up those who harm others," said Galkett.

Hulldar tossed a hand out. "So what if he's on this ship? We'll waste 'em."

"I don't usually agree with you on much, but on this, I do," said Jahl.

Galkett pointed at his console. "And what about that mysterious . . . anomaly . . . that popped in out of nowhere before that alien ship appeared? There was something else that came through and docked on the alien ship. It looks similar to Evaran's ship."

"Your eyes are playing tricks on you," said Hulldar. He slapped Hosk's arm. "Probably just a stray pilot. Not all of them can be Hosk."

"Damn right," said Hosk in a gravelly voice.

Galkett shook his head. "The capture of the three most wanted was unusual, and now we have something unusual before us, and in all cases, Evaran's ship was around."

Jerzan could see Galkett's logic; it was one reason Jerzan liked Galkett. He had an analytical mind, but the lure of potentially high-value salvage, not to mention whatever else might be on the ship, was just too good an opportunity to pass up. Jerzan glanced at Galkett. "I understand your concern, but we're Bloodbores. We've got twelve highly trained mercs that can easily handle one person, mythical or not." He motioned at Jahl. "Any objection to hitting it?"

"None. Let's raid this bitch," said Jahl.

Jerzan tipped his head up at Hosk. "Take us in."

"Going in," said Hosk.

Galkett exhaled from his nose as he eased back into his chair.

"It'll do us all good to get off this ship, even for a little bit," said Jerzan. He eyed Galkett. "If you're going to be a problem, sit this one out."

"I'm fine," said Galkett.

"I'll be with him," said Hulldar. He grabbed his crotch. "If this Evaran guy shows up, I got something for him."

Everyone laughed.

"If you don't do him in, the smell will," said Jerzan. "All right, Jahl, make sure the others are aware of the situation, and geared up accordingly. It's time to collect."

Hosk, Jahl, and Hulldar whooped and hollered.

Jerzan nodded at everyone and exited the room. The thought of all the salvage they might get ran through his mind. If there was crew alive on the alien ship, then maybe another urge could be satisfied. There would also definitely be food and drink supplies, something they could stock up on. The alien ship was just what the Bloodbores needed, and Jerzan would make sure they took advantage of it, regardless of if Evaran was there or not.

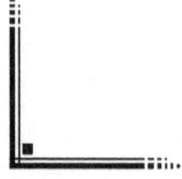

01

People do not normally walk through trees, as far as the laws of physics were concerned. Yet looking through his office window, Dr. Albert Snowden had seen it happen twice in the last hour. With his fair-skinned hands clasped behind his back, he observed the large, open quad area with its sprinkling of trees through his second-floor office window.

It was 2:00 p.m., Friday, March 1, 2013, and he was between classes that he taught at a college in Northwest Columbus, Ohio. There was only one class left on his itinerary for the day: Introduction to Astronomy. He sighed as he walked over to his office chair. After easing into it, he ran a hand over his balding head, with its two gray tufts. He hoped he was not losing his mind.

The glitches, as he was calling them, seemed to be increasing in regularity, and it was not just people walking through trees. It ran the gamut from people flying through the air to animals moving through cars. He knew those things should not be possible, but he had no rational explanation for the phenomena.

The thought of losing his mind was not something he wanted to entertain. There was so much more he wanted to do in life. He fiddled with his brown bow tie that sat over his white shirt and brown vest. At least he could still dress himself. He passed his hand over his well-trimmed beard.

Knock! Knock!

He exhaled sharply as he stood, smoothing out his brown twill pants. "Come in."

A middle-aged man, similar in size to Dr. Snowden at five feet eleven inches, entered the room. It was Dr. James Bryson, a fellow astronomer and professor, and also an old friend.

"Hey, ready for lunch?" asked Dr. Bryson.

"Sure. I wonder what monstrosity awaits us in the cafeteria today," said Dr. Snowden.

Dr. Bryson grinned. "To be fair, you get free food as a tenured benefit, so I wouldn't complain too much."

"You're right, you're right," said Dr. Snowden. He checked his pocket to make sure he had his card. "I'm good to go."

As they walked between campus buildings, Dr. Bryson cast a sidelong glance at Dr. Snowden. "You all right? You seem kind of out of it today."

Dr. Snowden sighed. "I wish I could say I was okay, but . . . I'm not sure, to be honest."

"Well, what's on your mind?"

"All right . . . Have you *seen* anything out of the ordinary lately?" asked Dr. Snowden.

"Besides Janet being on time to faculty meetings?"

Dr. Snowden laughed. "I'm being serious."

"I can't say that I have," said Dr. Bryson. "I'm assuming you have."

"Yeah . . . it's . . . hard to describe."

"Try me."

They began to cross the grassy quad area.

Dr. Snowden pointed at the tree he had seen earlier. "I saw someone sort of . . . phase out, then reappear in the tree, then pop back out of it."

"They walked through a tree?"

Dr. Snowden shook both hands out. "I know, I know, it sounds crazy, but I'm telling you, I saw it. Not just once, but twice today."

"I see," said Dr. Bryson. He eyed Dr. Snowden as they continued to walk. "How much rest have you been getting?"

Dr. Snowden shrugged. "It comes and goes, although I've pegged it at a three-week cycle. One cycle I can barely keep my eyes open, the next I can barely sleep or nap."

"And we all know how much you love napping."

Dr. Snowden chuckled as he swatted Dr. Bryson's arm. "That aside, I have considered that lack of sleep, or too much sleep, could be a cause of these . . . glitches." After a moment of silence, he said, "Crazy, right?"

Dr. Bryson bobbed his head. "Well . . . what you describe sounds like someone rubber banding."

"Huh?"

They crossed a sidewalk and stood outside the building with the cafeteria on the ground floor.

"You know I play games on my PC from time to time, right?" asked Dr. Bryson.

"Oh yeah."

Dr. Bryson smiled. "Sometimes players in a multiplayer game would rubber band. They would appear in one place and then reappear in another. It had to do with latency. You would get these hilarious situations sometimes, with players or objects doing things they weren't supposed to be doing."

"Like . . . flying through the air?"

"I've seen that. So maybe . . . the universe is a simulation, and you're seeing glitches for some reason."

Dr. Snowden rolled his eyes. "Not the universe-is-a-simulation thing again. We settled this at the Saint Louis conference."

"Give it time. There's still a lot of research to be done on it," said Dr. Bryson. He nodded toward the cafeteria. "Maybe some food will do you good."

Dr. Snowden nodded and slapped Dr. Bryson on the back. "Let's go."

After fifteen minutes, they had their food and were seated at an isolated table.

Dr. Snowden poked at the crispy chicken patty on his plate. "I *think* this is chicken."

"You never know," said Dr. Bryson, laughing.

Dr. Snowden enjoyed spending time with Dr. Bryson. It made everything feel normal, and hearkened back to a time when they were roommates in college, when there were no glitches or unusual sleep cycles. As Dr. Snowden looked up and around, he saw someone fall through the floor, then reappear a bit ahead back on the ground. His breathing went haphazard as his eyes widened.

"What is it?" asked Dr. Bryson, following Dr. Snowden's gaze. "You seeing another glitch?"

Dr. Snowden sighed as he drew his lips tight. "Yeah."

"You know what? You only have one more class for today. How about I take it, and you head home and get some rest."

"I . . . I think I'd like that," said Dr. Snowden. "I didn't mean to drop all of this on you today." He shook his head. "Today just seems . . . worse than the others."

"You should maybe check in with your doctor."

"I already did a while back. She said nothing's wrong and I just need more rest."

Dr. Bryson nodded. "Just like I did."

"You're both probably right. I need to call Emily before I start the drive home to give her an update," said Dr. Snowden. Emily was his niece and had lost both her parents. Dan, Dr. Snowden's brother, had died from cancer on February 4, 2011. Sarah had passed away giving birth to Emily. Dr. Snowden was the only remaining family member she was close with, so she was staying with him while she finished out her second semester of her senior year at the college where he taught.

Dr. Bryson rubbed his chin as he eased back into his chair. "How's she holding up now after Dan's death? It's been a while."

"She's still grieving, even after two years, but . . . I think she's handling it well," said Dr. Snowden.

"And you?"

Dr. Snowden's throat constricted. "I don't think you ever get over your big brother dying."

"Right, right," said Dr. Bryson. He cleared his throat. "All right, get going. Have a good weekend, and if you want company, give me a call."

Dr. Snowden stood and laid a hand on Dr. Bryson's shoulder. "I will. Thanks." As he walked out of the cafeteria, a wave of relief swept over him. Letting someone else know about the glitches besides Emily could be dangerous, but he trusted Dr. Bryson. Maybe it should have been discussed earlier. Dr. Snowden would update Emily on the drive home.

Emily sighed as she sat on a wooden bench on the platform surrounding a sand volleyball court. Her heart was still pumping from the pickup game she had played, but she felt like she could fall asleep at a moment's notice.

She felt bad when Brad, the captain of the other team, had come over to talk to her and then left after she was short with him. It was not his fault. She was just out of sorts. She ran her fair-skinned hand through her dirty-blond hair and then tugged on her ponytail. Her classes were done for the day, and a good rest seemed in order. Her eyes caught her girlfriend, Jennifer, approaching.

"Hey, that was a good game," said Jennifer, sitting next to Emily. Jennifer leaned in and kissed Emily on the cheek.

"I guess."

Jennifer tilted her head. "Everything all right?"

"I'm . . . not sure. I'm really tired."

"The three-week-cycle thing?"

Emily nodded. She did not understand why she could barely keep her eyes open sometimes, while others, she was wide awake. She had hoped caffeine and other stimulants would be her best friends for the last week, but nothing seemed to help. It scared her to think that there might be something wrong with her.

"Anything I can do to help?"

Emily shook her head. "I'm fine." Her cell phone played an incoming call sound. "I have to take this. Don't go anywhere."

Jennifer smiled as she nodded.

Emily put the cell phone up to her ear. "Uncle Albert? You're calling early."

"Yeah . . . I'm going home," said Dr. Snowden.

"You're having a bad day."

"Unfortunately, worse than any I've had in a long time. Something's *different* this time."

Emily swallowed hard. "Different how?"

"I can't put my finger on it but . . . more glitches, and everything seems . . . off," he said in a wavering voice.

"Okay. How about I make us a good dinner? I'm done here for the day, so I can head home," she said.

"Up to you. I don't want to ruin your day with mine."

Emily's throat constricted. "It's fine. I'll see you soon." Living with Dr. Snowden for the last two years had brought her closer to him, and she could not imagine her life without him. The thought that Dr. Snowden might pass was troubling.

"Your uncle having another bad day?" asked Jennifer.

"Yeah. I probably should head home and see how he's doing."

Jennifer nodded. "Okay. I know you probably want to be alone, but if you need me for anything . . ."

Emily leaned in and gave Jennifer a deep kiss.

After they pulled back, Jennifer smiled. "That'll hold me."

They shared a chuckle.

"All right, I better get going," said Emily. She exhaled from her mouth as she lightly squeezed Jennifer's hand. "I'll see you tomorrow. I think tonight will just be settling down Uncle Albert."

"I'll see you then," said Jennifer, rising as Emily did.

Emily watched Jennifer head out. Although Emily wanted Jennifer to come over, Emily was not sure what the environment would be. Dr. Snowden sounded almost panicked on the call, something she never associated with him. Short-tempered, sure, but she could not recall the last time she heard him so unsure of himself.

An hour later, she was home and ready to spend the rest of the night relaxing. She saw Dr. Snowden napping on his favorite recliner, but opening the door caused him to snort and wake up.

"Oh, that was quick," said Dr. Snowden.

Emily raised an eyebrow. "You were napping hard."

He chuckled. "Yeah . . . but it's not helping much. I bet you're as tired as I am."

"Yeah, I am," she said. She took a seat next to him. "So you saw more glitches?"

"Three this time. Two were someone walking through a tree. The third was someone falling through the floor. How about you?"

"Just one," she said. "At my volleyball game, I went to spike a ball over the net, and I swore I hit it. I know I did. But . . . everyone around me said I missed it. When I went to look for the ball, it was where it would be if I had missed it."

He tilted his head. "Huh. At least I know I'm not crazy, I think. The fact that you're getting them makes me think there's something wrong with the environment."

Emily looked around. "What do you mean?"

"Everything seems . . . less. Like . . . a little less colorful."

She chuckled. "Like it's losing power or something."

Dr. Snowden rubbed his chin. "That's a good analogy, actually. Maybe over the weekend, we could plug ourselves in."

She swatted his arm. "Now you're being silly. You have any plans for the weekend?"

"Just grading papers."

"Ahh. Jennifer will be over tomorrow."

Dr. Snowden nodded. "It'll be good to see her. I'm glad she makes you happy."

She laughed. "I'm glad she makes me happy too. Anyways, how about I make us some burgers and fries, your favorite," she said, grabbing his hand.

His eyes lit up as he tapped her hand with his free hand. "I could go for that."

It did her good to see Dr. Snowden in a better mood. "Okay, you rest up then. I'll bring it out to you when it's ready."

"All right."

Although her stomach was still churning at the thought that something was wrong, not just with Dr. Snowden, but with everything, she would focus on making dinner. She was not sure what she could do to help with the glitches. Maybe they would pass, but she had the sinking feeling that it would only get worse. At least a good dinner would be had.

02

Dr. Snowden gazed out the living room window with his hands clasped behind his back. It was Sunday morning, and the bright melting snow outside made him squint. With winter finally ending, he knew the snow would go. One aspect he loved about wintertime was that fewer people came by the house, and there were more opportunities to nap undisturbed, even if the naps did not actually make him feel more rested.

He shuffled toward his favorite recliner in the living room, hoping that maybe a change in sleeping venue might help. It probably would not, but at this point, he was willing to try anything. He still wore his clothes from the previous night, when he had fallen asleep grading papers at his desk in his study, and there were spaghetti stains spattered on his shirt. That could be dealt with later. A smile crept across his face at the thought of napping for the rest of the afternoon. Hopefully this time he might actually rest, although his gut told him he probably would not.

He plopped down onto the recliner, glancing around while wiggling his toes and gripping the recliner arms. The chair was like an old friend just waiting to comfort him. He was ready for his nap.

Emily bounced into the room from upstairs. She was wrapped in a bathrobe and running her hands through her damp hair. The smell of scented shampoo permeated the air.

Dr. Snowden reminisced about how much Emily was like Sarah, standing around five feet nine inches with dirty-blond hair and a face deep in thought. Despite that, she definitely had her father's disposition and personality traits. It sometimes felt as if he were talking with his brother.

"Uncle Albert, I'm going to the store here shortly to pick up a few things. Need anything, like coffee?" asked Emily.

"I'm fine. Actually," said Dr. Snowden, stroking his chin, "we're running low on coffee. Can you pick that up? Make sure to get ground coffee, not that instant stuff. You don't need to get creamer again either. You know I only drink my coffee straight black."

She gave him a critical look. "You stayed up late grading papers again, didn't you? And what happened to your shirt?"

"Yes, I stayed up, but I did get all the papers graded. As for my shirt . . . I just devoured your spaghetti, sometimes even got it into my mouth," he said with a smile. "At least now, I have the whole day ahead of me, and I can now enjoy studying a nap, for what it's worth. I'll be fine. You worry too much. Have a safe trip."

Emily shook her head and sighed. She turned and bounded up the stairs.

He appreciated her concern for his well-being, but it could be overbearing at times. It was her way of keeping him close after Dan died. Dr. Snowden enjoyed having her around, as she made the house feel more alive. She also reminded him of what was gone. With a final look around the living room, he reclined the chair and closed his eyes.

Knock! Knock!

His eyes popped open. He had not expected anyone today that he could remember. It better not be Jehovah's Witnesses, like the ones Dr. Bryson sent last week. While Dr. Snowden enjoyed a good prank, three times in a month was a bit much. He rose from the recliner with an audible sigh and lumbered over to the front door, pausing to peep out the peephole.

A Caucasian man in his mid-thirties stood outside, with dirty-blond hair, a chiseled chin, and piercing blue eyes that seemed to penetrate the peephole. The man had on a dark-blue-and-silver pinstripe suit and polished black shoes. His hair was short, with a small wave jutting out the front and to the side. The sides were shaved, giving an overall clean-cut profile.

Dr. Snowden narrowed his eyes. This was definitely not a Jehovah's Witness. He had put up a No Solicitors sign last year and made sure it was displayed prominently. There was no way this man could have missed it. He either ignored it or was there for another reason. Either way, Dr. Snowden was going to find out. He cracked the door open a bit.

"Dr. Snowden?" said the man in the doorway in a calm, emotionless voice.

"Yes . . . can I help you?"

The man bowed with his left arm across his stomach. "My name is Evaran, and I am here to save you."

Dr. Snowden smirked. Great, another religious nut, just what he needed. He had tangled with people pushing various philosophies on him all his life, and he had developed a mental checklist of tactics to refute many of their claims. Although he tried to avoid confrontations if possible, he knew that once a person made up their mind, they rarely changed their view. However, when cornered, he did not back down either. "How'd you know my name? Did Dr. Bryson send you?"

"I do not know a Dr. Bryson."

"How'd you know my name then?"

Evaran pointed to a package sitting on a chair on the front porch. "You have a package from the college with your name on it."

Dr. Snowden stepped back a bit and opened the door all the way to see the package. It was several feet wide by several feet tall. He did not remember hearing a package delivery last night. "Hmm, that's odd. Okay, well, thanks for stopping by. It's been great. Take care."

"Wait!" said Evaran, extending his left hand, palm up, toward Dr. Snowden. A vertical ten-inch screen appeared, hovering above a ring on Evaran's middle finger. On the screen was a decrementing timer, and it showed around ten minutes.

Dr. Snowden crossed his arms and raised his eyebrows as he scrutinized the display. He was not aware of any type of technology capable of producing a free-floating screen, especially from a ring. Typically, he would already shut the door, but the screen intrigued him. He pointed at the display. "Okay, tell me what that is, and I'll listen to what you have to say. Deal?"

"Curiosity. That trait befits you. It is a deal then," said Evaran with a nod. "At a high level, the screen is a holographic projection emitted by my ring. The ring also emits ultrasonic radiation for tactile feedback. The ring itself, however, is really just a relay for a much more powerful system. Does that satisfy my part of the deal?"

Dr. Snowden pushed his glasses up. He had never heard of technology combined like that before or seen anything so advanced. It could be some type of optical illusion. He was not even sure he fully understood what he had heard, but he could not deny what was in front of him. A deeper examination was needed. He pointed at the screen. "Yeah, I guess, although I'd like to touch it."

Evaran extended his hand farther toward Dr. Snowden.

Dr. Snowden poked at the display and felt resistance, like touching a rubber sheet. His lips parted as he pulled his head back. The applications a technology like this could power did not escape him. He closed his mouth after realizing it was still open. This was far beyond anything he had expected. He pulled his hand back and looked at Evaran. "That's . . . pretty amazing."

"I am glad you think so. Are you ready to hear what I have to say now?"

"Sure, why not," said Dr. Snowden, shrugging. He had many questions, and maybe he could ask them after hearing what Evaran had to say.

"Very well," said Evaran. He raised a finger. "I am here to save you from your current predicament. The world around you is an illusion . . . and I need to prepare you for an awakening." He pointed to the timer with his right hand. "In around eight minutes, this world will disappear, along with you in it. When it does, I will be there to guide you through your awakening."

Everything about this encounter seemed unusual to Dr. Snowden, from the high-tech screen he was seeing to the impeccable suit Evaran wore, which was not normal for a door-to-door solicitor. Dr. Snowden harrumphed. "That's an extraordinary claim. Do you have extraordinary proof to confirm this claim?"

Evaran lowered his hand to his side, making the screen go away. "Ahh, the scientist in you speaks. I like that. I do have some evidence that you may find interesting. Let me ask you, have you had dreams of being in a space that you knew was a medical room of some type but did not recognize as any medical room you have seen before?"

Dr. Snowden's heartbeat ramped up. He had only told Emily about the dreams, dreams she was having as well. How Evaran knew about them was a mystery. "Yeah . . . I've had a reoccurring dream about a medical room."

"Did the room have six beds, six stalls, a large screen with strange symbols on it, and an unusual-looking freestanding console in the corner?"

Dr. Snowden crossed his arms and leaned forward a bit. He pondered what he had just heard. Evaran's description of the room was too exact to blow off as pure chance. "How'd you know about that?"

Evaran placed both hands together in front of him, touching at the fingertips. "This world is a virtual simulation, a program that tries to approximate the real world. You are a virtual representation of yourself, an avatar. Your physical body is still in the real world, actually in the room I just described to you. You have been here for about three weeks. Occasionally, your body needed to be moved for research and maintenance. I am guessing that was most likely done with you in a sedated state. Your dreams would then be glimpses of the real world."

Dr. Snowden scrunched up his face. He understood what Evaran was saying, but it seemed unrealistic. "You would have to be an outside observer to know this, like standing next to my body then."

Before Evaran could respond, the sound of Emily descending the stairs made her the point of focus. She wore a light shirt, jeans, and comfortable shoes, and her hair was pulled back into a ponytail. After putting her left arm around Dr. Snowden, she smiled at Evaran. "Wow, nice suit! Who are you?"

Dr. Snowden perched his left hand on his chin and gestured with his right hand toward Evaran, indicating for Evaran to introduce himself.

Evaran tilted his head. "Ahh, yes. I am Evaran, and who might you be?"

"I'm Emily, Uncle Albert's niece. Am I interrupting something?" asked Emily, glancing at Dr. Snowden.

Dr. Snowden grinned. "No, not at all. He was explaining to me that we have a few more minutes before this world, which is a virtual simulation, disappears and we awaken in the real world."

"I see," she said, giggling.

He knew she would find it comical in the way he presented it, but he was beginning to believe Evaran's claim might have some merit.

Evaran extended his left hand again, showing the screen from his ring to both of them. "It is down to four minutes now."

"That's awesome! How're you doing that?" asked Emily.

Dr. Snowden drew his lips to the right. "Holographic projection, he says. He also seems to know about our dreams."

Emily's eyes sank as she grimaced. She took a step back with her hands clasped together tightly in front of her. "How does he know *that*?"

"A good question," said Dr. Snowden. He cast a sidelong glance at Emily, then eyed Evaran. "You say this is not the real world but a virtual simulation, and your only evidence so far is the mention of dreams. That could've been a lucky guess, although a very good one. What other evidence do you have?"

Evaran half smiled. "I understand your skepticism, and I was hoping it would not come to this. I am standing between the beds you both are on in the medical room I described. To prove it, I will gently squeeze both your shoulders. Tell me if you feel anything."

Dr. Snowden's heart pounded as he watched Evaran freeze in an unnatural manner, as if the pause button had been pressed on a remote control. After a few moments of silence, Dr. Snowden retracted with surprise from Emily as she jumped. He had felt the light squeeze too, which could not be possible. There was no object or force nearby that could have caused it. His skepticism was diminishing as Evaran's evidence seemed to keep mounting.

Evaran moved again and smiled at them. "Did you both feel that?"

Dr. Snowden's left shoulder tingled as he rubbed it and processed the squeezing sensation. "How . . . how's that possible?"

Emily whipped her head back and forth between Dr. Snowden and Evaran. "This is freaking me out!"

Dr. Snowden's fingers trembled as he analyzed the situation. The two points of evidence were undeniable. The scientist in him would not let him dismiss it. "Why didn't we feel anything when we were moved then?"

"Your physical sensations were neutralized. The virtual simulation is winding down, meaning your mind is now processing external physical sensations, as you just felt," said Evaran.

"I guess if this virtual simulation ends, that'll be the final proof."

Evaran pointed to the timer again. "You will have your proof then when the virtual simulation deallocation begins in two minutes. When the time comes, close your eyes and focus on clearing your mind. The sound of the deallocation will be all around. No physical harm will occur. Remember that. When it is over, both of you will be in the real world, in that medical room from your dreams. All I can do at this point is be your guide."

Dr. Snowden and Emily poked their heads outside, surveying the environment.

Dr. Snowden expected there to be something to lend credence to what Evaran was saying. Not seeing anything, he cocked his head at Evaran. "Assuming this is all true, are we the only ones in this virtual simulation?"

Evaran stared at the ground. "There are two others. I was not able to visit them due to time constraints. I had to make a decision, and I chose you and Emily. I got to visit both of you at one time, and you both appear to be fairly level-headed. For the other two, when they awaken, their experience will be vastly different from yours."

Dr. Snowden wondered who the other two were, assuming this was not some elaborate hoax.

"So what now?" asked Emily.

Evaran cleared his throat and looked back up at them. "We wait. I accessed quite a bit from the medical room's logs. When you are both awake, I will try to explain everything."

"Wait, were our names in those logs?" asked Dr. Snowden.

"Yes, they were."

"So you knew who we were all along then!"

Evaran half smiled. "You are correct. However, I felt it would be better to get your attention first before exploring that aspect. The holographic projection worked as I predicted it would. I knew you would be curious based on your profile. However, it is time. Prepare yourselves." He looked off to the sky in the west.

Dr. Snowden and Emily followed Evaran's gaze.

A loud boom shattered the silence, and the house shuddered as if an earthquake had hit it.

A jolt of adrenaline shot through Dr. Snowden. His breathing went ragged as he saw square chunks of the environment turning transparent, then fading to complete darkness. This must be the deallocation Evaran had mentioned. Why it was coming from the west was a mystery. The sound the deallocation generated was similar to radio static. Dr. Snowden rubbed the goose bumps on his arm and stepped out the front door in bewilderment. "You've gotta be kidding me!"

Emily followed Dr. Snowden and gripped his right arm. "Whoa!"

The deallocation crept faster toward them. Cars, houses, and streets disappeared before their eyes.

Dr. Snowden shielded with his left arm instinctively as he saw the wind toss the neighbor's lawn fixtures around.

"The deallocation is almost complete. Come stand by me. We will do this together," said Evaran.

Dr. Snowden moved to Evaran's left side and hunched over, with Emily in tow.

Evaran put his arm around Dr. Snowden while Emily maintained her death grip on Dr. Snowden's arm.

"This isn't real! This is preposterous!" said Dr. Snowden over the deafening noise.

"Dr. Snowden . . . focus!"

Dr. Snowden and Emily shut their eyes and focused on blanking their minds.

The deallocation was almost on them.

Dr. Snowden peeped out and braced for impact. Although he could feel no pain, he felt himself beginning to slip away.

Jay Beerman strummed his fingers on the steering wheel of his semi as he drove down a highway on another delivery. It was getting late, and his eyes were beginning to droop. Getting to a rest stop and lying up for the night was on his mind, and that was only a mile away. Trying to drive in the haze that seemed to cloud his mind was hard, and it seemed to be happening more.

He adjusted his red-and-white trucker hat with his fair-skinned hands and briefly looked down at his red puffy vest and the white shirt underneath. He grimaced at the stains from the chili dog he had picked up at the last rest stop. At least it did not get on his blue jeans. Looking up, his eyes widened.

A car appeared out of nowhere in front of his semi and phased through the cab.

He swerved to the side as his heartbeat shot through the roof. Half expecting a crash, he braced for impact. After a moment, he peeked out and saw that he was still moving at the same pace he had been, and there was no sign of a car. Looking around in confusion, he checked his mirrors. His breathing went haphazard as he reached the rest stop and pulled in. He took a moment to normalize his breathing. With a trembling hand, he shut off his semi and leaned back in his seat.

A foul odor permeated the air.

His nose wrinkled as he realized he had crapped his pants. Shaking his head, he stepped out of the truck and took a deep breath. Although he wanted to light up a cigarette, there were other pressing things to consider.

He leaned against his truck and closed his eyes. Death should have claimed him, yet somehow, the car disappeared just as fast as it had appeared, and it was like he had never swerved. This was not the first time he had seen something that should not be possible. All through the week, he had seen things. Impossible things. Things that had no basis in reality as he knew it. He sighed as he began to calm down. It was time to clean up.

Another semi pulled in and stopped next to him.

Jay grabbed a change of underwear and pants and then started off toward the rest-center building. Although he would normally hang out and chat with the truck next to him, he was not in the mood for conversation.

As he approached the visitor's center, several people wrinkled their noses when they passed him. When he got to the bathroom, he found an open stall. He stripped off his pants and underwear and then cleaned himself up. It was not as bad as he thought it would be. His eyes popped open when the stalls disappeared, leaving him standing half-nude in the open.

A man washed his hands in the sink next to Jay's stall.

Jay thought the man would say something, but it was as if he did not see anything unusual going on. It did not take long for Jay to get cleaned up, and by the time he had slipped on his change of underwear and pants, the stall had reappeared.

He sat on the closed toilet and put his head in his hands. Something was wrong. Very wrong. The first few times something had happened, he chalked it up to maybe being buzzed. This time, though, he had no alcohol in his system. He stepped out of the stall and tossed his old underwear and pants into the garbage.

A loud boom came from outside.

He looked at another person taking a leak, half expecting them to be as surprised as he was. The person did not seem to have heard it. How that was possible bewildered Jay. He dried his hands and exited the building. The wind had picked up, and anything not nailed down seemed to be flying past him to the east.

His eyes were immediately drawn to the unusual event to the west. It was like rectangular chunks of the sky were lighting up, then disappearing. He grabbed the arm of a man that was walking by and then pointed up. "You seeing that shit?"

The man's gaze followed where Jay was pointing. "Seeing what . . . exactly?"

Jay closed his eyes and exhaled from his mouth. Maybe it was just him. He let the man's arm go and then opened his eyes.

The disturbance was getting closer, along with the weird static noise. The wind had also picked up speed.

Jay began to sweat profusely as he realized that he was the only one able to see what was coming. Looking toward his truck, he was not sure he could even make it there in time before whatever was happening in the sky would claim him. He took off running toward the rest-stop exit. When he reached the highway, he peeked back.

The disturbance had reached the rest stop.

His breathing went erratic when he could see nothing but pure darkness beyond the disturbance. It was like the night itself was reaching out to claim him. He grimaced when his truck was devoured.

With a final look, he spun around and ran as hard as he could. The wind whipping around him told him that whatever was coming would reach him. He sighed, then stopped. After turning his hat backward, he clenched his fists as his face turned red. "Well, c'mon then, you pussy-ass darkness."

As the disturbance converged on him, he swung and kicked out. Whatever it was, he would go out fighting.

The disturbance reached him, and everything went black.

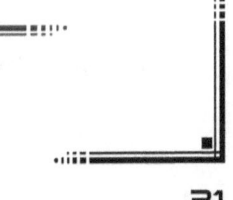

Sanjay Chandrakar knew that when compiling a program, he should see what was being compiled and if there were any errors or warnings. What he did not expect was seeing his monitor show live television for a moment. He also did not expect that his outfit of casual dress shoes with khakis and a tan buttoned-up short-sleeve shirt would dissipate, leaving him completely nude. His legs closed instinctively as he brought his arms together over his chest.

Looking around, it seemed none of his classmates in his computer-science class at a college in Cincinnati, Ohio, had noticed anything. After a moment, the screen changed back to the black and green colors he was used to, and his clothing had returned. He swatted his classmate's arm. "Chris, did you just see anything happen?"

Chris looked around and then shook his head. "No . . . What am I looking for?"

Sanjay sighed. Sweat had consumed his face, and he was not sure what was going on. Previous instances of unusual events had occurred, but they were limited to when he was out and about. Usually it was someone walking through a building. Other times, it was like everything disappeared, leaving him in some dark void, but then everything came back just as quickly as it had gone. He thought maybe it was his eyes playing tricks on him, or possibly lack of sleep. This was the first time it had happened in class.

Chris wrinkled his eyebrows. "You all right, man?"

"Yeah. I'm . . . okay," said Sanjay. He smiled and nodded. "Just tired, you know."

"I do know," said Chris. He leaned back in his chair. "We had a raid last night, and your healing was *way* off."

Sanjay sighed. Although he enjoyed playing massively multiplayer role-playing games, some of the events were tiresome. One event was a raid, and they involved various amounts of people and could take up to six hours to complete. The one he did the night before was twenty people, and everyone had a role. He was a healer, and there were several times when the monster they fought had talked to him directly. That should never happen. "I know. I got distracted is all."

"We're hitting darklark dungeon again tonight. You in or . . ."

Sanjay shook his head. "I have to study. Too much going on."

Chris nodded. "I probably should too."

It was 4:30 p.m. and Sanjay's eyes were drooping. He could have fallen asleep without much effort. After saving his code and exiting out of his integrated development environment, he said, "I'ma go home, rest up. Not feeling too good."

"Cool. I'm going your way anyways. Let's get out of here," said Chris.

As they walked toward their apartment complex, a growling and snarling bear appeared in front of them.

Sanjay froze while Chris walked through the bear.

The bear disappeared.

Chris stopped and turned to face Sanjay. "You sure you're okay?"

Sanjay's breathing went all over the place as his stomach churned. "You . . . didn't see that?"

"See what?"

Sanjay squinted hard. After a moment, he opened his eyes and shook his head. "I think I'm sicker than I realize."

Chris narrowed his eyes. "You're telling me you're hallucinating now or something?"

"I don't know. I think I just need a good dinner and maybe some rest."

They continued on. As they approached the apartment complex, a loud boom from the west filled the air.

Sanjay froze again as Chris kept walking.

Chris stopped. "What now?"

Sanjay pivoted to the west to see what had caused the sound. His eyes popped open when he saw rectangular chunks of the sky shimmer, then turn dark. He pointed at the disturbance. "You don't see that?"

Chris looked at where Sanjay was pointing. "No . . . I just see a clear sky. What should I be seeing?"

A static noise permeated the air as the wind picked up.

"That!" said Sanjay, pointing emphatically at the disturbance.

"I don't see shit," said Chris. He tilted his head. "You been taking any meds or something . . ."

Sanjay's legs wobbled as the disturbance reached the ground and began to fade anything it touched into darkness. He gathered his senses and began to run away from it.

"Where the hell you going?" asked Chris.

Sanjay's heartbeat had gone nuclear, and he could barely control his breathing. The disturbance was moving fast, and when he got to his apartment complex, he realized he would not be able to outrun whatever was coming. His hands went cold when he saw the disturbance devour Chris. Sanjay took off down the street.

The wind picked up, and the static noise became deafening.

He tripped on the curb when he peered back. Spinning onto his back, he raised his arms and screamed as the disturbance reached him.

Everything went black.

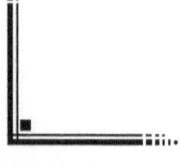

03

Dr. Snowden winced as pangs shot through his body. They passed as quickly as they came, but it was enough to make him try to open his eyes. He immediately shut them due to the blinding light. His nostrils flared as the smell of sweat poured through them. He could almost taste it.

Trying to talk was a failed endeavor since his throat did not move. His stomach tumbled, and disorientation had set in. He tried to move his arms and legs, but they were heavy and unresponsive. At least he could hear.

The recognizable voice of Evaran cut through the silence. "Do not try to move just yet. Your bodies are readjusting after a few weeks of being under. Even with the periodic maintenance done to you, your bodies are still in need of repair. The nanobots inside you are restoring your bodies now. It will be a few minutes or so."

Prickles ran throughout Dr. Snowden's body. His hip region had the most intense tingling sensations, and his mind swirled as he tried to focus on Evaran's comment about nanobots. It seemed as each second passed, Dr. Snowden was able to move more.

Squinting hard, he peeped out, letting his eyes adjust. The environment around him became less blurred, and sounds became clearer. Emily coughing and moving around on her bed caught his attention. At least she was there with him. The pace of recovery struck him as odd, like a cold car engine warming up.

"These nanobots are a remarkable accomplishment," said Evaran. "They can repair damage and fight off diseases, and they even have rudimentary sensory aspects to them. I have seen other nanobots before, but never this advanced. They have integrated themselves quite efficiently. Interesting. I will need to download the schematics for these before we leave."

Dr. Snowden was not sure what Evaran was talking about. Nanobots were not a new concept for Dr. Snowden, but it seemed they were in him doing something. His focus was trying to regain control of his senses. He attempted to open his eyes completely but could only get them halfway there. His throat had unclenched, and the initial disorientation was passing.

He tried sitting up, but his arms gave out. The prickle sensations were gone now, and in their place was a warmth spreading throughout his body. He knew these feelings were real. In the virtual simulation, his aches felt disconnected from the realization of them. He heard two men groaning. They must be going through the same thing he was.

After several minutes, he tried sitting up again. His vision was sharp now, and he could move his body around better than he could ever recall. Going from a debilitated state to one of such strength was puzzling. He sat up without a trace of weakness and swung his legs off the side of the table. One hand rested on the cool slab, while the other ran over the metallic dots on his white robe. The chill of the slab cut right through the robe to his naked body underneath.

Looking to his left and across an aisle, he saw two others moving around on metallic slabs like the one he was on, and both had on similar robes. One appeared to be a fair-skinned man in his mid-thirties and the other a tan-skinned man in his early twenties.

Dr. Snowden turned around and saw Emily beginning to get up. She wore the same robe that he and the others had. He turned back around and saw Evaran, but the blue suit with silver pinstripes was gone. In its place was a very different outfit. Dr. Snowden's breath slowed, and his eyes widened.

Evaran's outfit looked like a padded light-armor suit. It was pale gray with highlights of blue, white, orange, and silver. The suit covered his whole body except for his head, neck, feet, and hands. What intrigued Dr. Snowden was that the dark-gray pads were spread out across the suit in various patterns and sizes. The ones on the chest and legs were larger than the ones on the arms, and shins. The suit also had a metallic utility belt, boots, forearm covers, and a neck guard.

The silver segmented utility belt had various attachments on it. In the center of the belt was a dark-gray buckle with a button in the middle. Dr. Snowden saw what appeared to be a cardholder on the right side. Behind that, a cylindrical rod hung off the utility belt. It was metallic and had intricate designs on it with several buttons. He thought it looked like the grip of a sword, but without the rest of the parts associated with a hilt. On the left side of the belt, various small metallic pouches and orbs were attached.

Dr. Snowden slid off the slab and scrambled over to Emily. She was sitting on the edge of her slab and looked frozen in place as she surveyed the environment. He verified that this was the medical room he recalled in what he thought was a dream. It was apparent this was not a typical medical room.

Emily slid off the slab and grabbed his right arm as she hunched over. In a wavering voice, she asked, "Uncle Albert, what's going on?"

He wiped the sweat from his hands on his robe. His right arm tingled as Emily's shallow breathing coursed over it. With his left arm, he cleared the sweat off his face. Evaran had said this was where they would be when they awakened. Dr. Snowden cleared his throat. "I don't know, but this is the medical room from the dreams."

The two men on the other slabs had sat up on the edges of their slabs. They rubbed their eyes and looked around.

The older man slipped off the slab. His face contorted. "What the *fuck*, man?"

Dr. Snowden stepped in front of Emily with her still gripping his right arm. It was evident this man was unhinged.

The younger man also slid off the slab. He jerked his head around and took off past the older man and Evaran. When he reached the end of the lab, he pounded on a light-blue smoke-filled doorway. In a light Indian accent, he said, "Help! Someone help, please!"

Evaran glanced at Dr. Snowden for a moment, then softened his look as he turned to the older man. With a raised hand, Evaran said in a calm voice, "Jay, please calm down. You are safe here. No one will hurt you."

Jay focused on Evaran and walked aggressively toward him. "Damn right, they won't. Who the fuck are you, man?"

Evaran stepped back. "I am Evaran. You have been through a traumatic experience, and I am here to help you."

The younger man stopped screaming and slid down to the floor with his back to the shielded door. While grimacing, he pulled his trembling balled fists close to his chest.

Dr. Snowden licked his lips as he watched the two men's actions. These men were clearly in distress. He did not want to interfere, but it was apparent they were not forewarned about this awakening like he and Emily had been.

Jay stepped toward Evaran and then tried to push him, but he didn't budge. "I said, who the *fuck* are you!" He tried to push Evaran again.

Evaran sidestepped the push effort and brushed Jay's arms to the side.

Jay stumbled.

Evaran spun Jay around and lightly pushed him to the nearest slab.

Jay hit the slab, and his upper half spilled across it. He glanced at Dr. Snowden with a wild look. Jay stood back up and wheeled around to face Evaran, placing both hands on the edge of the slab.

Dr. Snowden noted that the push was fairly light, but Jay hit the slab with far more force than the push should have generated. It would be impossible unless Evaran's strength was off the charts. Dr. Snowden figured Jay must have calculated this too, based on his expression. Although Evaran appeared to be human, his strength was not in line with that of a normal human. Dr. Snowden winced as a pain shot up his arm. He glanced over at Emily, who was trembling and white as a ghost, and then tapped her hand.

Emily looked up at Dr. Snowden and relaxed her grip. She moved behind him, put her arms around his midsection, and then buried her face in his back.

He remembered she used to do that as a kid when there was a big bug flying around the room.

Evaran turned halfway around and glanced at the younger man at the other end of the lab. "Sanjay, please join Jay by the slab." Pivoting back, he motioned for Dr. Snowden to come forward. "Dr. Snowden, please come over here with Emily."

Emily released her midsection hug on Dr. Snowden and grabbed his left arm as they inched toward where Jay was.

Dr. Snowden stopped at the end of the slab and then eyed Jay and Evaran. Standing close to anyone at this point seemed like a bad idea.

Evaran twisted around toward Sanjay again and pointed to where Dr. Snowden, Emily, and Jay were standing. "Sanjay, these three are in the same predicament you are in. I can explain this, but I would prefer to do it once with everyone together. You are not in any immediate danger. Please, come stand by the slab."

Sanjay rose to his feet while staring down Dr. Snowden, Emily, and Jay. While creeping toward the slab, Sanjay flattened himself against the wall as he passed Evaran and arrived at the slab opposite where Dr. Snowden and Emily were.

Evaran raised his finger. "Before I begin, let us pause for a few moments and focus on breathing. Your adrenaline levels are high." He held out his hand directly in front of him. "When I raise my hand, breathe in. When I lower it, breathe out."

Dr. Snowden felt more relaxed after a few minutes had passed with Evaran raising and lowering his hand.

Sanjay was no longer hunched over, but standing straight. His face showed a mix of confusion and contemplation.

The lines on Jay's face had settled. Gone were the wild looks from earlier.

Emily loosened her grip on Dr. Snowden's arm.

Dr. Snowden glanced at her and noticed her skin had returned to its normal tone, and she seemed more settled. It was hard to believe just breathing in a controlled manner could have such a drastic effect. His heart had slowed, and his breathing had returned to normal. Everyone seemed calmer.

He was eager to find out what was going on, but tempered his expectations. What was real, and what was not, was on the forefront of his mind. With a deep breath, he awaited what Evaran had to say.

Emily was not sure what to make of everything going on. Although initially confused, her senses had calmed down, and at least Dr. Snowden was there with her. She did not know what to make of Jay and Sanjay, as Evaran had called them. They seemed confused and unpredictable. Her heart was still beating fast, and a tingling sensation swept through her body. Whatever it was, she sensed that it was trying to calm her down. She was curious about what Evaran had to say.

Evaran addressed the group. "Good. You should all be feeling a bit more relaxed. Now, I know this is rough, but I believe introductions are in order." He pointed to himself. "My name is Evaran. I would be what you term an alien, but it is more complicated than that. I am a traveler, and I help those in need, such as yourselves."

Jay shuddered and glanced at the others, then flung his arm into the air as he turned toward Evaran. "You're an alien? Are you fucking kidding me?"

"I assure you I am not kidding you, and I am not done yet. Bear with me," said Evaran with a hand raised out toward Jay.

Jay exhaled sharply through his nose.

Evaran pointed at Dr. Snowden. "This is Dr. Albert Snowden, a professor of astronomy at a college in Columbus, Ohio, and to his right," he said, pointing to Emily, "is his niece, Emily Snowden, who is a history student at the same college." Pointing at Sanjay, he said, "This is Sanjay

Chandrakar, a computer-science student at a college in Cincinnati, Ohio." He then pointed to Jay. "And finally, this is Jay Beerman, a former military member who is now a truck driver and lives in Southern Indiana."

The emotionless tone of Evaran's voice was oddly calming to Emily. She was glad Evaran was there, as Jay seemed like he could be dangerous, and Sanjay seemed unpredictable. She studied Evaran as he stared at the ground.

After a moment, Evaran looked back up. "This is going to sound incredible, but here is the situation. On February 4, 2012, around 6:00 p.m., you were all abducted from a small stretch of Interstate 70 by an alien race known as the Krotovore. They put everyone into a virtual simulation for research purposes. Your minds were altered so the transition was seamless. While in the virtual simulation, they injected nanobots into everyone to help maintain your bodies. Then on February 25, 2012, three weeks later, they sustained some damage before entering a space-time rift that instantly took them to the Andromeda galaxy. However, it ended up being one year into the future as well, March 2, 2013. I followed them through the rift and boarded their ship, and here we are."

Jay snorted. "Now you're just messing with us!"

"I am not."

Emily's shoulders slumped as she looked down. Although she was unsure of what she had just heard, the dates had sentimental value to her. It was the second anniversary of the day her dad died. He had been buried in the town he grew up in. The day he died had been one of the hardest days for her, but this day was shaping up to be a close second. She frowned and in a weak voice, said, "They abducted us on our way back from Dad's grave."

Dr. Snowden gritted his teeth as he put his left arm around Emily and gave a light squeeze. His eyes blinked rapidly as he fixed his gaze on Evaran. "That's utterly ridiculous."

Evaran extended his hands in a calming motion. "That is the current situation, and I have no reason to lie to you. You will be able to verify for yourself once we leave this room."

Dr. Snowden's eyes narrowed. "You want us to believe that?"

"I do. I know you have questions, and now is a good time to ask them."

"What the hell is a virtual simulation?" asked Jay, rubbing his left cheek.

"A computer program, right? That tries to simulate reality?" said Sanjay, motioning with his right hand as if shaking an imaginary ball.

Everyone turned to look at him.

Evaran half smiled while tilting his head toward Sanjay. "That is correct. You were all connected to it."

"I think a more likely explanation is that we're part of some failed drug experiment. Maybe a government thing," said Dr. Snowden.

Jay nodded his head and wagged a finger at Dr. Snowden. "Yeah, yeah. I'm with Doc on that. I've heard about shit like this in the army."

Dr. Snowden drew his lips flat and shot Jay a look.

Emily knew Dr. Snowden hated being called Doc.

Evaran sighed and addressed Dr. Snowden. "How would I have been able to appear to you and Emily in the virtual simulation then?"

"I don't know. Maybe it was a shared hallucinogenic effect or the power of suggestion or something," said Dr. Snowden, shrugging.

"No, and I do not think you believe that either."

Sanjay eyed Dr. Snowden. "You saw Evaran? In the virtual simulation?"

"Emily and I did, yeah, assuming that was what it was," said Dr. Snowden, clearing his throat.

"I didn't see him either," said Jay. He waved a finger between himself and Sanjay. "Maybe we weren't special enough."

Dr. Snowden shook his head at Jay.

"Why didn't me and Jay see you?" asked Sanjay, looking at Evaran. Sanjay bobbed his head and pointed at Dr. Snowden and Emily. "It woulda been nice to get a heads-up like they did."

Evaran nodded. "I was short on time. The systems sustaining the virtual simulation were ending. I decided to get at least two of you, rather than just one. It was nothing personal, more a matter of efficiency. I figured the nanobots would have helped you and Jay adjust quickly. It took a little longer than I expected."

"I see," said Sanjay. "I do feel calmer. More stable than just a few minutes ago anyways."

"The nanobots are engineered to protect your body. You do not have anything to fear from them, and your well-being is their main goal. They sensed your heightened states when we paused earlier to breathe and tried to normalize it," said Evaran.

"I'm not sure I like the idea of these things in us," said Emily as she looked at her hands. She could almost feel them swimming around.

"They don't sound harmful. Nanobots are just tiny machines at the nanometer scale," said Sanjay. He looked at Emily while putting two fingers together with a small gap to indicate *tiny*.

Emily glared at Sanjay. "Uhh . . . yeah. I know what a nanobot is." She was not sure she liked Sanjay.

"Don't worry," said Dr. Snowden, chuckling. "I don't think there are nanobots inside us making us magically feel better."

Evaran shrugged. "Whether or not you believe they are there is not relevant. Any doctor would be able to confirm their presence. I did not think you would dismiss your healing rate so easily. As I mentioned earlier, you will feel stronger and faster along with some other side effects from here on out."

A small metallic orb with a blue indented groove that criss-crossed it vertically and horizontally flew to the right of Evaran's shoulder and, in a monotonic voice with a digital rasp, said, "Correction. They are functioning at one hundred fifty-six percent of optimal human operating capacity."

"Whoa," said Emily.

"What the heck?" said Dr. Snowden, leaning back a bit.

"Now what the fuck is that?" asked Jay, pointing at the orb.

"Oh, wow," said Sanjay, leaning forward.

"That," said Evaran, pointing at the orb, "is my variable utility artificial intelligence orb, but his shortened name is V. Think of him as a mobile assistant, and also my friend."

Jay turned toward Dr. Snowden. "Doc, you ever seen shit like this before?"

"It's Dr. Snowden to you, and no, I haven't," he said with a clenched jaw.

"I would imagine not," said Evaran. "V took a while to build, and the voice synthesizer still needs some work, but V is highly functional and, more importantly, very handy and a good traveling companion."

"Is he a strong AI? Or weak?" asked Sanjay.

"A very good question. V is self-aware and what you would classify as a strong AI."

"That's impressive," said Sanjay.

V's lights glowed a bit brighter.

"I am glad you think so," said Evaran. "Let us take a moment to breathe and relax. Think about what you have heard so far and consider any questions you might have. Although time is of the essence, it would be good for you to gather your thoughts."

Emily did not realize she needed a break until Evaran mentioned it. She did not know much about artificial intelligence, but it seemed Sanjay did. It looked to her like Sanjay was trying to butter up Evaran.

She was still unsure of everything that was going on and was not even sure if what she was experiencing was real or a deeply complex hallucination. V seemed cold, but most machines and computers did. Although Evaran had referred to V in terms of a male, she did not think V had a gender. All of this was a bit much for her, and it was stressing her out. She exhaled from her nose as she awaited the next round of questions and answers.

04

During the few minutes everyone absorbed everything, Dr. Snowden had been assessing V, who was impressive, assuming the situation was real. Evaran seemed calm and level-headed, something Dr. Snowden appreciated. Sanjay seemed like a smart kid, and Dr. Snowden could see that Sanjay irritated Emily. Jay was another story, although given the situation, maybe he was acting differently. So far Dr. Snowden had not been impressed. He was appreciative of the fact that Evaran gave them a minute to let it all sink in because what had been said so far seemed incredible.

"Okay, let us continue," said Evaran. "We left off discussing V."

Jay snorted and crooked his thumb at V. "Enough about ol' Blue Ball. If all this shit you're saying is true, then who're these assholes that abducted us?"

"Designation Blue Ball has been added," said V.

Jay crinkled his eyebrows, with the left side of his lips upturned as he looked at V.

"Do you wish to see your abductors?" asked Evaran.

"Yeah . . . yeah, I do. They got an ass whooping coming," said Jay.

"Very well. Your abductors are an alien race known as the Krotovore. V, display Krotovore species."

"Acknowledged. Displaying Krotovore species," said V. He flew out a bit and then projected a holographic display of a three-foot-tall creature.

The creature had six eyes on a bulbous head; two were larger than the four surrounding them. Where a mouth would be, a short proboscis protruded. The body looked like a kidney bean covered in short hairs. The back had segmented armor plates while four legs supported the body. Two arms on each side of the body hung to the side and each arm had a hand section with three slim fingers, one of which was opposable. Small antennae extended from the head, which had small bumpy ridges around the top.

"That looks like a large flea!" said Emily as she stepped back and wrung her hands.

"It's probably *not* a large flea," said Sanjay.

Emily snapped her head around to glare at him.

He ducked his face and looked away.

Dr. Snowden figured it would freak out Emily. She did not like bugs. When she was a kid, he and Dan performed a bug check in her room before she went to sleep. "You want us to believe large, sentient, flea-like aliens abducted us?"

Evaran pointed at various objects in the room. "This is their lab. Would you conclude that the equipment design in this room was meant for humans?"

Dr. Snowden followed Evaran's pointing and concluded that the freestanding console in the back of the room was designed oddly. The big screen to Evaran's right also had an unusual interface to it. "Maybe it isn't, but why'd they pick us?"

"I am not sure. It could be random, maybe not. There is not a lot of information in the logs I looked at, but there may be more elsewhere. I plan to find out."

Dr. Snowden shook his head. "How convenient."

Evaran's eyes softened. "You are an astronomer, and I believe you would refer to their home galaxy as the Sombrero galaxy. These Krotovore, however, do not exist yet in this time period. They are from the future, about six hundred thousand years or so."

"The Sombrero galaxy? That's around eight point six megaparsecs away, roughly. Are you telling me they can time travel too? That's impossible."

"Mega what?" said Jay.

Dr. Snowden circled his right hand in front of him. "Umm . . . that's . . . twenty-nine million light-years or so."

"The fuck is a light-year?" asked Jay with a crooked mouth.

"An Earth metric that defines the distance light can travel in one year in a vacuum, roughly six trillion miles," said Evaran.

"Right . . . ," said Jay, nodding his head.

Evaran tilted his head at Dr. Snowden. "They did not do it on purpose. They traveled through space-time rifts, which makes travel instantaneous."

"Like a wormhole, right?" asked Sanjay.

Evaran nodded. "Conceptually they are similar. There are different types of rifts. The one thing they all have in common is that they can connect two points wherever they might be, and travel is instantaneous. For instance, a space rift would allow travel from one galaxy to another. A time rift would allow one to go forward or backward in time in the same position in space. The ones the Krotovore used were space-time rifts, meaning they could travel to a different point in space in a different time."

Dr. Snowden shook his head. "No. That's simply not possible."

"To your species perhaps. At least not yet. Any other questions?"

Sanjay glanced at Dr. Snowden, then at Evaran. "Going back to the virtual simulation, you said it was March 2, 2013, now, which was also the date in the virtual simulation. If the travel to Andromeda was instant, then we have only been in the virtual simulation for three weeks. How did we spend a year in the virtual simulation but three weeks out here? Time dilation or something?"

"Your knowledge is surprising, and you are correct again," said Evaran. "In the virtual simulation, time moved much quicker from your perspective. Three weeks in reality was roughly one year in the virtual simulation. The day and night cycles in the real world did not match up well with the virtual simulation's cycle. Trying to sleep in the virtual simulation when your body in the real world was awake made it appear as if you had insomnia in the virtual simulation. In contrast, when your body in the real world was tired, it would appear as if you were drowsy in the virtual simulation. One day in the real world would be about two to three weeks in the simulation. You would have died of old age in there, at least based on the simulations I ran."

Emily's lips turned down. "So my senior year wasn't real."

"That is correct," said Evaran.

"That's ridiculous," said Dr. Snowden. He tossed a hand out. "You're saying it's been one year and three weeks since my brother died and not two years?"

"I am," said Evaran.

"Makes sense to me," said Sanjay.

Jay glanced at Sanjay. "How you understanding all this shit, Chief?"

Sanjay clenched his jaw and bobbed his head as he faced Jay. "Firstly, my name is Sanjay. Secondly, you have the wrong Indian. Thirdly, I watch and read a lot of science fiction. These things are covered quite a bit. It does require having the ability to read and listen, so I understand your confusion."

Jay snapped his head back and narrowed his eyes.

Sanjay gulped and turned away from him and faced Evaran.

Dr. Snowden rubbed his chin. No wonder he was having trouble believing any of this. It did sound like science fiction to him. "Okay, well, if we're on an alien ship, how is it that we can breathe?"

"The air actually has a slightly different composition than what you are used to," said Evaran. "There is less nitrogen and more oxygen. Your nanobots have adjusted to that."

It seemed to Dr. Snowden that Evaran had an answer for everything.

Emily stepped out a bit from Dr. Snowden as she faced Evaran. "How do you know all this?"

Evaran pointed at the console on the far side of the room. "It is all in the system logs over there."

"This ain't happening, man," said Jay, dipping his head and rubbing his temples with his right hand.

"I am afraid it is," said Evaran.

"Why'd you help us?" asked Emily.

Evaran raised a finger. "I have been on Earth for quite a while now, studying your species, and I have grown quite fond of it. On the day of your abduction, my ship noticed a temporal signature on the Krotovore scout ship. That was cause for investigation, as is any type of temporal activity. I did not know they had abducted you at that point and only found that out when I boarded their ship and accessed the specimen list. It was corrupted and had only the names and basic descriptions intact. Although I did not know where most of the specimens came from, I did know where you came from, and from what time period. I decided to interfere, and here I am."

Emily's eyes softened as she glanced at Dr. Snowden.

Evaran placed both hands behind his back. "Before I answer any more questions, you should put on the clothes you had before you were abducted. We only have about ten minutes before the shields in this room drop." He walked over to the slab Dr. Snowden had been on and pressed a lower panel built into the slab, which then slid out with a slight whooshing sound. "Your clothes are in the lower panel facing toward the doorway of this room. There are stalls in the back of the room you can change in."

"Correction. The shields will drop in ten minutes and twelve seconds," said V.

"V, silent mode."

"Acknowledged."

"Does everyone understand this?" asked Evaran.

Everyone acknowledged Evaran and then went to their slabs.

Dr. Snowden studied the first stall that he had entered. With clothes in hand, he was ready to get out of his robe. The sterile smell was in stark contrast to the rest of the lab as it hit him in the face. Maybe the nanobots gave him a better sense of smell. He could almost visualize where the most sterile spots were in the stall. A small shelflike structure jutted out at chest level. He set his clothes on it and began to change. After he got his pants on and had half his shirt buttoned, he heard a soft knock at the stall door. "Who is it?"

"Evaran. Do you have a moment?"

Dr. Snowden opened the door.

Evaran leaned in. "You may not believe you have nano-bots, but so you know, the nanobots have removed your prostate cancer completely."

Dr. Snowden tensed up as he swallowed hard.

Evaran nodded at him and closed the door as he leaned back out.

Dr. Snowden turned around and continued getting dressed. His thoughts turned toward what Evaran had said. Dr. Snowden had never told Emily about his prostate cancer. It had been diagnosed in the early stages, and he had been undergoing effective treatment. Dan had died from a different cancer, and Dr. Snowden remembered the day Emily found out Dan had cancer. She had descended into a bad place. Dr. Snowden did not want to burden her with that while she was finishing college, especially when the chance of remission was high according to the doctor.

It dawned on him that the treatments in the virtual sim-ulation were not real, so he would have been behind in his treatments. However, it appeared that was no longer needed. He also found it interesting that Evaran mentioned this pri-vately instead of saying it aloud in front of the others. Maybe he did it because he knew Emily did not know about it.

Dr. Snowden rubbed his hips, thinking about the prickle sensations he had felt in that region earlier. He had no way of verifying it was gone and would still have to tell Emily at some point, a conversation he was dreading.

After he was fully clothed, he tapped his pocket, causing his key ring to jingle. He ran his hand across his back pocket and verified his wallet was still there and then stepped out of the stall.

Looking around, he saw that he was the first one out. He walked back to the slab that he had been at before and a few moments later, Emily joined him, then Jay, and then Sanjay. Emily had on her jeans, loose shirt, and comfortable shoes. Jay wore work boots, jeans, a white shirt with a red puffy vest of some type, and a red-and-white trucker hat. Sanjay emerged in casual dress shoes with khakis and a tan buttoned-up short-sleeve shirt. Evaran was studying a large screen on the wall.

Evaran turned to face the group. "The shields are about to drop, so we must leave now."

"What's so important about the room's shields dropping?" asked Emily.

Evaran pointed to the large screen. "Come over here, and look at this."

Everyone assembled around Evaran.

Evaran took a credit-card-like device from his belt and placed it vertically next to the console by the large screen. It snapped into a hovering position one inch from the console. An unstable blue light appeared between the card and the console, but after a few moments, it stabilized and emitted a steady light. He then interacted with the air in front of him, moving his fingers around and pressing buttons, like there was an interface only he could see.

The large screen on the wall began displaying different-looking creatures.

"You were not the only specimens on board," said Evaran. "This ship has sustained damage and is currently hurtling toward a planet. Impact is in two hours. Thankfully, the shields in this room lasted as long as they did, as the other specimen rooms' shields have dropped already. Those specimens, as seen on this screen, are now freely roaming the ship. That is why the crew is dead."

"This is so fucked up, man," said Jay.

Dr. Snowden's stomach rolled as he examined the screen. The creatures he saw looked like nightmares come to life. They had unusual symbols laid out around them, and the screen would show one for five seconds, then move on to another creature. Some of them looked humanoid.

"Why do you keep tapping the air in front of you?" asked Emily.

Evaran half smiled at Emily. "Human curiosity. How I so enjoy it. You would refer to it as augmented reality. The universal interface card, or UIC," he said, pointing at the card on the console, "connects me to whatever it is attached. An augmented reality interface, or ARI, that only I can interact with appears around me. In this case, I am able to control the large screen we are looking at."

"You don't have glasses on, though. Contact lenses?" asked Sanjay.

"Something like that," said Evaran.

Jay shrugged and shook his head. "Augmented what?"

"I can explain later when we get to my ship."

Sanjay wrinkled his eyebrows. "How does the UIC know how to connect to the—"

A high-pitched beep filled the room. The shields covering the front entrance were beginning to turn transparent and flicker.

"I will also explain that later. For now, it is time to go. Just stick close to me," said Evaran.

Dr. Snowden cleared his throat and cocked his head at Evaran. "I don't think we've established that we're going anywhere with you. I've listened to your explanation, and I'm not buying it. Now you want us to follow you," he said, shaking his head, "to who knows where."

Evaran eyed Dr. Snowden. "The bridge is where I am going. We need to change this ship's trajectory there by adjusting the thrusters. Otherwise, the ship will crash into the planet.

We have two hours to do it. After that, we need to turn on the main engines in the engine room."

"I'm going with him. He's the one with answers," said Sanjay, gesturing at Evaran.

Jay crooked his thumb at Dr. Snowden. "I'm with Doc and Hot Pants. If they ain't going, I ain't."

V flew over to Emily and shot a yellow beam over her pants. "Correction. Emily has pants within an acceptable temperature range."

Sanjay chuckled as everyone else stared at V.

Emily glared at Jay and then at Sanjay.

V flew back to Evaran.

Evaran shook his head and looked at V. "I thought you were in silent mode."

"Acknowledged. Silent mode engaged."

Dr. Snowden sighed and then faced Jay. "I'd appreciate it if you didn't call my niece Hot Pants, and again, my name is Dr. Snowden, not Doc."

Jay raised both hands toward Dr. Snowden. "All right, all right, damn, man."

Evaran interacted with his ARI.

A large creature appeared on the screen.

Evaran pointed to it and looked at Dr. Snowden. "This is a dungol. It is an apex predator on the planet it comes from." He pointed toward the door. "It was two hallways over from here, and the shields to its room are down. That means it is wandering around somewhere out there." He then wagged a finger at Dr. Snowden. "How will you deal with that?"

Dr. Snowden studied the dungol. It looked like a large boar with a huge mouth and a rhinoceros horn. "If it isn't real, then I won't have to."

Emily tugged at his arm. "Uncle Albert, I think we should go with him."

"What? Why?" asked Dr. Snowden, snapping his head toward Emily.

"Because it's what Dad would do. You told him there were those who research and those who do. He was a doer, and so am I. If we sit here doing nothing, what do we gain? I think it's safer to explore what's out there as a group instead of split up."

Dr. Snowden sighed. She was right about Dan. He would have slapped Evaran on the back and taken this as a challenge. Dr. Snowden could see it in Emily as well. However, he was not used to her questioning his decisions. Maybe it would be better to have numbers in an unknown situation. He dipped his head and flung his right arm up. "Fine. We go."

Evaran paused to look at Emily, then slowly nodded at her.

"How will we defend ourselves?" asked Sanjay, tilting his head.

Evaran pulled the cylindrical device from his belt. "This is my utility handle and what I will use for defense. It has the ability to shoot heat, stun, repulsion, and grappling beams. It can also form various shapes via morphable metal."

Sanjay looked around at the others, then back at Evaran. "Care to . . . show us?"

"Once again, your curiosity is refreshing. Although we are limited on time, I can do a quick demonstration so you are not startled if I do use it," said Evaran. He tapped a button on his handle, which extended morphable metal out one end in the shape of a baton.

"Whoa," said Jay.

The end of the baton glowed orange as Evaran pointed at the doorway. "This is a heat beam." An orange beam shot out, then dissipated. "It is used for utility purposes."

The baton end glowed blue and then shot out a beam. Blue electrical arcs jumped around the fading shielded door.

"That is the stun beam," said Evaran. "It only works on beings susceptible to it. For a human, it would knock them out." He changed the baton end to glow white.

Boom!

Everyone but Evaran and V jumped.

"What the hell was that?" asked Jay, with his left arm raised in front of him.

"A repulsion beam. I use it to repel those who would do harm," said Evaran.

"I like it," said Sanjay.

Evaran nodded. "The last beam is a grappling beam, as noted by a yellow glowing end, and it functions as you would expect." He extended his left forearm, which now had a glowing semitransparent rectangular shield with a hex pattern. "This is a resizable energy shield used to reflect any beam or projectile that should come our way."

"Pretty advanced," said Sanjay.

"And more than enough to handle anything on this ship," said Evaran. "Come, let us go to the bridge then. V, scout mode." He grabbed the UIC from the console on the wall and put it into the cardholder on his belt. When he got to the entrance, he turned to face V. "V?" He sighed. "Silent mode off. I really need to fix that."

"Acknowledged. Scout mode engaged," said V.

Dr. Snowden noted that Evaran walked with confidence, his head held high and shoulders squared, as if this was an everyday thing for him. The utility handle and shield were way beyond anything Dr. Snowden had seen. The one thing that stood out to him was that when the repulsion beam fired, there was no recoil. Either Evaran was insanely strong or the recoil was absorbed by the handle. Also, everything seemed nonlethal. Maybe that was on purpose.

Everyone followed Evaran to the doorway, where the light-blue smoke over it had dissipated.

V flew to the doorway and shimmered briefly before vanishing.

Dr. Snowden was not surprised at V vanishing. Impossible was becoming routine to him.

05

D r. Snowden followed Evaran along with the others out of the medical lab. Although Dr. Snowden was still unsure of everything, he did not see any harm in entertaining Evaran and seeing where this went. If this was a hallucination or a dream, it was well crafted.

Everything Dr. Snowden had seen so far seemed more real to him than in the virtual simulation. He was still coming to grips with having a year of fake memories. A part of him wondered if he was maybe in another simulation. That would at least make the current situation more plausible.

The dimly lit hallway was large, and a faint mist permeated the air. The ceiling was about twenty feet high, and there were two entrances across the hallway and one to the right of the doorway they just exited. At the end of the hallway was a larger entrance.

Alongside each room opening was a high-tech workstation with unusual equipment on the side. The walls were covered with metallic panels, broken up every now and then with a screen and elongated, flat, U-shaped tubules with a red-spotted flesh-like texture jutting out every few panels or so. Several feet from the ceiling on all sides was a glass-like black strip outlined with gold borders that wrapped around the whole hallway.

Jay waved his hand in front of his face. "Damn, smells like a wet dog up in here."

"The Krotovore probably had a similar reaction entering your room," said Evaran.

Jay cocked his head as if to say something, but shrugged his shoulders and looked around.

Dr. Snowden wrinkled his nose. He had a similar thought about the smell. Coming from the well-lit lab and into the dimly lit hallway sent chills through him. He waved his hand through the mist that seemed to float above the ground. There did not seem to be an obvious source for the mist. Focusing ahead, he noted that the other entrances did not have shields on them, which made him wonder if others had been in there. Looking up, he pointed to the barely visible strips. "What're those?"

Evaran tilted his head up to look at the strip. "It is a holographic projection strip, similar to my ring from the virtual simulation, but the strip is much more advanced. If they were working, I would be able to show you a holographic representation of a Krotovore AI."

"How convenient they're busted," said Dr. Snowden.

Evaran paused to look at Dr. Snowden, then turned and waved for everyone to follow.

They continued out into a hallway. At the end of it, they stepped into a large cylindrical area with an open center.

Dr. Snowden did not see a floor or ceiling in the middle, but the walkway they were on, and those above and below, extended around the edges in a full circle. It was difficult for him to see too much, as the mist seemed to be denser. Four half-cylindrical columns were evenly spaced on each walkway, and he figured they were some type of support structure. The whole area reminded him of a large, hollow missile silo, and they were quite a ways up. He moved to the walkway's edge and looked down a few levels, then up. "How big is this? I can't see the floor or ceiling."

"It is several miles each way. We are on level 546 out of 1000 or so levels. We need to go up to level 555, where the main bridge concourse is. There is an elevator system nearby we can use," said Evaran, pointing to the nearest half-cylindrical column.

Jay laughed. "Several miles? In a building? C'mon, man . . ."

"You still believe this is a building?"

"Yeah, I do," said Jay, glancing at Dr. Snowden.

Dr. Snowden nodded his head at Jay. "Until proven otherwise, I agree with Jay's assessment."

Evaran narrowed his eyes for a moment. "Okay."

They reached the featureless half-cylindrical column.

Evaran placed his UIC on the wall console and interacted with his ARI, causing the half-cylindrical column to rotate, exposing a spacious interior with gray walls. "In we go then."

After stepping inside, Dr. Snowden examined the interior. It was featureless except for one console. He was not sure where the light was coming from, but it was everywhere. The symbols on the console looked like rubbish to him.

The elevator doors slid shut, and after a few moments, they reopened to level 555.

Dr. Snowden was amazed at how fast it went up nine levels. After stepping out, he recognized that this level was about three stories high, much different than the other levels he had seen. He jumped as a shrieking sound rang out from far away. It sounded like something in pain. Between that, the mist, and the low lighting, the ambiance was beginning to get to him. Real or not, this place was ominous. He rubbed the goose bumps on his arm.

After a few minutes, they reached main bridge concourse entrance.

Dr. Snowden took a moment to examine the archway. The border of the entrance had thick segmented blocks ringing it. Each segment had a circle on it, with an alien symbol in the circle. It was elegant in its simplicity, and he wondered what material it was made out of. He could barely see the end of the main bridge concourse. "This is a pretty big room. How far to the bridge?"

"Approximately one mile," said V, appearing next to Dr. Snowden.

Dr. Snowden flinched. He had forgotten V was flying around. "Umm . . . thanks, V."

"Acknowledged," said V. His lights glowed a bit brighter as he flew to Evaran.

"V, map the concourse," said Evaran.

"Acknowledged. Mapping mode engaged," said V. He flew off toward the end of the main bridge concourse, emanating a two-dimensional circular red light that expanded to all sides of the room.

"When V gets back, we will have a three-dimensional scan of the room. I just want to make sure it is clear before we proceed," said Evaran.

"You think there might be other specimens in there?" said Emily, watching V fly down the main bridge concourse.

"Possibly. It is a large area, which has some tactical disadvantages for us," said Evaran, raising a finger.

"What else would V be scanning for?" asked Sanjay, looking at Emily.

Emily shot a look at Sanjay. "I don't know. That's why I asked."

Sanjay ducked away to the other side of the arched entrance.

Dr. Snowden did not think Sanjay was trying to be confrontational, although his curiousness could be construed as aggressive. Emily seemed to think so. Dr. Snowden walked over to one of the segmented blocks on the entrance border. An interface projection appeared in front of him and displayed the unusual alien symbols, but this time, he understood what they meant. It was a map interface for the main bridge concourse. "Hey! I can understand this!" he said, turning to look at Evaran.

"Ahh, good. The universal translator has kicked in," said Evaran.

Everyone gathered around Dr. Snowden.

Sanjay studied the map interface. "Are the nanobots doing this?"

"They are involved," said Evaran, gazing down the main bridge concourse. "I was able to get them to accept translation requests from my ship. I was unsure how long it would take to kick in, but it appears they have completed integration."

"Translation requests? You mean we're connected to your ship through our supposed nanobots?" asked Dr. Snowden with raised eyebrows.

"Yes, the *supposed* nanobots can communicate with the ship's universal translator. Typically, I would offer you a temporary set of nanobots. As you already had nanobots inside you, I decided to see if I could interface with them, and it appears to have worked. Your nanobots now have a new protocol to check with the ship's universal translator if they cannot translate something. If it cannot translate something directly, it will use the nearest term, even if it is slang," said Evaran, turning to look at Dr. Snowden and Emily.

"Does it make others who don't have universal translators understand us? Like, if I were to speak to a French person, would it come out as French?" asked Emily.

"Yes, and your lips would move to compensate. Although you would still see French in text and the other person's lips move in sync with French, you would understand what it meant," said Evaran.

"I find that very unlikely," said Dr. Snowden.

Jay shook his head. "That's messed up."

"The evidence is staring you all right in the face," said Evaran.

"Does this mean the ship has access to our thoughts then?" asked Sanjay.

"Temporarily during the translation it does, but it does not keep an audit trail. The universal translator protocol came with my ship, and all I know about it is how to access it remotely and configure some of it," said Evaran.

"So it has some privacy security built in. I like that," said Sanjay.

Dr. Snowden could see that Sanjay was into the situation, but Dr. Snowden could not bring himself to so easily believe what Evaran was saying. The conclusion Dr. Snowden had reached in the medical lab was no longer as secure as he thought it was. He watched as V flew back. Dr. Snowden calculated that since V had not been gone long, he must be able to either fly quickly or skim across the top and scan forward as opposed to only the sides Dr. Snowden had seen initially.

V flew next to Evaran and projected a three-dimensional overview of the main bridge concourse. The projected map had more detail than the displayed one from the segmented block.

Evaran began walking around the projection with his hands behind his back. "V, report."

"Analysis. No active life-forms detected. Multiple inactive life-forms detected. Eighty-seven entrances, seven thousand hatchways—"

"I think that will be enough. Let us go," said Evaran.

Although Dr. Snowden had been able to keep his fear down, knowing this all might be real kept badgering him. Emily was about as he would expect her, and Sanjay and Jay seemed real. Dr. Snowden exhaled from his nose. Being on an alien ship in the Andromeda galaxy due to flea-like aliens abducting him was not what he had envisioned being wrong with him just a day ago, yet here he was. Hopefully this was a big hoax. He sighed as he trudged after Evaran and the others.

⸻

As the group moved down the main bridge concourse, Dr. Snowden took note of the architecture. The sides had walkways accessible by ramps at evenly distanced intervals. There were various areas sectioned off in the main walkway that contained stands with unusual devices. Benches with strange shapes and an occasional odd-looking plant dotted the floor.

The concourse was definitely larger than he had expected. The most unusual aspect was the small hatches high up on the walls. There were three rows, each row having roughly five feet between each hatchway. The rows seemed to span the length of the concourse.

After thirty minutes, they reached the middle of the main bridge concourse, and the bridge door could be seen in the distance.

"This is something you all may want to see," said Evaran, pointing to something on the ground.

Everyone assembled around Evaran and examined where he was pointing. On the ground was a dead Krotovore. It was missing a leg and two arms, and half of the chest armor was gone with teeth marks around the edges. Green liquid had solidified around it.

There were other aliens near the dead Krotovore that Dr. Snowden did not recognize.

"It looks part eaten," said Sanjay.

"It was one of the security forces of the ship. You can tell by the designation on the chest plate," said Evaran, motioning at the mangled chest armor. "Whatever got to it was strong enough to peel apart the armor. That is probably something we want to avoid."

"Ewww. I think I'm gonna be sick," said Emily as she grimaced and put a hand on her stomach.

"I've seen better props than this," said Dr. Snowden.

Jay shook his head. "I dunno, man, looks pretty real to me." He rubbed the back of his neck while looking up. His head snapped back as he pushed Dr. Snowden down. "Watch out!"

"What the—" said Dr. Snowden as he rag-dolled to the floor. A spiderlike creature landed where he had stood just a second ago. His eyes widened, and his heart began to race.

"What the *fuck*?" shouted Jay as the creature jumped at him. He caught it in midair and threw it to the ground and then stomped it.

Several more creatures landed near him.

Jay kicked the nearest one, sending it tumbling back.

Another one jumped at him.

He dodged it, and when the creature landed, he pivoted and stomped it.

Another creature fell on his arm.

He shouted out in pain as it careened off him and crashed to the ground. His face turned red. He stepped back and kicked the creature into the air. After turning his hat backward, he balled his fists and shook his head at the one he kicked. "Well, c'mon then, you little shits!"

Sanjay took off running with four creatures in pursuit.

Evaran had turned to help Jay, but then turned back around to run after Sanjay.

Dr. Snowden scrambled to his feet. Emily screaming caught his attention.

Two creatures had landed near her, and another was already trying to bite her.

Emily held the one trying to bite her in place with her outstretched arms.

Dr. Snowden bolted over and kicked the first one.

Its sides busted open, spewing guts everywhere.

Dr. Snowden stomped the second one, causing its organs to fly out the back end. He yanked the third one off Emily and threw it to the ground.

It landed on its back.

Dr. Snowden's eyes flared as adrenaline surged through him. It tried to flip over, but he got to it first, kneeling to slam his fists into its soft underbelly.

It shuddered as black blood spattered out.

Dr. Snowden grunted as his vision blurred, and he raged that they would threaten Emily. He grabbed a leg.

Rip.

And another.

Rip.

And another.

Rip.

The creature stopped moving. The nauseating smell of guts permeated the air.

Dr. Snowden turned as he heard the thump of another one landing near him. He reached out and grabbed it. His fists slammed into the creature's multi-eyed face, crushing it.

A sharp pain shot up his leg where another had bitten him. He grunted as he pulled it off him. Using his right hand, he flipped and crushed it.

It shrieked and then gurgled. Black blood oozed everywhere.

Dr. Snowden picked up the body and ripped it in half. He turned to look at Emily, who was violently shaking.

She had fallen back some and was dodging one of the creatures while kicking at it.

It avoided her blows and continued to circle her.

Dr. Snowden scrambled to his feet and rushed over. He dove at it, slamming both fists into it.

It flattened out.

Dr. Snowden let out a primal scream as he jackhammered the lifeless corpse.

Evaran had returned and laid a hand on Dr. Snowden's shoulder. "Dr. Snowden."

Dr. Snowden kept hitting the dead creature. Tears ran down his face.

"Dr. Snowden!" said Evaran.

Dr. Snowden stopped and put his fists against his temples and squinted his eyes. His jaw was clenched and his breathing ragged. He whimpered as he looked back to Emily, who was frozen in fear. Looking around, he saw Evaran and Jay, both covered in guts, staring at him with dead creatures lying around them. Peering back, he glared at the thing he had mutilated. There was no way a creature like this existed on Earth for many reasons. He knew any aggressive bugs that could evolve to this size would have easily swept the planet. They were definitely real and not props.

"I believe it is dead," said Evaran.

Dr. Snowden took a deep breath. He splayed out his arms as he leaned forward and dry heaved. The taste of the creatures' blood was in his mouth. Some of the entrails that had shot onto his face slipped off. After a few moments, he turned his head to look at Evaran. In a quiet voice, Dr. Snowden said, "This . . . this is real."

Evaran's eyes softened as he nodded at Dr. Snowden. "Yes, it is." He lightly squeezed Dr. Snowden's shoulder.

Emily walked over and put her trembling hand on Dr. Snowden's other shoulder and whispered, "Uncle Albert?"

Dr. Snowden turned to face her. His body shuddered as more tears ran down the sides of his face. In a cracked voice, he said, "I was wrong." He looked down and squinted hard. His lips drew down. "I was so wrong," he said in a hushed tone while looking at Emily.

"It's okay," whispered Emily as she knelt to hug him. She sniffled and wiped a tear off her face.

Jay looked around, then at Evaran. With clenched fists, he said, "Sanjay ran away! That lil chickenshit!"

Evaran sighed and turned to face Jay. "It was a rough situation. Do not judge him harshly. Nonetheless, we need to move. Those were draug. The ones you saw were just the scouts, and the smallest of their type. Some escaped back to their brood."

"Ohhh, that's just fucking great, man!" said Jay, tossing his right arm into the air.

Dr. Snowden stood up with the help of Emily. He looked at the ground as the warm sensation of embarrassment washed through him. His heart slowed down as he measured his breath. Thoughts ran wild in his mind. Being wrong on this level bothered him.

He put his hand on the bite on his leg. It was just a minor surface wound, but it stung. To add to the uneasiness, the smell of the corpses was overpowering. He walked to Jay.

Jay slapped Dr. Snowden on the back. "Damn, Doc—I mean, Dr. Snowden. You literally kicked the shit out of them, man. Fuck yeah."

Dr. Snowden exhaled sharply and nodded at Jay. His push was timely, and the situation could have been much worse. When it came to fight or flight, he was all fight. Dr. Snowden cleared his throat. "Call me Doc."

"All right then," said Jay, nodding at Dr. Snowden.

Evaran tilted his head while raising his hand. "The brood has arrived at the entrance. We must move. *Now.*"

Dr. Snowden rubbed the goose bumps on his arms. The intensity of Evaran's face startled Dr. Snowden back to reality.

V had flown off back toward the main bridge concourse entrance per a motion from Evaran.

It took the group twenty minutes to hustle to the main bridge door.

When they arrived, Evaran placed his UIC on the console next to the entryway.

"There you are, you son of a bitch!" said Jay, approaching Sanjay, who was curled up next to the door.

Sanjay used the door to slide up into a standing position. A urine trail snaked down his slacks. "I was scared, okay?"

"Fuck, man, we're all scared. Doesn't mean we don't watch each other's back," said Jay.

"Jay, this is not the time for this," said Evaran.

Jay shook his head and exhaled sharply. "God, what a pussy." He walked away from Sanjay.

Evaran interacted with his ARI and then pulled out a small orb device from his utility belt. He tossed out the orb, which then hovered a few feet off the ground. After interacting with his ARI again, a projection shot up showing creatures running through the entrance. They were pouring in, not just on the ground, but on the walls and the ceiling.

"Shit, more of those things," said Jay, his mouth slightly ajar. He turned his hat back around.

"So many of them," said Emily, grimacing.

"That is a full-on draug brood. We can discuss it more when we are in a safer position," said Evaran.

"Goddamn," said Jay.

Emily grabbed Dr. Snowden's arm.

Dr. Snowden could feel her trembling echo through him. He had a lot of thoughts running through his mind, but the projection of the draug mesmerized him. The draug had different body types. Although they were all mostly mottled brown in color, there was a remarkable diversity of shapes. They reminded him of ants somewhat.

There were larger ones with four legs, a thorax behind them, and an upper plated body. The face had two large eyes and large pincers where a mouth would be. The upper body had two powerful-looking arms that ended in claws. Those must be the soldiers. Then there were two smaller types running around the larger ones. The first one was the type they had just run into. It was a darker brown than the rest of the draug. They also seemed to move much faster than the rest. The second one reminded him of a pill bug, except with armored plates that had spikes on each segment. It had a tube of some sort coming from its face. Those must be specialized workers.

As V began flying back, there was a wide shot of them.

A large one towered over them all. The body reminded him of a large praying mantis, but this one had arms ending in large claws instead of praying forelegs, and there were all sorts of protruding spikes on it. Dr. Snowden figured it was the size of an elephant, and the face reminded him of a spider's. It had multiple eyes and large fangs projecting from its mouth. He had no idea what that creature represented, maybe an overseer or something. The clicking sounds were getting louder. He guessed they knew that there was food in here. At least there were no flying ones.

"Umm . . . how's the door coming?" asked Sanjay.

Evaran reached out, and after the projection orb flew into his hand, he put it back on his belt. His UIC had established a blue light between it and the door console, and after interacting with his ARI, he said, "Opening it now."

The doors pulled back into the sidewalls, revealing a large bridge.

They burst through as Evaran pulled the UIC from the door console, causing the doors to move.

V flew in as the doors closed.

Thumping sounds emanated from the door a few moments later.

Dr. Snowden barely registered the thumping. A jumble of thoughts was waging war in his mind. He was not used to being this wrong and realized how foolish he must have looked to Evaran and, more importantly, Emily. Dr. Snowden vowed to learn everything he could.

06

Dr. Snowden slumped down against the wall just inside the bridge entrance. He could not believe what had just happened, yet it had been right in front of him. This was real, and he knew he had to adjust to it or he would not survive. Having Evaran around made things a bit easier, and Dr. Snowden was coming to trust Evaran more.

Dr. Snowden closed his eyes as his breathing normalized. It was sinking in that not only was everything real, but they were in a potentially very bad place. He looked to his side when Emily sat next to him and then linked her left arm with his right. She was probably worse off than anyone so far, and he would try to put on a brave face for her to hold on to.

Jay leaned against the wall on the other side of the bridge entrance. He looked up at the ceiling and took a deep breath. "Damn, I could go for a smoke 'bout now."

Sanjay went ahead a bit and stood by one of the workstations in the room. He drooped his head and slid his hands into his pockets.

Evaran walked out in front of the group. "Any longer out there and we would have been another meal for them. While I could handle them, I would not be able to guarantee your safety. Nonetheless, they will not be breaking through that door. It has shields and is physically very durable. Relax a bit. I am going to work on the bridge consoles. There are sustenance replicators to your right. You can get some water there, but I would recommend not trying to select any food items." He looked at Jay. "Or cigarettes."

"Figures. Any place to get this crap off?" asked Jay, pointing to the draug bits and pieces on his boots.

Evaran nodded and pointed to their left. "There are some cleaning rooms over there. Just step in, wait for the door to close, and undress. If you need to use the bathroom, they have a structure for that in there as well. Once you are ready, just press the large green button, and it will scan and then clean everything in the room."

Jay smirked as he walked over to the first cleaning room. "A shit scanner."

"I suppose so," said Evaran with a half smile.

Emily tugged on Dr. Snowden's arm. "Uncle Albert? You okay?"

"I'm fine," said Dr. Snowden, sighing. "I . . . need to think for a bit. Why don't you go get cleaned up?"

She stared at him for a moment. "Okay." She got up and walked toward the cleaning rooms.

Sanjay followed after her, giving her ample time to get into one of the rooms before he went in one.

Dr. Snowden began to sort out his thoughts in more detail. He decided to focus on why he did not believe Evaran initially. Evidence was all around, and Dr. Snowden had dismissed it out of hand because he did not believe in the premise. It was not easy for him as a scientist to accept the situation, especially given the lack of verifiable facts. He concluded that Evaran was just being brutally honest.

Next, Dr. Snowden began going through what he knew. One, there was Evaran. The first alien that Dr. Snowden had met while conscious. Evaran was apparently able to hack into an alien virtual simulation. On top of that, he had his own starship and a flying orb with artificial intelligence. He also seemed to have an understanding of time travel, space-time rifts, and their abductors, the Krotovore. Dr. Snowden figured maybe this could be a learning opportunity. Evaran did not have to rescue them, but he did. That said a lot about his character. Dr. Snowden concluded that Evaran had their best interests in mind.

Dr. Snowden's thoughts turned to the Krotovore. They abducted four people along a lone stretch of I-70, but the why eluded him. Evaran said there was sparse information in the logs and that he planned to find out more. Maybe there would be additional information here on the bridge. Dr. Snowden filed it away as something to ask Evaran later.

The fact that aliens existed at all was exciting, but what they did was inexcusable. Life was already hard for Emily, and now she had to deal with this. It saddened Dr. Snowden that meeting aliens for the first time was not in an effort of cooperation, but a violation of his very being. He tried to subdue those thoughts, but they simmered in the back of his mind.

Then there was the virtual simulation. It felt real. The sensations he felt now were much different, and the sudden onset of insomnia now made sense. One hour awake in the real world was probably a day or two in the virtual simulation. No wonder trying to sleep in there was so hard. Other times he could barely keep his eyes open. Evaran mentioned that death was a real possibility, and for these Krotovore, it would have been just another failed experiment.

Dr. Snowden looked at his hand and flexed it. He imagined the nanobots swimming around in there. They cured his prostate cancer, and he felt like he was twenty-one again. He had doubted their existence, but he could feel their effects on him when fighting the draug, and even now, he felt a bit calmer, despite knowing that he should be going out of his mind about the situation. If they kept his body in this shape, he was not sure he wanted them out.

Evaran had mentioned the nanobots had sensory functions, but Dr. Snowden did not know what that meant. Emily would definitely want them out, but maybe after hearing what they did, she would change her mind. Dr. Snowden planned to let her know about his prostate cancer before then. The last thing she needed right now on top of all this was to learn that he had any type of cancer.

Dr. Snowden's mind wandered to Jay. His machismo was off-putting at times, but Dr. Snowden saw a certain charm in it. Jay had saved Dr. Snowden from having one of those creatures fall on him. He admired Jay's resilience, and although Jay was probably as scared as the rest of them, anger was his reaction to the situation.

Sanjay was a mystery. He seemed to be a bright kid, but crippling fear caused him to run at the first sign of trouble. Not once, but twice. His awakening had been rough like Jay's had.

Dr. Snowden was glad Evaran had visited him and Emily. The next plan of attack was to learn as much as possible. If this was real, Dr. Snowden needed to know the lay of the land. Evaran seemed willing to share some information, so Dr. Snowden would take advantage of that. He stood up and walked over to the cleaning rooms. There were six of them, and three were active.

After entering an open room, the doors closed. Like in the stall in the medical lab, Dr. Snowden was hit by a strong scent, except this one smelled like vinegar. He undressed and placed his clothes on a table that jutted out from the wall.

The structure Evaran mentioned was a hole in the ground with a set of movable limbs extending out over it. Dr. Snowden adjusted the limbs and locked them in place, then sat on them and relieved himself. Once finished, he stood up and pressed the large green button near the entrance.

A greenish mist filled the room.

It was difficult for him to see anything, but the mist massaged his body. He enjoyed the sensation over the next few minutes. The grime fell off like skin from a molting snake. Once the mist dissipated, a sweet fragrance filled the air. He looked at his arm and ran his hand over it. The mist had cleansed him thoroughly.

He grabbed and inspected his shirt and noted there was not a trace of black blood or draug guts. How the mist was able to figure out what to remove was yet another mystery. This would be on his wish list back at home, assuming he could get there. He checked the toilet and noticed it was cleaned out as well. This room was efficient. He leaned back against the wall. It felt good to be in a place where he was not being threatened by crazy aliens.

Fifteen minutes later, Dr. Snowden exited the cleaning room. It was time to find out what was going on with the ship. He surveyed the bridge. Evaran faced one of the wall consoles and interacted with his ARI. His hands moved in the air like he was using a computer keyboard only he could see. Dr. Snowden refocused on the bridge. It was a mash-up of alien spaceship bridges he had seen on television growing up.

On the front wall of the bridge was a large single screen that covered almost the entirety of it. To the sides of it were multiple smaller screens. The room had two areas. The first area near the entrance they had come in from had three rows. Each row had consoles and unusual-looking chairs. A walkway down the middle separated the rows into equal parts, and a command chair loomed at the end of the walkway.

The second area was open in front of the front screen. The sides of the bridge had a continuous console with more odd-looking chairs distributed evenly. The center screen showed a planet, with readouts indicating distance and speed on the bottom right.

Dr. Snowden chuckled when he saw Jay trying to interact with Emily at the sustenance replicators. Emily was less than pleased to talk with him. Her lips, pulled to the right, gave it away.

Jay scratched his hand and moved over to Sanjay, who was busy interacting with one of the consoles and brushed off Jay's attempt to talk. He approached Dr. Snowden and sighed. "Maybe I shouldn't have been so hard on Sanjay. Your niece doesn't like me either."

"They're young, angry, and confused," said Dr. Snowden. He wagged a finger at Jay. "And you did call her Hot Pants."

Jay looked down and away.

Dr. Snowden tapped Jay on the arm with the back of his hand. "It's okay. This situation is . . . unusual. Let's see what Evaran's up to."

They assembled around Evaran.

Dr. Snowden pointed to the center screen. "Is that the planet we're hurtling toward?"

"It is," said Evaran, facing them. "The planet has primitive life but will not have any if this ship hits it."

Dr. Snowden noticed that Evaran's suit was cleaner than before. It must have had some type of slow self-cleaning aspect to it.

Emily had joined them and handed Dr. Snowden a container of water. She looked at the center screen. "It looks so serene."

Sanjay followed in after Emily.

Evaran glanced around at them all, then looked at Dr. Snowden with knowing eyes. "So, what questions do you have?"

Dr. Snowden smiled. He reflected on how odd it felt to smile. "That UIC, you said it allows you to connect to any system. How does it know how to connect to an alien system like this?"

"I'd like to know this too," said Sanjay.

Evaran nodded. "It is only important that you know it can. The how is . . . a bit deeper than I think you are ready to hear. The UIC can interface with any technological system, usually bypassing any security setup."

"Impressive," said Sanjay.

"I like to think so," said Evaran. He gestured at Sanjay. "Your studies involve working with software. Think of it as a low-level matter decompiler that works on technology. When it is accessing the system, it will snap a few inches from what it is trying to interface, and you will see a blue light begin to intensify. Once it has accessed the system, the UIC will emit a stable blue light, and I can then access it via my ARI. The Krotovore security system, which is fairly secure I might add, does not have countermeasures for a device like this. The only effective countermeasure is a security AI, and in this scenario, there is none."

Dr. Snowden furrowed his eyebrows. The idea that the UIC could access any technological system, except for security-enhanced AI ones, seemed implausible. The results, though, were obvious, and he could not deny that.

"Why would you need the ARI then? There's already a physical interface," said Sanjay.

"The ARI is a generic interface that works across any system. The ARI and the physical interface both access the same set of functionality," said Evaran.

Sanjay raised his eyebrows. "So the ARI is just another view essentially."

"Exactly. Imagine a sphere where the bottom is at your hips and the top is at your head. Inside that sphere surface live the interfaces. I get readouts on the surrounding environment from the UIC, or from V's scanning or mine as well," said Evaran.

"Damn, that's sweet," said Jay.

"Yes, it is."

Dr. Snowden shook his head. "I can't even imagine that. Could these nanobots inside us give us something like that?"

Evaran half grinned at Dr. Snowden. "Perhaps. I will investigate the possibility later."

Dr. Snowden's eyes lit up.

"I hate to interrupt, but these draug creatures . . . are they specimens like us?" asked Emily.

Evaran tilted his head at Emily. "Yes, they have been extinct for a very long time. Nasty creatures, and in following with the theme of the other specimens, apex predators of their world."

"Why'd these asshole Krotovore pick so many of them?" asked Jay.

"I do not think they picked up all the ones we saw. I am guessing they picked up a brood queen by accident. She would need considerable amounts of food to make that many, though."

Dr. Snowden gulped. "What're we going to do about them? If we go out there, we wouldn't stand a chance."

"To that point, I have been trying to access the Krotovore global security control system, but it is too far gone. However, I have been able to access the local security control system and reroute some functionality," said Evaran. He tapped at his ARI and directed them to look at the main screen. "You can see it in action for yourselves."

Everyone turned to the main screen and watched the draug roaming outside the door. The draug brood was feasting on the dead Krotovore and other dead aliens. A beeping sound rang out, and metallic spiderlike robots swarmed from the hatches and attacked the draug. The robots began dismantling the draug with incredible efficiency. The draug retreated with the robots in pursuit.

"Man, they kick ass!" said Jay.

"Those are security drones. They are strong and fast and can jump and scale walls, and they have numbers. They are also all networked to the ship, so they have a sensor advantage and can communicate instantly with each other," said Evaran.

"Where were they earlier? We coulda used their help," said Emily.

"They would not have distinguished us from the draug had they come out. In addition to that, they can only be turned on from here since the global security control system is down. It was one of the first systems to go down since it is a primary system. They will ignore us since we are now honorary crew members. I added us to their ship roster database when I reactivated the local security control system, and they have been updated. However, the update only applies to the ones outside this door. We will need to be careful if we see any outside the surrounding bridge area."

"Oh," said Emily.

Evaran raised a finger. "I did find some other information on your profiles in the system. It seems they kept a master copy of them here. It had information gleaned from the virtual simulation as well as the state of your memories from your initial entry into it."

They all turned back around to look at Evaran.

"Like what?" asked Jay.

"To start, it says you just had a son before entering the virtual simulation."

Jay swallowed hard. "I can't wait to get back to him."

"Sanjay is the first in his family to go to college in America."

Sanjay grimaced. "I wish I was back at college."

"Emily plays volleyball."

Emily sighed. "Be nice to be on a court instead of here."

"And finally, Dr. Snowden recently published a paper."

"I did," said Dr. Snowden.

Sanjay smiled at Emily. "I wish I had time to play sports."

She glared at him. "It's simple time management."

He averted his eyes and looked away.

Evaran paused as he interacted with his ARI. "It looks like there is more, but a bit personal. Okay, back to digging for me."

Sanjay went to one of the consoles and began interacting with it while Jay hit the sustenance replicators.

Dr. Snowden and Emily approached one of the consoles in the back row. A dead Krotovore lay sprawled out to the side of it. It was in similar shape to the one they saw outside. The odor of the rotting flesh wafted through the air.

Emily grimaced as she walked past it.

Dr. Snowden scrutinized the console. He reached out to touch the glass-like surface, tracing its multiple circular interfaces along the multicolored lines that connected them. It reminded him of a circuit chip with swirls. He ran his finger across each quadrant of the main circular interface, noting it lit up where his finger touched. Running his finger over a smaller circle displayed a series of menu options. The interface would probably work better with four eyes, given how spread out the information was. He was able to catch some of the words, but the interface moved too fast. It seemed like a mess.

"I can barely read anything on this," said Emily as she touched the screen. A golden circle lit up under her finger.

"I guess if I had four arms, more than two eyes, and the ability to process information at blazing speeds, it might make more sense," said Dr. Snowden. He bumped Emily slightly with his shoulder, causing her to smile. He was glad that at least in all the chaos, she was holding on. The sense of dread that pervaded him was not going away anytime soon, and the longer he was on the ship, the stronger it got.

Over the next fifteen minutes, Dr. Snowden perused the various workstations. Emily stuck close by, and he enjoyed discovering and exploring with her at his side. It reminded him of the camping trips they used to take. While Dan made dinner, Dr. Snowden and Emily would look around at various plants and trees and try to name animals and insects they saw. That was the one time when her bug aversion was not as strong. He got a similar vibe exploring the workstations with her, but he knew just how deadly the situation was.

Evaran addressed the room. "Who wants to hear a Krotovore speak?"

Although Dr. Snowden had an intense dislike of the Krotovore, the scientist in him still wanted to hear what they sounded like. He wondered about their culture, having ships this big. One thing was apparent: the Krotovore seemed to have little regard for life they considered under them. He wondered how many aliens woke up from their virtual simulation without the aid of Evaran. Dr. Snowden shuddered. Regardless, he was intrigued enough to listen to the Krotovore speak. "What'd you find?"

"The last visual log in the system. I will play it on the main screen," said Evaran, pointing to it.

Everyone turned their attention on the main screen.

Evaran swiped at his ARI, and the main screen changed from the picture of the planet to a Krotovore with a tight-fitting gray suit. Lights flashed in the background around the Krotovore, and a muted warning alert was firing off.

A tingling sensation rushed through Dr. Snowden's chest. He noted that the background looked similar to his immediate surroundings. Although he did not know Krotovore facial expressions, the rapid blinking of the eyes seemed to indicate nervousness. He wondered if they were the first humans to see a nonhumanoid alien speak. The Krotovore interrupted his thoughts when it spoke in a high-pitched and garbled-sounding voice.

"Kri'tokhaar reporting. Kri'tokhaar is the last surviving member of the crew. Kri'tokhaar doubts it will make it out of this alive. A majority of the main systems are down except for life support. The global security control main system is down along with most of the secondary systems. Bipedal creatures attacked us en route to the last rift we came through. The specimens are roaming the ship freely. Tertiary systems such as transports and replicators are still functional. Kri'tokhaar barely got into the bridge and sealed it. Ghaa'kiPruut was with

Kri'tokhaar and made it into the bridge, but Ghaa'kiPruut was mauled severely by a quadruped creature on the way in. Ghaa'kiPruut died shortly thereafter."

Dr. Snowden looked down at the Krotovore they had walked around earlier. Although he was saddened at the situation being described, he was also excited to see Kri'tokhaar speaking. Their odd speech made him wonder if this was how they truly spoke or if it was a glitch in the universal translator. Maybe the translator could evolve to make it sound more normal over time; then again, he doubted he would ever hear another Krotovore speak. It seemed when Ghaa'kiPruut was mentioned, Kri'tokhaar's eyes blinked slower and its voice slowed down. Maybe these Krotovore did have emotions.

Dr. Snowden cast a sidelong glance at Evaran, who had his hand on his chin and his finger on his lips. It struck Dr. Snowden again that for Evaran, this was probably nothing out of the ordinary. However, this was a once-in-a-lifetime experience unfolding before Dr. Snowden. He turned to look back at the display as Kri'tokhaar continued speaking.

"Kri'tokhaar doesn't know if anyone will ever listen to this, but beware the rifts. This journey through the rifts did not go as planned. It was to be a quick jump through and back. The probes that initially tested it went in and came back. They reported an unknown constellation on the other end. We thought it was stable but found that it is not."

The talk of rifts piqued Dr. Snowden's curiosity. Evaran had mentioned them earlier, and Dr. Snowden wondered if they were some form of an Einstein-Rosen bridge. He focused back on the screen.

Kri'tokhaar continued on. "We have been through eighteen rifts now, with each one placing us in an unknown location. However, we still did our mission, picking up species for study and researching every place we went. At our last pickup, we retrieved four bipedal creatures. That region appears to have an unusually high amount of bipedal forms. It took us three weeks to get to the next rift, and on the last week, we encountered an aggressive bipedal species that attacked us after failed communications. Although our ship had better defenses, they had more ships. We made it through another rift, but the systems damage had been done."

Dr. Snowden waved his hand at the display. "Can we pause for a sec?"

Evaran paused the playback.

"Who're the bipedal species they're referring to? I know it isn't us."

Evaran placed his hands behind his back. "Earth is part of a galactic community. The Krotovore ship was flying through the Kreagan Star Empire, which stretches over a vast area of space around both Earth and the space-time rift. The Kreagans are humanoid and aggressive at defending their space."

"As advanced as this ship seems, it sounds like the Kreagans must've been fairly advanced too," said Dr. Snowden.

"Not so much advanced as different. The Krotovore region of space in their galaxy only has one humanoid race, and they are primitive technology-wise. However, the Kreagans are far from primitive. They are the dominant power in your section of the galaxy. The Krotovore had no defense against some of their weapons, it appears, based on the logs I have read," said Evaran.

Sanjay raised his hand. "I noticed they referred to time in weeks. I assume the universal translator is translating that? To something we would understand?"

"Very observant, and you are correct. If it had translated it to fifty-nine tetritons, it would not make sense to you. Anything else?" said Evaran.

Dr. Snowden and Sanjay shook their heads.

Evaran interacted with his ARI.

Kri'tokhaar began speaking again. "Kri'tokhaar was able to guide the ship to the nearest planet, which seems to have primitive life. If the life pods can fire, there may be a chance of getting out of this. Kri'tokhaar is heading to the docking bay now." The sound of something hitting the door in the video startled Kri'tokhaar, who looked back at the door. "There isn't much time. If you are hearing this and are on the ship, be careful. Kri'tokhaar out." The video showed Kri'tokhaar reaching forward with two of his arms and touching the console screen.

The video went blank.

"I wonder if he made it to the docking bay," said Emily.

Evaran looked at the ground as if in thought. "Not likely. The ship reports all Krotovore life signs are gone, and none of the life pods were fired." He looked around at his ARI. "Nonetheless, it looks like the data retrieval still has some time left. I have changed the ship's trajectory, so we are no longer in danger of crashing into the planet. However, we need to get the main engine back online. I have downloaded the sequence needed to do so. We will need to head to the engine room after this data retrieval process is complete."

"What did you change the ship's trajectory to?" asked Sanjay.

"To the sun. The ship will continue toward it, but under its current momentum, it will be several weeks until it gets there. By turning on the main engines, we can shorten that time to seven hours," said Evaran with taut lips.

"You're gonna kill everything on the ship?" asked Emily with wide eyes.

"Unfortunately, yes."

"That's cold, man," said Jay.

Evaran looked down for a moment, then sighed as he looked back up. "This was not an easy decision. I feel for the creatures on this ship, abducted without a choice in the matter. However, the planet below cannot be interrupted by this timeline-changing event. This ship is larger than the asteroid that hit your planet sixty-five million years ago. The primitive life on the planet would not stand a chance."

"Okay, but why're we speeding up the ship to the sun?" asked Dr. Snowden.

Evaran gestured with his right hand. "We are deep in Bilaxian space. They are aware of this ship, and I am sure it has attracted the attention of others. This ship's technology is far more advanced than that of any of the civilizations here. It would radically alter the timeline to have this advanced technology fall into any of their hands. That must not occur. They would arrive before this ship hit the sun with plenty of time to scour it. Even now, there is a Bilaxian cruiser group approaching rapidly."

He gestured with his left hand. "Another thing. This ship causes timeline changes wherever it goes. It must be stopped. The very existence of these apex predators on this ship has already caused changes from wherever they are, just as your presence here has. If I had the time, I would capture every one of them and take them home. However, I do not know where they came from, save a few. I could try and guess, but that could make things worse. I had to make a choice, and I chose to save you four and direct the ship into the sun. I know where you came from and when."

"What do you mean by timeline exactly?" asked Dr. Snowden.

Evaran tilted his head. "Although I would not normally discuss this, I think we are past that point. Are you sure you wish to know?"

Dr. Snowden looked around at the others for a moment and then faced Evaran. "Well . . . yeah."

"Okay then. I am glad you are still curious after recent events," said Evaran. He raised a finger. "Now, on to my explanation. Your universe has many instances. Each instance has a defined chronological sequence of events, which is called a timeline. Let me give you an analogy. Let us say the Krotovore never abducted you and your life continued on as normal. A year after your brother's funeral, you meet the woman of your dreams."

"Hell yeah, Doc!" said Jay, nodding with a crooked smile.

Dr. Snowden cocked his head at Jay. "Hey! It could happen."

"Yes, it could," said Evaran. "We will call that the default state of the timeline at that point. Now along comes the Krotovore, and they abduct you before you meet this woman. Your future has now changed. Since your future has changed, anyone or anything that had interacted with you also changes. This is how the timeline maintains referential integrity. Any change in the timeline causes an update toward the future. This is referred to as a cascading timeline update. The point where you meet the woman of your dreams no longer happens now. She would go on about her life, never having met you."

"That assumes there is a future that exists and can be updated, though," said Dr. Snowden.

Evaran half grinned. "You are beginning to understand."

Dr. Snowden had heard some of these terms before but wasn't sure how they could be verified. "So when we go back to Earth, the timeline will reset back to the default state, right?"

"Not quite. You all are changed now, both physically and mentally, and your lives may be different because of this event. Back to the analogy. Say the woman was a doctor and you originally met her at a checkup. However, now that you are back, you can no longer go to the doctor since it would expose your nanobots. You would never meet her. It goes a lot deeper than that and would require extensive learning on your part to fully understand."

Dr. Snowden shook his head. It sounded crazy to him. "So . . . do these cascading timeline updates cross over to other timelines?"

"They do not. The timeline is one entity, and updates are localized to it. There are other timelines parallel to the one you are in, as I mentioned, and they do not intersect with each other. The timeline changes the Krotovore caused were isolated to this timeline."

"In these other timelines, is there a copy of us?" asked Sanjay.

Evaran half smiled. "There is in some, and they would refer to you as the copy. However, your timeline is one of the rare ones where your species evolved to dominate Earth. By rare, I mean several million timelines. That should give you an idea of how many timelines there are. In the last one I visited, Earth was dominated by a species you commonly refer to as Neanderthal. I do not want to give away more information on that than I already have."

Dr. Snowden sighed. He wondered what a modern-day Neanderthal society would look like. The very idea lit his mind on fire. There were many questions he wanted to ask, but he figured Evaran was not going to answer all of them. Dr. Snowden got the feeling that Evaran had already said more than he was comfortable with.

"There is some time left for this data retrieval process. Feel free to look around the bridge," said Evaran.

Dr. Snowden watched as everyone split off. He wanted to talk with Evaran more, but assumed Evaran suggested everyone look around as a means of distraction. With that in mind, Dr. Snowden decided to examine the bridge in more detail.

07

Sanjay went to one of the remote workstations near the front of the bridge. He felt like the outcast of the group, something that seemed to happen more often than not. He liked Dr. Snowden and could sense that in another time and place, they would get along well. Academics were always Sanjay's strong point, and dealing with professors was something he enjoyed.

He was unsure of Jay. He came off as brutish and crude. However, Sanjay admired how Jay did not flinch when the draug had attacked. Instead, Jay had flipped his hat back and gone into fight mode. Sanjay sighed. That was just not his style. Then there was Emily. She was attractive, and he did what he always did around pretty girls: stumble around and come off sounding weird. Even on an alien ship in the Andromeda galaxy, he could not escape his awkwardness.

Running his finger across the Krotovore console brought a smile to his face. Although he was scared, he felt safe with Evaran. Sanjay loved all the technology he was seeing, and he now had proof that aliens existed. He just wished they had asked him instead of abducting him.

With a sigh, he studied the console. He could tell that from a graphical user interface perspective, it was not built for humans. What intrigued him was that it looked like they had some type of command line interface in the bottom right of the console. He chuckled to think that some Krotovore preferred the simplicity and power of a command line interface versus a graphical one, a battle he knew all about from his studies.

"Hey," said Emily.

Sanjay flinched as he snapped his head toward her. He had not even sensed her coming up on him. "Umm . . . hey."

Emily sighed. "Look . . . I don't want you to think I don't like you. It's just . . . I'm scared. I'm trying to keep my cool, but it's hard. This whole situation is . . . messed up."

"Yeah," he said, looking down. "I wasn't trying to make fun of you or anything."

"I know. I can be defensive sometimes."

Sanjay smiled. "And I'm awkward around pretty girls."

Emily raised her eyebrows.

"Uhh . . . I mean . . . you know . . ." He sighed as he shook his head. "I did it again."

She chuckled. "It's cool. I just didn't know you as well back then, but . . . I think I have a better understanding now. What were you looking at when I came over?"

"Oh, just the console interface. I've developed some before and was curious how an alien one would look." He shrugged. "Looks like chaos is their design philosophy."

Emily laughed.

Sanjay was glad to see that Emily was not angry with him. He tossed a hand out. "So . . . I heard you met Evaran in the virtual simulation?"

"Yeah, and he had on a pinstripe suit."

"That's crazy. How did he inform you of what was about to happen?"

"He showed us a timer that was ticking down to our 'awakening,'" she said. "Then he said that we were in a virtual simulation and proved it to us by touching our shoulders in the real world. It freaked me out, to be honest. What about you?"

"I was walking to my college apartment with a friend, and then the sky began . . . disappearing. It scared the hell out of me."

"I bet. Did you see any glitches before that?" she asked.

He nodded. "Too many. I thought I was losing my freaking mind."

She chuckled. "Yeah, me too."

An awkward silence passed.

Sanjay looked her in the eyes. "I wanted to thank you for coming over. I know I can be weird, and it's hard for people to overlook that sometimes."

"It's all right," said Emily. She looked around, then back at Sanjay. "So what do you think will happen when we get back to Earth?"

"I don't know, but I do know I'm gonna stay with my parents in town for a bit. Being around family . . . will help with this. I'm not sure I want to be around my apartment anytime soon."

"Makes sense."

"What about you?" he asked.

She exhaled from her nose. "Probably sleep for a few days."

They shared a laugh.

"But honestly, I'll try to put all of this away in my head. Life is short, and there's a lot I want to do," she said. "I don't know how easy that will be. I mean . . . this *is*, by far, the weirdest situation I've ever been in, and now I have a year's worth of memories that aren't even real."

"You have your uncle here at least."

Emily glanced at Dr. Snowden. "Yeah. He keeps me grounded."

"At least you can talk to him about it. I would never in a million years tell my parents. They'd have me committed."

Emily's eyes softened. "Maybe we can all stay in contact. A . . . support group or something."

"I'd like that. If anything, it will remind me I'm not insane."

She laid a hand on his shoulder. "We'll get through this. I may be scared out of my mind, but for now, we have Evaran as a guide, a way off the ship, and a future ahead of us."

Sanjay licked his lips. "Yeah." The sensation of relief that he would not be alone with this experience made it seem less threatening. They still had to get off the ship, but he felt that Evaran was far more than he looked and would be able to get everyone to his ship. At least with Emily, things would be okay. Sanjay looked forward to the prospect of a support group. Maybe they could have outings. This would be a bond that he did not think anyone would forget.

Jay wanted to talk to Sanjay, but it seemed Emily was already talking to him. With everything going on, freaking out and taking it out on others was not going to be helpful. Jay sighed. He knew his aggressive personality painted him as an asshole sometimes, and this was a time everyone needed to be together. It reminded him of his service in the military. Things could get bad between members, but everyone always pulled together as a unit. He saw this as no different, although it took him a while to get there. Looking around, he saw Dr. Snowden examining the sustenance replicator. At least Jay could talk with him. He sauntered over.

"This sustenance replicator is interesting," said Dr. Snowden.

Jay studied the unusual-looking replicator. He had no idea how it could create something out of nothing, yet there it was. "Have you gotten it to work?"

"Yeah, watch this," said Dr. Snowden. He pressed a glowing green button on the nearby console. "Water."

A small container with water appeared on the replicator pad.

Jay wrinkled his eyebrows. "How . . . how'd you figure that out?"

Dr. Snowden pointed at the button. "That seems to be the only button on the interface. I guessed that in order to determine when to listen to what was being said, the button needed pressed. Sorta like a press-to-talk type thing."

"Huh," said Jay. "And . . . since we have these nanobot things in us, it translated water to whatever the hell these bug aliens speak."

Dr. Snowden nodded. He took a sip of the water. "Not bad. I guess you can't go wrong with H2O."

Jay shook his head. "I'm glad you understand all this shit."

"I'm still coming to grips with the fact that this is real," said Dr. Snowden. He sighed. "I'm trying to hold it all together, but . . . this place scares me to death. I wouldn't mind learning about alien culture in small, bite-size chunks, but we were tossed right into the mix."

"Yeah, I'm with ya there, Doc. This is a damn ship of horrors."

"You seem to be holding up well."

Jay shrugged. "I'm trying. I don't like being this amped up."

They turned around to face the front of the bridge.

Jay saw Emily and Sanjay share a laugh. It made Jay feel even worse about unloading on Sanjay earlier. Jay figured Sanjay probably had no formal training in how to handle high-stress situations. Unfortunately, he ran into one and Jay was less than helpful. He sighed. Keeping it together was what he needed to do, and although the bridge was safe for the moment, his anxiety was through the roof. Fighting the draug gave him an adrenaline boost, but thinking about them now made his skin crawl.

"They seem to be getting along," said Dr. Snowden.

"Yeah. I should talk with him after we leave here. I didn't mean to snap on him."

"It was a tough situation. I don't really think anyone plans what to do when you're attacked by cat-sized alien spiders."

Jay laughed. "I like you, Doc. Despite all this shit going on, you can make light of the situation."

"Losing my cool wouldn't help anyone."

Jay licked his lips and looked down. "Yeah."

Dr. Snowden swatted Jay's arm. "It did help fight the draug, though."

They shared a chuckle.

"While we're talking about Emily and Sanjay, I didn't mean anything bad about your niece. That was me just acting out," said Jay.

"It's okay. We have much bigger things to worry about than that."

Jay liked talking to Dr. Snowden. He brought a sense of calmness and assuredness that everything was going to be okay. It was similar to the feeling Jay got from Evaran. Maybe they were more similar than they knew.

"I know you have a son, but do you have any other family?" asked Dr. Snowden.

"No brothers or sisters, and besides my son, just my wife. I *thought* I was with them."

Dr. Snowden nodded. "They'll be happy to see you when you get back."

"What about you?"

"It's just Emily and I. My brother died a few years ago due to cancer, and Emily's mother died giving birth to her, so I watch over her now. She came up to live with me, and . . . here we are," said Dr. Snowden. He glanced at Jay. "Great job I'm doing, huh?"

Jay shrugged. "You're doing your best, man. That's all you can do."

"Yeah." Dr. Snowden shook a finger out. "You know . . . I bet these virtual simulation memories are going to be hard to deal with when we get back."

"I never really thought about that, but I could see it."

"Imagine going back and finding out you weren't married."

Jay shook his head. "We were married earlier than I guess whenever all this alien shit happened, but I could see mixing up conversations that are now just in my head. She'll have a field day telling me she never said things I thought she did. Some of them will probably be true."

Dr. Snowden chuckled.

Jay's muscles relaxed some. It felt good to talk knowing that the memories being formed were real. The fake memories from the virtual simulation would probably make things worse with his wife. He would need to watch what he said. This all assumed he would make it back. He looked in Evaran's direction. "So what do you make of this Evaran guy?"

"To me, it seems like his knowledge is even more advanced than the Krotovore. He said he built V. I don't know anyone that could have done that, although in time I suppose they could. All this talk of time travel, universes, and how he just seems to know more than he's letting on leads me to believe that Evaran is far more than anything we can comprehend."

Jay scratched his forehead. "Yeah. I barely understand half of what he's saying, but I think he means well. I do know he's strong as shit. He lightly tapped my back, and I went sprawling over a slab."

"Yeah, he's definitely strong."

As if on cue, Evaran turned toward the main screen and scrutinized it. After interacting with his ARI, he said, "My ship's external sensors have been activated. I have accessed the visual feed from docking bay three, the next bay over from where my ship is, and I am transferring the visual to the main screen. It appears we have visitors."

08

Jerzan's eyes narrowed as he stood in the command area of his ship. He surveyed the docking bay they had just landed in. They had flown through a light-blue shielding, and all indicators showed that the bay was pressurized. The flashing lights that washed over the docking bay made it hard to really see anything. "All right, let's see what this bitch has on her. Assemble outside."

"Don't need to tell me twice," said Hulldar. He jumped up and ran to his quarters.

Galkett nodded. "Same here."

Jerzan glanced at Hosk. "You seeing anything out of the ordinary?"

"I'm not sure yet. There's another docking bay connected through a hallway, and I can't make out any of the symbols on the walls. They don't match up with anything in our language database."

"How's the air?"

"Not bad. It might be rough, but breathable. Seems like there's less nitrogen than we're used to."

Jerzan rubbed his chin. "The Rybox brothers will love it then."

"Yeah, probably. I've deployed our defenses. Anything we don't like that comes near this ship, they'll get ripped to shreds. I've also sent a pulse to get a layout of the ship. I would have expected some defense against that, but the ship is having power issues."

"All right. See you outside," said Jerzan. He went to an area just a bit out from the bottom of the ship's exit ramp. The flashing lights had stopped, and only the sound of the crew moving inside and the quiet hum of the ship could be heard. Metallic containers were on the edges of the room, with some stacked on each other, obscuring his view. Two doorways stood out. One seemed to lead to the interior of the ship, while the other was a hallway entrance that led to the other docking bay. In terms of docking bays, it looked standard, although it was a bit more advanced in design. He could not make out what any of the symbols were on the containers or the walls but figured it was a language of some sort.

He double-checked that his medium-sized energy weapon was on his back, along with two energy pistols strapped to each thigh. Although he knew they were there, it was instinct to verify it in every new environment. His formfitting suit was ready to go. The suit's material could withstand medium blunt force, was tight, and could change color as needed. It was gray for the moment, which accentuated all the black straps holding various gadgets and weapons. His attention turned to the crew disembarking.

The first down were Goran and Doran, the Rybox brothers. They were Bilaxians, humanoids that stood seven feet tall and had blue skin and ritualized facial scars. Their outfits were pure black, typical of Bilaxian special forces, and combined with their size, they were a formidable sight.

The next down were the Dalruns of the crew: Hulldar, Galkett, Gaellus, Tostik, Henrital, Simas, and Rondall. They wore a mix of tactical gear, usually dark in color, and had a variety of weapons on them. Hulldar and Galkett stood out from the others. Hulldar wore baggy green pants and a sleeveless shirt, while Galkett had a tan suit covered by a trench coat and a wide-brimmed partially metallic hat.

The last two to come out were Hosk and his humanoid assault robot, G-85.

After everyone had assembled at the bottom of the ramp, Jerzan walked to the front of the group. "Listen up! This is a unique opportunity. We've never seen a ship like this before, which means it ain't from around here. That means there's the possibility of truly unique loot. We're going to do two passes. First one is to mark anything of value. Then we'll go collect it as a group in the second pass. Only mark shit that has value." He pointed at Simas. "Let me say that again. Anything of *value*. No partially severed legs."

The group laughed as Rondall slapped Simas's arm.

Simas harrumphed.

Jerzan continued on. "If you find any survivors, capture them and bring them back to the ship. If they prove not worth the hassle, kill them. Hosk has identified potential areas to check out, although it's just a guess as to what they are, but I trust his analysis. This ship is huge, so we're going to split up."

"Works for me," said Hulldar.

"I figured you'd like that," said Jerzan. "Now, on to the assignments. Jahl and Gaellus are with me, and we're going to hit the research labs, or at least what looks like it. Goran and

Doran, you two are together and can check out the engine room. Hulldar and Galkett, you two will check out the large areas Hosk picked out. Probably some type of storage. Simas and Rondall, hit the bridge area. Tostik and Henrital, there's a massive storage area down below you two can investigate. Hosk and G-85 will secure this area and the other openings to this room. Is everyone clear on what they need to do?"

"What about that other docking bay? We should secure that first while everyone's here," said Hosk.

"Good idea," said Jerzan. "Everyone not defending the ship, follow me."

The group went down the hallway to docking bay four.

Jerzan's eyes immediately trained on the odd-looking disc-shaped ship that sat off to the side.

"Damn . . . that's Evaran's ship, I'm telling you," said Galkett. "If I'm right, there'll be a shield around it that's impenetrable."

Shielding appeared when the group walked around trying to poke at the ship.

"Jerzan, whaddaya want to do with this?" asked Rondall.

"Hell if I know. I bet their crew is somewhere on board, though . . . ," said Jerzan. He snapped his fingers. "Gather round, assholes."

The men complied.

"We might have a crew loose on board. Standard rules apply. No killing, capture only, and," said Jerzan, pointing at Hulldar, "no sampling their entertainment value before they get to the ship. I hate sloppy seconds."

Everyone shared a laugh.

"You may get thirds," said Hulldar, slapping Galkett's arm.

"I got a bad feeling about this," said Galkett.

Jerzan shook his head. "You always have bad feelings. All right everyone, keep in contact every hour with Hosk and plan to meet back here in four hours. Let's move it!"

The group went back to docking bay three since docking bay four's hallway exit was sealed due to wreckage.

Jerzan noted that Hosk had begun the arduous task of setting up defenses around the perimeter of the ship. G-85 positioned itself near the front of the ship, with arms splayed outward. Jerzan chuckled as he watched Hosk grapple to a beam on the ceiling and set up a device that scanned the docking bay and the surrounding area for life signs. He would have his work cut out for him if things went bad. Jerzan looked to his sides to see Jahl and Gaellus ready to go, and then they all moved out.

It had been about fifteen minutes since everyone had split up, and Galkett's stomach was churning. Most runs were easy since they involved people. Dealing with an unknown ship in an unstable state was an invitation for trouble. The hallway they were in seemed bland, with metallic paneled floors, ceiling, and walls. The dim lighting and odd mist just made everything seem more sinister than it should. At least he was with Hulldar. As crazy as he was, when it came down to a fight, he was always the first in. Galkett sighed. "Hopefully we can get in and out quick."

"Will you relax?" asked Hulldar. "The life signs were weak and sporadic. Besides, we haven't been challenged since we arrived. I'm thinking . . . there's a vulnerable crew here."

Galkett shook his head. "Do you ever think out of the head on your shoulders?"

Hulldar laughed, and then his face went rigid. He pointed forward. "Some noise up ahead."

They pulled out their weapons and crept forward.

Galkett's eyes narrowed as a scaly creature on two powerful legs exited a room. It was bent forward and had a long tail. The snout filled with sharp teeth indicated it was a predator of some type.

The creature snorted and stomped the ground.

"Well, fuck you too," said Hulldar, opening fire with his energy-based assault rifle.

The beams reflected off the creature's scaled hide. It ducked back into the room.

They ran up to the room with weapons aimed forward.

Galkett could not see any sign of the creature and, after noticing the doorway on the other side, figured it had run way.

Hulldar laughed. "That creature was a bitch, all snorting and shit."

"Yeah . . . but I don't think that was a crew member."

"Probably not. Maybe it was a lost pet," said Hulldar.

"It could be. What type of alien species keeps predators like that as pets, though? Especially ones with reflective scaling?"

Hulldar shrugged. "If they wanted to stop us, they woulda showed themselves by now."

"I guess."

They entered the room and looked around, then continued on back toward their designated area.

After going a bit farther, Galkett spotted something on the ground. It was an alien with a suit on, and it reminded him of a large bug. Something had slashed through the chest armor, and green blood was pooled around. He gestured at the corpse. "Check that out. Looks like that was a crew member."

"How can you tell?" asked Hulldar.

"The markings on the armor are similar to what we saw in the docking bay," said Galkett. He narrowed his eyes and looked around. "I don't think the crew is alive . . ."

Hulldar shook his head. "If that's the species of the crew, then let's hope there are some other aliens I can play with."

Galkett laughed. "You'd still do a crew member if we caught it."

"Yeah, probably."

Galkett knew Hulldar's sexual appetite was voracious. It was not limited to just species with two legs. He did not differentiate if there was the potential for pleasure. The last few weeks had been rough for Galkett since he had his living quarters next to Hulldar, who was not shy about broadcasting what he was doing with his hands and his body up to three times a day. Galkett knew that if they saw a Dalrun-like female anywhere on board, Hulldar would do everything to get her, even risk his life.

After thirty minutes, they came to a large, dimly lit room.

Galkett could barely make out the cargo containers that seemed to fill the area. There were some unusual skittering noises that occasionally rang out, but for the most part, it was just the quiet hum of the ship along with its creaking.

"What do you think this room is?" asked Hulldar.

"Storage of some type," said Galkett. He motioned at one of the containers nearby. "Let's check to see what it is."

After entering the room, Hulldar kicked at one of the containers.

The skittering noises stopped.

Galkett looked around. "How about we not make a lot of noise?"

Hulldar grinned. "I was just checking if it was hollow. Seems full of something."

"Yeah. There's a console near the front, but I can't make out what it's saying. We'll mark it and come back with some equipment to rip it open."

Hulldar nodded.

They proceeded farther into the room.

Galkett narrowed his eyes. "The silence is creeping me out. It wasn't quiet when we came in."

"You worry too much. Anything comes close, I'll hack it up."

Galkett appreciated Hulldar's bravado, but something seemed off. Maybe it was just the bad feeling he got from being on the ship. After checking out a few more containers, he marked them and then pointed back at the entrance. "All right, I don't think we'll find much—" He tilted his head at the small bug-like creature with six legs at the entrance. "Now what do you suppose that is?"

Hulldar aimed and then shot at the creature, causing it to go limp. He laughed. "Something dead."

The skittering noises rang out from the hallway.

"Whatever that is, it's coming from the outside to the left. We should go right," said Galkett.

Hulldar pulled out an energy blade and a pistol and waved forward. "C'mon."

As they approached the entrance they had come in from, another bug-like creature appeared.

Hulldar shot it with his pistol. "How many of those damn things are there?"

Scraping sounds echoed out.

"Whatever's coming, it's coming fast. Move!" said Galkett.

They entered the hallway.

Galkett's eyes popped open at the swarm of bug-like creatures scurrying their way. Some were larger, with various appendages, while others were smaller and moving fast. There were some other types, but they presented a wall of teeth, mandibles, and claws and were approaching rapidly. "Let's get the hell out of here!"

Hulldar stood his ground and opened fire.

Some of the creatures fell but were replaced by others.

Galkett grabbed Hulldar's arm. "Quit playing around, man. Let's go!"

Hulldar fired off one last shot and then pivoted and ran.

Looking back, Galkett saw the creatures pouring into the room they had just left. Whatever was in there, those creatures wanted it more than he or Hulldar did.

"Now you know there's something of value in there," said Hulldar.

A large creature, bigger than the others, paused at the entrance and looked their way.

"Yeah, but we're not going to find out without backup," said Galkett. He could see that the large creature had no fear of them. It filled up the height of the hallway and looked menacing. The other creatures ran around it like they could not wait to get whatever was in those containers. Seeing the large creature's massive arms ending in claws, he did not think it would have any problems opening the containers or defending them.

"Damn bugs," said Hulldar. "We'll see how they like a flamethrower when we come back."

Galkett slapped Hulldar's arm. "I'll bring the fuel."

They left the area and continued on.

09

Dr. Snowden narrowed his eyes as the main screen shut down. The mercenaries he had seen were heavily armed and poking at Evaran's ship's shields. They looked like they would be trouble. He was not sure if the translator was working as expected, as it seemed odd they would say "sloppy seconds." It made him wonder what their native term was and why the translator chose that slang to use. Evaran had shut down the screen shortly after that. Dr. Snowden glanced at Emily. They would not get a chance to explore that with her, not while he could do something about it.

Emily swallowed hard. "Who . . . were they?"

Evaran rubbed his chin. "Jerzan . . . hmm."

"Analysis. Jerzan Graduul. Leader of the Bloodbore mercenary group. Wanted in five systems. Thirty-four counts of—"

"V, that will be enough," said Evaran, raising his hand. "I know of Jerzan and the Bloodbore mercenaries. They have hurt some of my friends. We will need to avoid him and his group, and once I get everyone to my ship, I will deal with them personally."

"How does V know who that is?" asked Dr. Snowden.

"I have traveled in this region before and have information from this time period," said Evaran.

"Oh . . . I see," said Dr. Snowden.

Jay snorted and shook his head. "Great. Now we gotta deal with these assholes on top of everything else. Where can we score some weapons?"

"The handheld weapons on this ship are designed to work for only the Krotovore," said Evaran. "I will deal with them if we run into them. We should head to the engine room now."

Jay shrugged. "Awesome, man. No weapons. Mercenaries *with* weapons. Dangerous creatures. Yeah, this'll go well."

"C'mon," said Dr. Snowden, slapping Jay on the back.

Jay sighed.

Everyone followed Evaran as he left the main bridge.

As the group walked back through the main bridge concourse, Dr. Snowden observed the security drones he had seen earlier that so efficiently sliced up the draug. The drones milled about but kept their distance. They were spraying a gel of some type on the dead draug. The gel converted anything it touched into a gelatinous substance that the drones then shot a vaporizing beam at. It seemed to be an efficient cleanup process.

There were other dead non-Krotovore aliens lying about that he had seen earlier. He had not had time to investigate them closely at that time due to being chased. What they were doing there and what relationship they had with the Krotovore was a mystery. Maybe they were researchers from other civilizations.

The main bridge concourse did seem to be a bit brighter, but that may have been from the lighter mist. The stench was bad before, but it was much worse now, and the smell of raw flesh wafted through the air. He jumped a few times at the random noises that filtered into the area. His pace quickened as they approached the entrance.

After an hour on the main bridge concourse, they reached the end of it and exited back onto the walkway in the large cylindrical area.

V flew out and then down into the open area. As they approached the elevator, he flew back up from outside the railing and toward them. He hovered by Evaran and then projected a display before them. "Analysis. Life-form detected on level 283."

The projection showed a large canine-looking creature. Black chitin-like armor punctuated the creature's silver fur, and it had a large head and jaw. The head was mostly mouth, with a set of four eyes. The ears stood up on each side of its head, and its body was very muscular. The creature looked up curiously with a tilted head when V scanned it.

Dr. Snowden thought it looked like a large hyena with black plate armor.

Evaran studied the display and then interacted with his ARI. "Interesting. It appears we have a krall on board. That would qualify as a dangerous creature. That may be the quadruped the Krotovore was referring to."

"You've seen this before?" asked Emily.

"Yes. This one is a little different, but a krall nonetheless. Krall are sentient creatures. They are not quite as intelligent as your species, at least from the time period this one is from. The Grimlyn Empire used them in the front lines, and sometimes used them for entertainment in pit fighting. Their descendants are still around in this time period, unlike the draug, and they have a sizable population spread out across the Andromeda galaxy. This is probably not something the

Krotovore should have picked up either, as the krall would see them as a threat. Come, we need to head to level 285 and go down a major hallway and then up a few levels in another central area like this one," said Evaran.

"Looks like a big-ass dog to me," said Jay.

Sanjay chuckled. "Same here."

"It is an apt comparison," said Evaran.

After taking the elevator to level 285, the group disembarked.

Dr. Snowden caught his breath at the dead bodies strewn about just outside the elevator. He was not used to seeing so much death. Not all the dead bodies were Krotovore, similar to the main bridge concourse. He did recognize the white robes with dots on some of the bodies, though. The stench was different here, as if the flesh had been cooked.

"Damn, it smells like rotten ass out here," said Jay, grimacing.

"Analysis. Is this a smell you have encountered often before?"

Jay drew his head back. "No . . . I don't often smell rotten ass."

"Acknowledged."

Sanjay chuckled.

V's interaction intrigued Dr. Snowden. It seemed like V was trying to be friendly, but it came out awkward. Dr. Snowden did not think V meant any harm and was probably just trying his best. At least V seemed to have some personality. Dr. Snowden gestured at the corpses. "Looks like a fight happened down here. Were these other aliens with the white robes specimens like us?"

"Most likely," said Evaran. "That is a specimen-specific robe. Some were other alien species traveling with the Krotovore, it would appear." He approached one of the corpses and scanned it with his ring. "Interesting. These were killed by energy weapons." He looked around.

"You think it was the mercenaries?" asked Dr. Snowden.

"Possibly. We are exposed here. Let us go."

The group continued down the walkway.

Dr. Snowden spun around as a noise caught his attention. He did not see anything, but was sure that if he heard it, then Evaran would have heard it. "Evaran, do you hear something?"

"Yes. A group of small creatures is following us. It is not the krall. I am sure they are specimens, although I am unfamiliar with the scent. They have decided not to show themselves, and I think if they were aggressive, they would have made a move by now. They have been following us since we got off the elevator," said Evaran.

"They prolly saw all them aliens get blasted and bailed," said Jay.

"Maybe," said Dr. Snowden, shrugging. Apparently, Evaran was not too worried about it, so Dr. Snowden would not give it a second thought. Emily had skipped ahead of him to walk with Evaran. She must not have wanted to be the last in line.

Emily studied the bodies as they walked around them. "Evaran, why aren't there more humanoids? There seems to be a lot of . . . bug-like ones."

Evaran stopped and glanced at the bodies Emily was standing by. "The humanoid form is actually common among the stars. What you see here is but a tiny fraction of the advanced races in their time period and region. These just happen to be mainly nonhumanoid. Unlike your galaxy, theirs has very few humanoid species."

Dr. Snowden glanced at Emily and then paused for a moment to reflect on what was just said. He tilted his head at Evaran. "I thought the chance of a species arising with the humanoid form and our level of intelligence or greater would be rare."

"I read that too," said Sanjay, glancing at Dr. Snowden.

"You are correct," said Evaran with a half smile. He turned back around and continued to walk toward a large hallway entrance.

Dr. Snowden increased his pace to keep up with Evaran. "Wait a minute! How can the humanoid form be common, yet the chance of it arising be rare?"

Evaran raised his finger up and out and shook it. "That is the right question to ask, and something I would like to know myself. I have encountered far too many humanoid species, including yours, for it to be merely coincidence. Tracking it all down takes time but is on my list of things to find out."

Dr. Snowden nodded. It was oddly reassuring that Evaran, despite his apparent knowledge, did not know everything. On the other hand, Dr. Snowden did wish that Evaran could have answered that. It must be greatly satisfying to travel through time and space and resolve mysteries like this one.

At least for the moment, and as much as Dr. Snowden's nerves were frayed, the group seemed to be safe. He hoped they did not run into any other creatures or mercenaries. At least Emily seemed calmer, as did Jay and Sanjay. Maybe they would get out of this in one piece and have a good laugh about it. Looking around, though, he was not sure he would ever have fond memories of this place. He exhaled from his nose as he tried to keep up with the group.

Rondall surveyed the room he and Simas were in. On the ground were dead bug-like aliens that looked like they had been killed in their sleep. The method of death seemed to be blunt trauma to the head. Although Rondall had seen brutal violence in his days as a thief for the black market, this was on another level. Whatever killed these aliens did it while they lay in their unusual-looking beds. It seemed death was no stranger here.

"I don't know what half of this shit means or does," said Simas, holding an object in his hand.

Rondall nodded. "Just tag it, and we'll move on."

Simas dropped the object and looked around. "Seems that's the story on almost everything we've seen so far. The alien weapons we saw earlier seemed to be busted, and," he said, waving a finger around, "it didn't do shit for these aliens apparently."

"Maybe so, but I'd like to study these things away from a place like this. The sooner we mark these things, the quicker we can get out of here."

Simas tilted his head. "This place bothers you, doesn't it?"

"Yeah . . . and it's nothing like the places we've been to before. Something's very wrong on this ship. I'm not sure what it is, but . . . just a feeling."

Simas eyed Rondall. "You had that same feeling when we robbed that weapons facility on Barakas Prime."

"Yeah, but at least we knew what we were gonna fight. Here . . . not so much."

Simas laughed. "You just don't like space in general."

"Planet-side cities is where it's at," said Rondall, shrugging. "C'mon, I don't think we'll find much in these living quarters."

Simas tapped at his palm, and as he pointed two fingers at each object, a highlighting beam shot out. "All right, marking done."

They exited the room and continued down a hallway with doorways off to various living areas. When they came to a four-way intersection with another hallway, they paused.

Rondall's eyes popped open at the hairy mass of flesh down a bit off to their left. A wall of bones, limbs, and odd-looking appendages completely filled the hallway. "What the hell is that?"

"I don't know," said Simas. He shot at it with his energy pistol.

The creature pulsed while emitting a loud groaning sound. The energy burn from Simas's pistol healed itself, and an appendage shot out toward them.

Rondall grabbed Simas and pulled him off into the hallway. "What are you doing?"

"Relax. It's not going to move. All it can do is shoot that tentacle thing out at us."

"Yeah . . . a tentacle thing that almost reached you. That shit pulls you in, I think you become a part of it," said Rondall. Simas making dumb decisions was not unusual, but in a place like this, it could be the tipping point. Rondall knew that Jerzan did not like Simas and only let him travel with the Bloodbores since it was a requirement for Rondall joining. He sighed. "We're thieves, not mercenaries. Shooting that thing is what Hulldar would do."

Simas looked down for a moment. "Yeah, that's on me, and yeah, I'm nothing like Hulldar. I hate that guy."

"Yeah, no shit. I think most do. He's a loose cannon. All right, c'mon, let's just mark some things."

After a while, they reached a room with massive shipping containers in it. The lighting was dimmer inside the room, and there was an odd chattering sound coming from a darkened hallway opposite of them. Busted displays hung on the walls.

Rondall performed a thermal scan. Outside of a few lights, there was not a lot of power to the room, but the temperature was higher than the hallway they were looking in from. Maybe it had something to do with the pod-shaped organic structures on the ground that caught his attention. A slimy substance covered the structures, giving them a sleek sheen. He tossed his hand out to the right, hitting Simas in the chest. "We're not going in there."

Simas looked around. "Those egg-looking things might be useful."

"We can mark them from here."

"You get another bad sense?"

Rondall narrowed his eyes. "This is a den of some type, and I *do* think those are eggs. That means whatever laid them is big, and probably nearby. Let's not provoke it."

Simas nodded.

They turned back and went down another hallway.

When they reached the end, they entered a massive cylindrical room with walkways ringing the edges and ramps going up and down to the different levels.

"Looks like a central access way to the rest of the ship," said Simas.

Rondall grinned. "Yep." His helmet picked up voices. Looking around, he spotted movement several levels up from where they were. He pulled Simas back. "There's something up there. I'm checking it out. Cover me."

Simas pulled out his two pistols and faced down the hallway they had just come from.

Rondall grabbed his sniper rifle and kneeled. After adjusting his rifle and activating its recording feature, he anchored himself and peered through the scope, which showed several Dalruns walking.

It was the Dalrun female that made Rondall grin. She looked to be younger than the others, with dirty-blond hair. Although he could only see the upper half due to the walkway's guardrails, she looked to be physically fit. That could be months of entertainment for the crew. There was another younger Dalrun male, although his skin was tan. That was not unheard of, but definitely unusual. He too could be part of the entertainment. The others could be sold on the slave market, assuming Jerzan decided to keep them for sale.

"What are you seeing?" asked Simas.

"Check for yourself. I think . . . you're gonna like what you see," said Rondall, standing and putting his sniper rifle on his back. He grabbed his dual pistols. "I'll cover."

Simas switched places, and after getting his sniper rifle out and peering through the scopes, he said, "Oh man . . . that *alone* is worth the trip. I call first night with the girl."

Rondall laughed. "We can switch when we're done with them, but yeah, we can claim first rights." He switched on group comms. "Jerzan, transmitting a video feed of what we found. Looks like a group of Dalruns."

"I see them," said Jerzan. "Go ahead and capture them, and . . . yes, you have first rights on whoever you want."

"Damn it," said Hulldar over group comms.

"Jerzan, I don't know about this," said Galkett. "That one in the front looks an awful lot like Evaran from what I read."

"Good, then we can capture him and put to rest this idea that he is some sort of long-lived hero," said Jerzan.

"This is a mistake," said Galkett.

"Quit being a pussy," said Gaellus. "Simas, Rondall, get some slaves."

"We're on it," said Rondall. He switched off group comms. "You heard the boss man, let's capture them." As he turned back around, he saw Simas take aim. "Simas, don't!" Rondall lunged forward and hit Simas's rifle, causing it to sway and discharge.

A tingling sensation ran through Dr. Snowden as he followed Evaran and the others toward the engine room. Dr. Snowden was not sure if it was just due to the stress or maybe a reaction to the environment. The thought that there might be mercenaries around every corner saturated his thoughts. What the group would do in that situation was unknown to him, but Evaran had said he would deal with it. How that would work with just a utility handle for defense was a mystery.

After walking for a bit, the group came within viewing distance of the large hallway entrance that led away from the open cylindrical area they were in. It was arched, like the main bridge concourse, but a lot smaller. Unlike the main bridge concourse, this entrance looked heavily guarded. Turrets protruded on every other segmented block and were swiveling around.

"Some pretty interesting stuff, huh?" said Sanjay, turning his head toward Dr. Snowden.

"Yeah. I'd love to research all this," said Dr. Snowden.

"Me too. Maybe when we get home, we can compare notes. At least we'll be in a safe place to do so."

Dr. Snowden nodded.

Jay caught up to them and turned to Sanjay. "Hey, man, about back there when we fought those draug things . . ."

Sanjay raised his hand. "It's okay. I deserved it. I just panicked, and I was thinking of myself instead of the group. I won't—"

Zzzt!

A beam hit the back of Sanjay's head, punching a perfect hole through it. His face shot out, hitting Emily in the back.

She stumbled, turned around, and then screamed as she swung her arms wildly to scrape off the bits and pieces of Sanjay's face.

Sanjay's body fell forward. Blood oozed out onto the ground.

Dr. Snowden and Jay dropped to the floor.

Evaran ran past them while raising his left arm and activating his shield.

Emily began hyperventilating and knelt down with her hands over her head.

"Oh, *shit*!" said Jay.

"Go!" said Evaran, pointing to the hallway entrance.

Dr. Snowden scrambled to his feet with Jay in tow. When they got to Emily, Dr. Snowden grabbed her arm, dragging her to her feet.

They ran in the direction Evaran had pointed.

Dr. Snowden peered back and saw a beam connect with Evaran's shield that sent him sprawling back.

Evaran motioned at V.

V flew toward the hallway entrance and stopped just inside the entrance.

Evaran got up and ran past V and then caught up with the rest of the group that was fleeing down the hallway. "V is going to lead them away. We need to get to the other central area and up to the engine room now!"

"Sanjay . . . he's . . . ," said Dr. Snowden with his lips turned down. A lump formed in his throat.

"He is no longer with us," said Evaran with creased eyebrows.

Dr. Snowden sighed as he struggled to make sense of what had just happened.

"Keep moving. We can discuss it in a safer place," said Evaran.

Dr. Snowden's eyes misted as he nodded. Death seemed to be popular today.

They got to the end of the hallway and ran to one of the elevators. The group rushed in after Evaran activated it. When the elevator reached its destination, everyone charged out and down the walkway. After a few minutes, they reached an entrance similar to the main bridge concourse and entered.

Dr. Snowden's eyes adjusted to the dimly lit hallway he found himself in while he heard an eerie sound penetrating the air.

After a short run, they reached a main chamber.

It was the largest room Dr. Snowden had seen so far outside of the main cylindrical area. The room was spherical, and in the center was a black orb surrounded by a mass of metal rings that stood still. There were three curved metal pillars evenly distributed around it, shooting a red beam at the rings. There was a corridor at the opposite end of the room, and one on each side.

They stopped to the right of the chamber entrance.

Evaran raised his hand. "They are following V's projection of us down a different path away from here. He will be back shortly. Let us rest for a moment."

Jay rubbed his forehead and squinted hard while grimacing. He walked over and put both hands on the wall, then leaned his forehead against it.

Dr. Snowden could hear Jay's short, anger-filled breaths. After what had just happened, that was understandable. Dr. Snowden went over to Emily, who had tears running down her face as she sat slumped with her back against the wall. He sat down next to her and put his head in his hands.

She leaned against him.

He could not believe Sanjay was dead. It happened so fast. One moment there, the next, not. A tidal wave of anger swept through Dr. Snowden. Sanjay didn't deserve this. He just wanted to go home like the rest of them. Dr. Snowden was really beginning to like Sanjay. Why Sanjay was targeted was a mystery. Maybe whoever did it was aiming for someone else and just a lousy shot.

Evaran turned toward them as V flew into the room. "V, status?"

"Analysis. I led them to a large creature. They did not survive."

"Replay," said Evaran, circling a finger in the air.

V projected a holographic display showing two men firing at a large shelled creature. The creature launched itself at one of the men, crushing him against the wall. It then lashed out with green tentacles through its shell, grabbing the other man. It pulled the man close and squeezed him until he went limp.

Evaran narrowed his eyes and interacted with his ARI. "A Cepharus." He tilted his head. "It would seem the men were from Jerzan's crew based on their gear, unless there is another pack of mercenaries on board we are unaware of."

Jay faced Evaran and took a deep breath. "We're not gonna make it, are we?"

Evaran looked at the ground for a moment before glancing at Jay. "I have failed Sanjay, but we will make it. I underestimated the mercenaries. That will not happen again."

Jay turned and kicked the wall. *Fuck!* He faced Evaran. "How can you assure it won't happen again? That shit came out of nowhere!"

"I understand your anger, and I will do my best to prevent something similar from happening again."

Jay shook his head.

"As unfortunate as that was, we still need to turn the engines on. Dr. Snowden?"

Dr. Snowden looked up. He took off his glasses and wiped his puffy eyes. "I'm here."

Emily sniffled and wiped her face. Her voice cracked. "I'm here too."

Evaran nodded at them and interacted with his ARI. "V, display engine room layout."

"Acknowledged."

V projected a layout of the area they were in. It showed them as *X*'s in the main chamber. Hallways leading off to the right, left, and opposite end of the room were colored. They wound around several rooms and other hallways, ending in small rooms.

Evaran traced his finger along the colored hallway leading to the left. "I do not want to split us up, but for this, we will need to. Dr. Snowden, you and Emily will take this route. There will be signs on the wall leading to the control rooms. They are clearly marked, and there is also a colored line on the floor leading to them." He traced the colored hallway off to the right. "Jay, you and V will take the right one." He traced the one on the opposite end of the room. "I will take this one."

Jay guffawed. "Sanjay just got *wasted*, man! You don't seem to really give a shit. Now you want to split up?"

Evaran pointed to the red beams in the center of the room. "Those red beams need to be disabled, and shutting them down is a manual process. It requires at least three people per the Krotovore security protocol. I have already disabled all the security checks and door locks here, so we just need to get to the control rooms. If there was another way, we would be doing it. I cannot physically be in three places at the same time. I hate having to ask this of you, but there is no other choice. I do not like what happened to Sanjay, but we cannot change it, only try to prevent it from occurring again."

Jay snorted. "Whatever, man."

Dr. Snowden stood up and crossed his arms while slightly bending forward. Splitting up did not sound like a wise decision after what had happened, and he agreed with Jay's assessment. Evaran seemed almost indifferent to Sanjay's loss, or maybe emotion was not something Evaran showed easily. It seemed odd how he expressed emotion, very constrained. Then again, he was an alien, or something else, so maybe it was different for him.

"V, display the unlocking panel," said Evaran.

V projected a wall in the control room. It showed a panel cover with a screen above it. The screen had an image of three red dots in a triangle with a button in the middle and the word *unlock* in green on it. There was a status label under it, indicating "Locked."

"I have to turn it off in the main control room," said Evaran. "When I do, the top dot will turn green. When it turns green, there is only a five-minute window to get both the others unlocked. To do that, press the button in the middle. The button will appear disabled, and the panel cover underneath it will slide back."

V projected the sequence, showing the panel sliding back. A cylinder with a handle was embedded in the wall.

"The status will say, 'Pull.' You will pull out the cylinder, turn it until the status on the screen says, 'Push,' then push it back in. Once it is back in, the status will say, 'Ready,' and the button will be enabled with the word *lock* on it. Press the button. The panel will slide forward to close, and the red dot corresponding to your control room will turn green. When all three are green, the engines will fire," said Evaran.

V projected the final steps.

"Everyone clear?"

Dr. Snowden's eyes dulled, and his shoulders slumped. "Sounds kinda simplistic for a ship this advanced."

Evaran nodded. "You do not have to deal with the security checkpoints, automated scans backed by turrets, stun beams, shielded sections, biometric scans on the unlocking mechanism, or door locks. The manual process is just a backup in case the main automation system goes down. We are activating the secondary systems. Simple perhaps, but far from easy if the ship was not damaged."

Dr. Snowden sighed and shook his head. "Doesn't sound like we have a choice. C'mon, Emily." He reached toward Emily.

She grabbed his hand and stood up.

"I will get to the main control room before you do," said Evaran. "V will let me know when you get to yours, Jay. The time to get there should be about the same for you, Dr. Snowden. Remember to only begin the process once the top red dot is green. Okay, we meet back here once it is done. Good luck."

Jay sighed. "Fine. C'mon, Blue Ball, let's get this shit over with."

"Acknowledged."

Jay and V moved off to the right.

Evaran walked to the opposite side of the room.

Dr. Snowden squeezed Emily's shoulder as they walked over to the left hallway. Sanjay's death was still reeling in his mind, but getting the engines on was a helpful distraction. Death was not something Dr. Snowden ever got used to seeing, and having it happen right in front of him was more than he wanted to deal with for the moment. Whatever was needed to get off this deathtrap, it would be done.

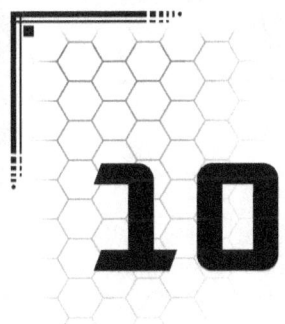

10

Jerzan's blood boiled listening to Simas and Rondall over group comms, screaming that they were chasing down a group, then hearing their death cries. Although Jerzan was not sure what they ran into, he had pinged their location and was on his way with Jahl and Gaellus. The Rybox brothers were close and on their way as well. Jerzan ordered Galkett, Hulldar, Henrital, and Tostik to continue marking since they were too far away to help.

As they rushed down a hallway, Jahl said, "Those cries . . . it sounded like they were being beat to death."

"Simas and Rondall are tough. Whatever coulda done that musta been tougher," said Gaellus.

They burst into a room and charged to the other side.

"We'll find out," said Jerzan. He had already heard the reports from the others out and about. This ship had creatures on the loose, and the alien crew had been slaughtered. Usually, that meant easy picking, but these creatures defied explanation. There had not been one that anyone could identify.

That meant these creatures were from somewhere else, but where, he did not know. Maybe it had something to do with the anomaly that the ship came through.

After twenty minutes of hard running, they arrived at where Simas's and Rondall's location beacons were broadcasting.

Jerzan was not sure what he was seeing. It was a bloodbath. Simas had been ripped in half, and Rondall looked like he had been flattened against the wall.

"Damn . . . Nothing but a puddle of guts here," said Gaellus, grimacing.

Jahl extended his forearm and scanned the area with a device on his forearm. "I got their location beacon history. They seemed to be running this way, and then . . . into whatever did this."

Gaellus pulled out his medium weapon. "Then we waste it, whatever it is."

Jerzan bent over and picked up Simas's location beacon. He nodded at Jahl. "Get Rondall's beacon. We can analyze this later."

"You think Evaran and his group did this?" asked Gaellus.

"I don't know," said Jerzan. He tilted his head and over group comms said, "Galkett, you hearing this?"

"Yep," said Galkett.

"Has Evaran been known to do this type of thing?"

"Nothing I read indicated he would do something like that," said Galkett. "He tended to turn people over to local justice. I don't recall reading anything where he killed someone."

Jerzan glanced around. "So he handles things like he allegedly did with Dolgus Kree and the others."

"That would be his style."

Jerzan sighed. "Then we may be dealing with another merc crew."

Jahl shook his head. "I'm not sure about that. Whatever killed Simas and Rondall was not Dalrun, Greer, or Bilaxian."

"Probably one of these crazy-ass creatures running loose," said Gaellus.

Everyone focused on the arriving Rybox brothers.

Goran knelt and rummaged around in Simas's guts.

"What the hell are you doing?" asked Gaellus, stepping forward.

Jerzan laid the back of his hand on Gaellus's chest. "It's a Rybox Clan thing. It means he's covering his hands with the blood of a fallen member. It's symbolic and means he will avenge them."

"I never heard of that ridiculous shit before," said Gaellus.

Doran stepped up to Gaellus.

Gaellus raised his head a bit. "You got a problem with that?"

Jerzan stepped between them. "This is not the place for that shit." He glanced at the Rybox brothers. "Get whatever you can off their bodies that's salvageable and take it to the ship, and join up with us later."

Doran and Goran nodded.

"Let's go," said Jerzan, waving forward.

As Jerzan and the others trudged to the research labs, Galkett said over group comms, "I highly doubt that was the work of Evaran now. It was definitely something else."

"I'd like to see whatever did that to Simas and Rondall try that shit with me," said Hulldar over group comms.

Gaellus laughed. "You and me both, brother. We'll be the butchers of an unknown alien ship."

Jerzan shook his head. "All right, you two, cut the love fest out. We got shit to do. If anyone sees Evaran and his group, call for the others. Don't try to take them on by yourselves. Everyone hear me?"

Everyone acknowledged over group comms.

"Good," said Jerzan. His nose flared as the haunting last words of Simas and Rondall went through his mind. Jerzan did not know Simas and Rondall to be intimidated easily, at least not Rondall, but his last words were surprising. Although it pained Jerzan to lose Rondall, breaking down in front of the others was not an option. Jerzan's chest was heavier, and his eyes had sunk a bit. Rondall was not just a regular member of the crew; he was also a close friend. Whoever or whatever did this, Jerzan vowed that they would pay.

Tostik shut off his group comms after listening in on the situation with Simas and Rondall. This ship was more deadly than it appeared, and although he thought there might be potential slaves here, that seemed less likely the longer they were on the ship. He and Henrital had entered what looked like a massive warehouse of some type. Per Hosk, there were several of these chained together by hallways, and his best guess was they were storage or maintenance facilities of some type. Tostik shivered. "Damn it's cold in here."

Henrital grinned. "Nothing like Cooris IV."

"Ahh . . . How I miss that place. One of our better slaving raids, and it was warm there."

Henrital nodded. "You just liked having a new personal slave each day for five months."

"And you did too," said Tostik, laughing. "Amazing what a bit of technology can do to pacify the locals." He fondly remembered finding a technologically primitive civilization, and between their slave ship and weapons, they easily handled the forces arrayed against them. The locals were similar to Dalruns in form, but as he and Henrital found out, the local populace's bodies worked well for pleasure. Tostik was not sure why the bipedal form seemed to be so common, but he was not complaining. It was just more bodies to sell.

Henrital pointed at a row of cubes on the right side of the room, each with a transparent window sitting on a side face and a console wrapped around the window.

The cubes were about four feet wide and four feet tall. There were other rows that went to the left, and the cubes got larger in size. Creatures were visible in some of the cubes.

Tostik counted about seven rows. "This looks like some type of specimen storage room." He walked up to the first cube. The creature inside had three spherical armored body parts, all connected by a thick muscle. Tentacle-like appendages hung off the orb parts. "Not sure what the hell that is, but maybe someone would buy it for research."

Henrital slapped Tostik's arm. "I'll let you have that for the morning."

They shared a laugh and moved over a row.

Tostik noted the larger cube held a quadruped creature covered in scales. It had sharp claws and looked like a predator. "I'm getting the sense that these specimens are top predators from where they come from."

"That one is a bit small, though."

"That could be due to the planetary conditions or even . . . a point in time in the planet's history."

Henrital laughed. "You think they're jumping across time and collecting these things?"

Tostik shrugged. "Maybe across space too. This ship *did* appear out of nowhere."

"Maybe. You been listening to Galkett too much."

There was a rustling sound on the opposite side of the warehouse.

They raised their weapons.

Tostik waved forward as they crept down the aisle with weapons aimed forward.

"Detecting two life signs," said Henrital.

"I see 'em," said Tostik. He saw that the life signs were weak but matched a Dalrun-sized creature.

As they approached, Henrital called out, "Come out, whatever you are."

A catlike humanoid with blue-and-orange fur and white stripes stepped out from behind one of the cubes.

"Hold it right there," said Henrital, aiming at the alien.

The alien paused.

Tostik glanced around. "There should be two." He stepped to the left and used the angle to see that there was another alien behind the cube. "The second is back here."

The alien uttered some sounds.

"Translator doesn't work with whatever these are, but they appear to be sentient," said Henrital.

Tostik gestured for the second alien to step out.

The second alien complied.

Henrital smiled. "Looks like the first one is male, based on its size. The other . . . seems to be female."

Tostik laughed. "You just want to try blue fur."

The male alien stood in front of the female and uttered more sounds.

"Not sure what the hell this thing is trying to say," said Henrital. "Cover me." He lowered his weapon and let it hang from his shoulder as he reached behind him and pulled out two magnetic wrist restraints and a collar.

The male alien adopted a defensive stance.

Henrital tossed the restraints and collar before the male alien and then raised his weapon. With a motion toward the restraints and collar, he said, "I don't know if you can understand this, but put those on."

The male alien picked up the restraints and sniffed them, then tossed them on the ground. When he picked up the collar, his eyes flared. He uttered a low growl and then jumped left toward Tostik.

Tostik tried to fire, but the alien was too fast.

The alien knocked Tostik's weapon out of his hand and then kicked him back. With a second leap, the alien was on Henrital, slicing up his face and then his neck.

Henrital gurgled as he fell to the ground. His weapon discharged, hitting the female alien.

The male alien crushed Henrital's head, then rushed over to the female, who was bleeding everywhere.

Tostik's eyes widened as he scrambled up. He wanted to go for his weapon, but it was near the male alien. With a quick jump, he ran out of the room. He figured the male alien would be attending to the female. His throat constricted when he saw the last signs of life fade from Henrital's face. He was dead. Tostik's heartbeat went wild as he heard a loud growl echo out from the warehouse. He tapped at his group communicator. "Jerzan! Henrital's dead! Some alien killed him, and it's after me!"

"What?" asked Jerzan. He sighed. "We'll meet up. Hosk, what's the nearest point we can meet?"

After a moment, Hosk said, "I've marked it for both of you."

"All right, meet there," said Jerzan. "Goran, Doran, you're both near that spot, meet us there. The rest of you continue doing what you're doing."

"Hurry!" said Tostik. "I think we killed this alien's mate. It's pissed."

"Great," said Jerzan. "Simas, Rondall, and now Henrital." He sighed. "Damn it! This shit's starting to piss me off now. When we meet up, I want that alien dead."

The group acknowledged Jerzan over comms.

Tostik ran as hard as he could. His breathing was already rough, but it was even harder now. Running was not something he did often. Taking a quick peek back, he did not see anything, but he could hear the claws of the alien hitting the metallic floor. It was getting closer. Looking at his mini map inside his helmet, there was a storage room where he was to meet up with Jerzan and the others. It was some distance away, and he knew if he did not reach it, he would be dead.

Once he arrived, he entered and ran to the right and then down a bit. He sat still behind a shipping container of some sort as he tried to minimize his breathing. Hopefully Jerzan and the others would arrive before the alien did. Taking a quick look over what he had defensively, he noticed that his weapons belt had been sliced off when the alien attacked. At least his knife on his thigh was still there. He grabbed it and held it tight.

A silence spread out over the storage room.

He closed his eyes and laid his head back. Even if this all worked out, Henrital was gone. Tostik always knew that was a risk as a slaver, but Henrital had been his closest friend. Now he was gone in a random encounter. Tostik sighed as he waited.

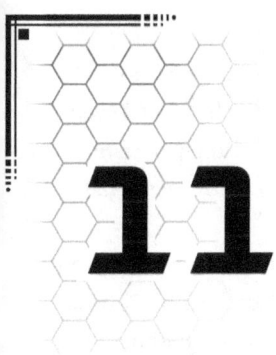

11

Dr. Snowden sighed as he paused at the entrance to the hallway that had been assigned to them. He could see Jay and V entering their hallway, and Evaran had just gone into his. Dr. Snowden refocused on the hallway before them. It had low lighting, and the mist was unusually heavy. Emily seemed to be holding it together, but her nervous movements had not gone unnoticed. She had latched on to his arm and was frowning. He patted her hand and said, "You ready for this?"

"Not really," she said in a quiet voice.

"We can do this," he said. "We've come this far, and Evaran seems to think we'll be okay."

"You trust him?"

"After what I've seen so far . . . yeah. I mean . . . I didn't at first but . . . this is real."

She nodded as she pulled her arm back. "Okay. I'm good to go."

"All right," he said. He could see she was still shaken up after Sanjay, but so was he. It bothered him that less than a half hour ago, Sanjay was alive, and now he was not. Dr. Snowden clenched his teeth as they entered the hallway. Several minutes in, he paused at hearing the same pitter-patter noise from before. He cocked his head at Emily. "You hear that?"

Emily sniffled. "I don't hear anything."

He held out a hand toward Emily and stopped to listen intently. After a few moments, he exhaled sharply. "Something is trailing us." He swallowed hard as they continued on. Whatever was making that sound was now behind them. He wondered if it was the group of small creatures Evaran had mentioned earlier.

Another round of small footsteps echoed through the hallways.

Dr. Snowden turned and looked around again, but did not see anything. Whatever they were, they would not lay a finger on Emily, of that he was sure. It was probably some lost specimens or something.

The dimly lit hallway made it hard to make anything out in detail as they continued on.

He saw the signs on the walls with directions, but the colored lines on the ground were hard to see due to the mist. The noises he heard earlier were also more distinct. It sounded like the footsteps of children intermixed with occasional banging against something. He estimated they were about a few bends away. A chill ran through him. He briefly peered back while shielding his torso but did not see anything. Maybe the nanobots were malfunctioning. He clasped his hands together and rubbed them.

Emily swatted his arm. "Uncle Albert? Am I a bad person?"

He wrinkled his eyebrows and glanced at her. "Why would you say that?"

"When others need compassion, I seem to fight them," she said with a grimace.

"Where's this going?"

Emily's chin quivered as she looked at him. "Sanjay died, and although I *think* we made up, I feel bad about how I treated him initially. Same with Dad when he was close to death."

Dr. Snowden let out a measured breath. "Those are slightly different situations. You can't control how other people are going to act. All you can do is be yourself in the moment. You were angry at life when Dan was close to passing. It happens."

"If that's true, then being myself is fighting others when I should be helping them," said Emily.

"Or that you're just headstrong," said Dr. Snowden as he put his left arm around her and squeezed.

A chattering noise breached their discussion.

His heart skipped a beat. He peeked behind him and saw nothing. "We need to pick up the pace."

They hustled down the various hallways and ramps and, after fifteen minutes, reached the control room doorway. A console to the right of the door had various options, one of which was to open the door.

He pressed it, and the doors slid open. They walked into the bare control room, and he pressed the close option on the inner console. The first thing he saw was a table that stood in the center of the room surrounded by consoles lined up against the wall. There were no loose items anywhere in the control room. Maybe that was an intentional design decision. Another possibility was that something had looted the room clean. He walked up to the table and looked around for the locking panel. After finding it on the wall to the left of the room's entrance, he verified that the dot at the top was red, so he figured Evaran must not have started the process yet.

Three slow knocks rang out from the door.

Emily moved behind Dr. Snowden.

He froze as another three knocks rang out. Whatever it was, it was knocking, so it must have some semblance of intelligence. He walked up to the door and turned to Emily while pointing to the unlock panel. "Watch that panel."

"What're you gonna do?" asked Emily as she walked over to the unlock panel.

"I'm not—"

The door slipped open.

A small red-skinned humanoid alien stood in the room's entrance.

Dr. Snowden swallowed hard and drew his head back. The alien stood about three feet tall and had large black eyes, and its grayish hair stood upright in a frizzled pattern. The mouth was excessively large for the face. He wondered why a small alien would need such a large mouth. The ears, eyes, and nose had bone-like piercings, and it wore a chest piece that also looked like it was made of some type of bone. Below the chest piece was a belt with what appeared to be various other bone pieces held in place by leather strips. It reminded him of a Pygmy headhunter. Maybe it was just as frightened as he was. He figured he would try to communicate with it.

Emily gasped with wide eyes. "Uncle Albert! What is that?"

He gulped. "I don't know." He approached the alien and placed his trembling left hand over his chest. "Hello. I am Dr. Albert Snowden."

The alien tilted its head at him and put its hand on its chest.

Dr. Snowden waved his right hand in front of him, and the alien responded by waving its hand at him. This alien seemed to be sentient, as he had thought. Then he saw that there were two more behind it, gazing intently at him. Their big black eyes shined in the dim hallway. His chest tightened, and his fingers went cold. He pushed up his glasses.

This did not seem right. It felt like they were sizing him up. Maybe he could show them he was not a threat. He raised both hands in front of him.

The aliens tilted their heads and then looked at each other. With a sharp, piercing cry, the first one turned around and lunged at him. It revealed a mouth full of sharp teeth.

He sidestepped the charge.

The first one slid to a stop. The second one rushed at him.

He grabbed it by its hair when it was within range and slammed it against the wall.

The first one jumped on the table behind him.

Emily screamed.

The third one rushed in.

He ignored the third one and went for the first one. With a quick motion, he grabbed it off the table and slung it at the second one, which was just getting up. Looking over at the unlocking panel screens, he saw that the dot was now green. "Emily! Unlock it!"

Emily gritted her teeth and began the unlocking process.

Dr. Snowden turned at the sound of bone scraping. A pain shot up his right leg as the third one he had ignored stabbed him. Adrenaline surged through him. His vision blurred as his face turned red. These things meant to kill.

The third one faced Emily and swayed as it approached her.

Dr. Snowden snatched it by the hair with his right arm, pulling it back toward him. Rage bubbled inside at the thought it would try to hurt Emily. After placing his left arm around its throat, he pulled hard to the right, snapping its neck. The smell of sweat and blood saturated the air.

The first and second ones shrieked as they ganged up on him.

He wheeled around and kicked the first one back down with his left leg.

The second one dodged his kick and pulled out a bone knife. It positioned itself near his left leg.

Stab!

He howled as he fell to the ground.

"Uncle Albert! It's set!" said Emily, trembling.

His breathing went ragged as his speech slurred. "Get out of the room!"

"I'm not leaving you!" shouted Emily.

He kicked out at the second one.

It dodged him again and then raised its arm toward his right leg.

Stab!

His jaw clenched as he grunted when the bone knife lodged itself near the first wound. He tried to stand up using the table but fell back down. *"Go!"*

"No!" screamed Emily as she pushed the second alien away. She pulled the knife out of Dr. Snowden's right leg.

The second one staggered back up and rushed her.

"No!" She stabbed it in the eye.

It howled and fell back into the wall. The first one jumped at her.

"Get away!" she said with tears running down he face. She punched it midair, sending it sprawling.

It hit the wall and slid down. When it was on the ground, it whimpered as it put both hands on its head.

She grabbed Dr. Snowden by the arms. *"C'mon!"* She dragged him out of the room and hit the close option on the console on the way out.

The doors slid shut. Thumping sounds emanated from the other side.

She helped Dr. Snowden up and put her arm around him.

They took off toward the main engine room.

The adrenaline was still pumping through him. He struggled to keep his eyes open, and his breathing was ragged. Looking down, he massaged the three stab wounds with a free hand. They must have poisoned him. His voice slurred. "It won't . . . take . . . them long . . . to get out."

"I know. Let them come," said Emily with a clenched jaw and a guttural voice.

He did a double take. Emily's face was strained, and her eyes had a look of defiance, just like Dan's did when he was backed into a corner. Dr. Snowden had never seen her like this before. Whatever was happening, it was hard to concentrate, and he was not sure he was going to make it. He exhaled from his mouth as he concentrated on trying to move.

━━━━━━━━━━━━━━━━━━

Jay sighed as he tapped the lock button. Other than odd noises here and there, it had been a quiet trip to his control room. V had tried to initiate some conversation, but Jay's mind was still tumbling thinking about Sanjay. His death was senseless, but at least those responsible paid the price. He glanced at V. "All right, Blue Ball, I think this is done."

"Analysis. The three dots are green, so Dr. Snowden and Emily must have set theirs as well."

Jay nodded. "Let's get out of here."

"Acknowledged."

They exited the room and were on their way back to the main engine room.

"Query. I understand you are upset about Sanjay. Do you blame Evaran?"

Jay tossed a hand out. "Nah. As powerful as I think he is, he can't know everything. That shot that took Sanjay was from below. How could Evaran have known about that? By the way, good job on leading those assholes to that cephy thing."

"Cepharus."

"Yeah, that. How'd you find it?" asked Jay.

"I was not looking for it. Based on the Cepharus's approach, I calculated that it must have heard the commotion and come to investigate."

Jay looked down. "Karma's a powerful bitch."

"Query. For what reason?"

Jay shook his head. "It's just a figure of speech. It means you do bad shit, it comes back to you. In this case, they took Sanjay's life, and in the end, their lives were taken."

"I see."

Jay paused as he picked up the sound of small footsteps. "You hearing that shit?"

"Analysis. It matches the sounds from when we were near the elevator. I will investigate," said V. He shimmered and flew ahead.

Jay paused to look around for a moment. A thought popped in his head that if Evaran and V had not come, this might be what it would be like: alone, hearing weird sounds, and scared half to death. He could not imagine trying to survive in that situation and knew he would have probably died a brutal death without fully knowing what was going on. With a sigh, he continued to trudge on.

Small footsteps echoed out a bit ahead.

He froze. Whatever was making those sounds was just a bend or two away. He scouted the area to see if there was anything he could use to defend himself. V seemed fragile in his little orb, and Jay doubted V would be able to help. Jay turned his hat backward. Whatever was coming would learn that he would not be an easy meal.

Three small red humanoids burst around the corner and paused when they saw Jay.

He narrowed his eyes. The aliens reminded him of head-hunters, just shrunken. Their intent was obvious by the way they were staring him down and gripping what looked like bone knives. Still, he was twice their size and had combat training. He gritted his teeth. "Well, c'mon then!"

The aliens rushed forward. The first one raised its arm as it neared Jay.

Jay ran forward and kicked it back into the others.

It dropped its knife.

Jay picked up the knife and rushed up to the other two. With a swift motion, he sliced the third one's neck.

It gargled as it tried to move away.

The second alien had jumped up and stepped back and was joined by the first.

Jay's eyes widened when a Cepharus appeared behind the aliens.

The aliens spun around and froze.

Jay rushed forward and stabbed the first one in the back of the chest, then kicked it away.

The second alien jumped to the side in surprise.

Jay's adrenaline surged. He was tired of everything trying to kill him.

The second alien waved its knife at Jay while keeping an eye on the Cepharus.

The Cepharus slid forward, causing the second alien to react.

Jay stepped to the side and knocked the knife out of its hand, and then while holding its hair, he slit its neck.

The alien fell to the ground as the Cepharus dissipated.

V flew over to where Jay was. "Analysis. They are all dead."

"Yeah . . . thanks to you, Blue Ball. You did good."

V's lights glowed a bit brighter.

"Why does every damn thing want to kill on this ship?" asked Jay. He took a moment to catch his breath.

"Perhaps they were hungry."

Jay snorted. "This is one meal that can fight back."

"I have updated Evaran. He is on his way back to the main engine room."

"Good," said Jay. "Let's get the fuck out of here." Although his heart was still pounding, a wave of relief swept over him. He knew that the engine should be up and running, meaning the only thing left was to get to Evaran's ship. No more splitting up or going to other places. He cast a sidelong glance at V flying by. Jay was glad to have V on this trip. Hopefully this was the last fight they would get into before leaving.

Dr. Snowden could barely recall the trip to the main engine room, but they had reached it. His mind was fogging over, and it felt like a war was waging in his body. He could tell Emily was struggling to keep him up, and several times he had faltered and fallen to the ground. Looking at his watch, he saw that it had taken them about fifteen minutes to get back to the main engine room. Although he had initially heard the aliens shrieking, there was only one doing it now. The second one with the stabbed eye must not have made it.

The shrieks got closer.

Looking around the main engine room, he did not see anyone else. His vision was still blurred, so he was not seeing everything clearly. It did not help that nausea was running wild in his body, which caused a massive headache. He tried to focus for a second look around. The red beams had been disabled, and the blades were whirling around. At least the engine was back on.

He grimaced as he massaged his stab wounds again. The tingling feeling he felt was probably the nanobots trying to counteract the poison. These nanobots just signed a renewal contract.

His muscles tensed up as he heard a deep growling noise coming from the entrance to the main room. Time seemed to slow down as he turned his head and saw the krall standing in the doorway, gazing at him. His heart went ballistic as he realized just how bad the situation had become. The approaching sound of the alien's high-pitched screaming snapped his mind back to reality. How he had missed something that big when looking around surprised him.

Emily helped him toward the hallway Evaran had gone down. She got Dr. Snowden about halfway there before helping him lie down. She called out for Evaran several times. After no responses, she put herself between Dr. Snowden and the krall and adopted a defensive stance. She shot him a look filled with unbridled rage. "Don't you *dare* leave me!"

The krall moved closer to them.

It was just a blob to him at this point. He heard the alien burst out of the hallway entrance and figured this must be the end then. There was no way he could help Emily fight the alien and the krall, not in this state. They might have had a shot with the alien, but not against the krall. The krall was much larger than V's projection showed. This thing was the size of a grizzly.

He turned on his back and sat up after deciding he was going to go out fighting. They had come too far to give up. Tears streamed down his face, and his head drooped. He heard the muted sound of Emily calling out to him. Dan had said to watch over her, and Dr. Snowden had failed to protect her. His head bobbed. He wondered what would become of Emily once he had passed. His breathing slowed, and he crashed to the floor.

Everything went black.

Twenty minutes passed, and Dr. Snowden awoke with a headache, but his vision had cleared. Everything was quiet around him. He jumped at the sound of Evaran's voice behind him.

"It did not see you as a threat. You should be thankful for that."

Dr. Snowden sat up and rubbed his temples. He scanned the room for Emily and saw her over by the krall, petting it. The mangled body of the alien lay near it. "Evaran! How long have you been standing there?"

"I heard Emily's shouts and came as fast as I could, but it looks like she had everything under control. She is more resilient than I expected. It appears you met the krall. Despite their appearance, they are actually quite friendly," said Evaran.

Emily rushed over to Dr. Snowden and gave him a big hug. "Uncle Albert!" She helped him to his feet.

He eyed the krall, which had gone back to the dead alien and was munching on it. "I thought you said it was a dangerous creature."

Evaran nodded. "It is a dangerous creature, if it sees you as a threat. Your humanoid form and size resembles that of a Grimlyn. It most likely figured you could help it. When it saw the alien rushing to attack you and Emily defending you, it reacted. Emily seems to have formed a bond with it. It looks like you two were able to deactivate the beam, though," he said as he walked over to the krall and patted it on the side.

The krall appeared to enjoy the contact, and its eyes relaxed.

Dr. Snowden noticed Evaran had the bone knife in his hands. "Those aliens stabbed me in the leg three times with a knife like that, but it appears to be healing. I think they poisoned me too. I guess the nanobots took care of that."

Evaran's eyes narrowed. "It would appear so. I used my ring to close your wounds, but that is only an external fix. Internally there may be some pain as it heals." He spun the bone knife around in his hands. "This is a Grynge tribal dagger. You can tell by the decoration. That is very unusual, as there should be no Grynge here."

"Why not?"

"Let us just say that they are not a part of *this* reality."

Dr. Snowden swallowed hard. He figured Evaran would elaborate if he wanted to, but he did not. "Where's Jay? He got his unlocked, it seems."

"He did, but he is not back yet. V said they are almost here."

After a few minutes, Jay walked back into the main room but hesitated at the entrance when he spotted the krall and mangled alien. He looked at Dr. Snowden with dull eyes and flattened lips. "I killed them."

Dr. Snowden wrinkled his eyebrows. "Killed what?"

Jay pointed at the alien on the ground. "Its friends."

"But you survived," said Emily, walking over and giving Jay a hug.

Jay creased his eyebrows and hugged Emily back listlessly with one arm as he pointed to the krall with the other. "That the krall?"

"Yeah, it protected us," said Dr. Snowden. "I got stabbed in the leg three times and was poisoned, but I'm okay now. Thought I was gonna die."

"You're a tough son of a bitch," said Jay. He walked over to the wall, slumped down, and put his head into his hands.

"Everything okay?"

Jay grimaced and looked up at him. "Just thinking about Sanjay. That shit's still burning a fire in my head."

"Yeah," said Dr. Snowden, lowering his head and drooping his shoulders.

"Also thinking about my son possibly never knowing his dad," said Jay, looking off into the distance. "That and I never killed . . . ," he said as he twirled his hands in the air, "something smart like us before, not even when I was in the army."

Dr. Snowden sighed. "I know the feeling." He looked up at Jay. "I got one back in the control room."

Emily looked down. "I did too, I think."

"Why couldn't they just leave us the hell alone? Instead they gotta fuck with us," said Jay. He snorted and shook his head. "Credit to Blue Ball, though. He did one of them light shows behind them. It gave me the distraction I needed. Not sure it would've turned out as well without him."

V's lights glowed a bit brighter. "Acknowledged."

Dr. Snowden, Emily, and Jay shared a look and then nodded at each other.

Jay stood up and put his hands in his pockets. "So . . . what now?"

Evaran interacted with his ARI. "With the main engines online, we have a little less than seven hours to get to my ship. We can head there now. Before we go, though, I need to check something." He walked in front of the krall and then balled up his right fist and put it on his chest. With one continuous motion, he extended his fist toward Dr. Snowden, then to Emily, then to Jay.

The krall watched Evaran's actions intently.

"Everyone, extend your right arm, palm up."

Dr. Snowden extended his hand slowly, and the krall walked up and nuzzled it.

The krall then walked over to Emily and nuzzled her hand.

She reached out and patted it on the head.

The krall went over to Jay and nuzzled his hand. It slowly blinked, then walked back to Evaran.

Dr. Snowden had seen it blink slowly like that with Evaran. It made him think the krall was happy to not be alone.

"Umm . . . why's it doing that?" asked Emily.

Evaran scratched the krall behind the ears. "The krall understands a limited set of hand motions. The collar on the back of its neck gives it enhanced intelligence. The nuzzling was confirmation that you three are its friends."

"You just happen to know krall hand signals?" asked Dr. Snowden.

"Not quite, but the collar has an interface. I just tapped into it and downloaded the hand motions while you lay unconscious. Another interesting feature is it can project a shield in front of it. Quite useful when charging enemies with ranged weaponry. Now, let us head to my ship," said Evaran.

Jay exhaled sharply. "What about them mercenary dudes running around out there? They already got one of us."

"I have V set to continuous scanning. If we find a group of them, I will deal with it and retrieve information from one of their data devices. Most mercenary groups in this region have a crew location beacon of some type that we might be able to use as well. That should give us a tactical advantage, knowing their general locations."

Jay sighed. "A shotgun would work better."

Evaran half smiled at Jay and then walked toward the engine room entrance.

The group followed behind Evaran.

As they were walking out, Evaran turned to the krall and extended his right arm with a horizontal flat hand toward Emily.

The krall moved over to Emily and walked beside her. She patted it on the side.

Dr. Snowden could see that the krall would protect Emily. It could probably do a better job of that than he could. He limped along as he massaged his legs. The poor Grynge. Pulled from wherever they were, to this ship, confused, lost, and hungry. They probably attacked out of desperation. Now they were dead, just like everything else he saw on this ship.

The krall, though, was able to feed at least. It had saved his life, and he felt safer with it on their side. Just a bit ago, he thought it was going to be his death. Now it was protecting them and seemed to have bonded with Evaran and Emily. Maybe it saw what he saw in Evaran: hope. Hope that Evaran can maybe lead them out of this hell.

Dr. Snowden was relieved to leave the engine room, but all the death he had seen still lingered around in his mind. Although he was a bit calmer, he was beginning to realize the full impact of it in his thoughts. His stomach tightened up at the thought of running into more mercenaries. Hopefully the next leg of the trip was uneventful.

12

Galkett's muscles tensed as he and Hulldar moved down a hallway. So far, Galkett had only seen corpses and crazy-looking creatures. Although he had been marking items for salvage, he was not sure what half of the items were. It seemed the ship was doing its best to let him know it was truly alien. After hearing of Henrital's death, and Simas's and Rondall's before that, Galkett was beginning to think they should just cut their losses and leave.

"I know that look," said Hulldar.

Galkett sighed. "Nothing about this feels right."

Hulldar shrugged. "Just another alien ship to me."

"Yeah . . . but we've lost three crew already."

"That's on them. Maybe we're better off cutting deadweight."

Galkett shook his head. "Man, c'mon. They carried their weight."

"Whenever we had a firefight . . . who was getting hurt all the time? Simas always seemed to pick the worst choice and then do it. Rondall was okay . . . but his weakness was defending Simas. As for Henrital . . . I don't like how he always kept to himself. Same with Tostik."

"That's a slaver thing. They almost always work in pairs or small groups."

"Then why join up with a larger group in the first place?"

Galkett chuckled. "You don't have much empathy, do you?"

"Empathy's a weakness. It lets your guard down, and then you get your shit pasted."

"I don't know about all that."

They paused at the entrance to a massive corridor. Along the sides were entrances to other rooms. They chose the first entrance on the left.

Galkett figured the room was some type of cafeteria. What looked like replicator stations lined one wall, and a series of unusual-looking tables and chairs were spread throughout the area. A massive cracked screen resided on one side of the room. What surprised him was how clean the room was. He pointed at one of the replicators. "Let's see if we can get one of those to work."

They went over to the replicator.

Galkett studied it for a moment and then said, "Doesn't seem too obvious to me." He touched the console and pressed around on it.

"Broken, like most of this ship is," said Hulldar.

"It could be voice activated, but probably restricted to whatever language the crew spoke."

"I guess. It's not like we can pull one and take it. It's not worth marking," said Hulldar. He grinned as he gestured at some panels across the room. "But maybe there's something worth marking over there."

When they got to the panels, Hulldar tried to pry one open.

Galkett noted that although the panels had a console, there did not seem to be any handle to pull them open. The console had gibberish on it, and Galkett had no idea if it was even a language or a picture.

Hulldar tried to pry a panel open from the edges. After a moment, he stepped back in a huff. "Shit. These things must be magnetically sealed. Can you do anything with the console?"

"I don't think so," said Galkett.

"All right. Stand back," said Hulldar.

Galkett complied.

Hulldar pulled out his weapon and fired at the console.

The console fritzed, and after a moment, the panel slid out.

"That's how it's done," said Hulldar as he began to rifle through the now-exposed container attached to the panel.

Galkett peered in but did not recognize the cube-shaped packages. They were wrapped in a golden cover, with various symbols on them. Some had a green icon, others blue.

"Man . . . what the hell is this shit?" asked Hulldar.

Galkett laughed. "No idea. Maybe they're food seasonings or spices or something." He scanned them with his forearm device. "Looks like there's something organic in it."

Hulldar pulled a few of the cubes and put them in his pocket. "We can come back and get more of these then. Figure it out on the ship."

"All right."

They exited the room and paused in the hallway.

Looking down the hallway, Galkett said, "I count about ten of these rooms. I bet they're all the same."

"Won't hurt to check them out. Maybe we'll find some crew taking a break."

They shared a look and then laughed.

"Yeah . . . I don't think anything is taking a break on this ship," said Galkett. He appreciated Hulldar's sense of humor.

As tense as Galkett was, it helped ease the situation some. It was not the creatures, or even potential mercs that might be on board that gave him pause, it was the fact that he was sure Evaran was on board. Simas and Rondall had interacted with Evaran, and it cost them their lives, even if Evaran was not directly involved. A confrontation would be the worst-case scenario. Hopefully they could scan the rooms, mark up a few items, and then get off the ship. A sinking feeling in his stomach reminded him that things were probably just going to get worse.

⸻

As Jay walked out of the engine room, he instinctively peered around. When Sanjay was killed, Jay had no idea it was coming. Although he prided himself on being aware of his sur-roundings, the environment they were in was messing with his mind. He thought he was getting adjusted, but then between Sanjay's death and having to kill several of the Grynge, as Evaran called them, Jay felt off. He knew if it came down to fight or flight, he would fight like he always did, and proba-bly die in the ensuing altercation.

He sighed as he watched Evaran motion for V to fly out and then gesture for the others to cling to the wall. Evaran then took a step or two away from them. Jay understood it to be a defensive formation and appreciated Evaran's under-standing of the environment. Although Jay had been unsure of Evaran, that was not the case anymore. It seemed like he was far more than he appeared, although trying to figure out his emotions was hard to do.

Jay was not sure what to make of the krall. At least it was something friendly, but he could see it was not something you messed with if given a choice. It reminded him of a dog in some regards, and he could sense that it was probably just as confused as they were. The fact that Evaran could communicate with it showed it to be semi-intelligent. It also seemed to adopt Emily. As it strode next to Evaran, Jay could not help but think the krall considered the group its pack now.

His thoughts turned toward V. The ability to fly, cast holograms, and analyze things made him stand out. Jay was not fully sure he understood what a strong artificial intelligence was, but he figured V was a smart machine. During the fight with the Grynge, V's holographic distraction worked well, and it seemed he did it without a prompt but with more of an awareness of the situation. Maybe after this was all over, Jay could learn more about V in a less deadly environment.

Jay could see that Dr. Snowden was still in pain. He was rubbing his upper thigh and limping. It surprised Jay to know that Emily had stepped up to the plate, but since it was family under attack, maybe it ignited something in her. He thought about his wife and son for a moment. If he ever got out of this, he would spend as much time with them as he could.

His thoughts shifted back to Sanjay. Jay did not even know if Sanjay had any living relatives, and now, they would potentially never know what happened. If there had just been a few more minutes, Jay could have come to an understanding with Sanjay. Jay sighed.

Dr. Snowden glanced over at Jay. "You all right? A lot of sighing going on over there."

"Yeah . . . just . . . thinking, you know?"

"About Sanjay?"

Jay nodded. "It's so messed up. If I get my hands on any of those mercs, it's lights out for them."

Evaran raised a finger. "We should avoid any contact with that group if possible."

"I know . . . and they got weapons. I probably wouldn't get close to them before getting blasted," said Jay. He shook his head. "I was a dick to Sanjay and didn't have time to resolve that."

Evaran tilted his head at Jay. "I think he knew that you are a good person, and this is a stressful situation. Everyone reacts differently."

Jay swallowed hard as his eyes searched the ground. He would make an effort to be a team player, although he felt naked without anything to defend himself with. Even though Evaran was tough, Sanjay's death showed that anything could happen. Jay glanced at Emily. "If I came across as an asshole to you, I'm sorry."

"It's okay," said Emily. "This place . . . it's just wrong. It'd make anyone not be themselves."

Jay nodded.

"Hopefully we can get to Evaran's ship without any more issues," she said.

"That is the plan," said Evaran. "We are not too far from it now, assuming we do not run into more trouble."

Jay hoped so too.

After fifteen minutes of walking without incident, they reached a large hallway and entered it. On the sides were doors leading off to other areas.

Jay was again mesmerized by the size. It looked like it could easily sustain a large amount of traffic. With the lower mist density and brighter lights, he could see quite far. The random far-off shrieks and noises of creatures disturbed him, but he knew there was nothing he could do about that.

V flew back from scouting ahead and projected a map.

It showed one of the smaller side doors off to the right side leading to a large room, which was highlighted. Past the large room was a series of rooms connected to each other with two red dots highlighted in one of them.

"Analysis. Two humanoid life-forms detected ahead. Ninety-three percent match on visual profile indicating mercenaries."

Evaran narrowed his eyes. "Although I said we should avoid them, it looks like we have an opportunity to get some data, assuming they are Bloodbores."

Dr. Snowden bent over and took a deep breath.

"Uncle Albert?" said Emily as she rushed over to him.

Dr. Snowden held his hand up to her. "I'm fine. Just walking with pain is all." He glanced at her and smiled while exhaling sharply through his nose.

Emily tilted her head at him. "What?"

"Just glad you're headstrong," he said with a cracked voice. He straightened up, and Emily put her left arm around his shoulders.

Jay could see that they were close. If they were not before, they would be after this. He was thankful it was just him and not his wife and son present. Keeping it together was hard enough as it was.

The group reached the door V had highlighted earlier. It opened into a small hallway that ended at the entrance to another room.

Evaran pulled out his utility handle and formed a baton with a glowing blue end. "It is time to meet the Bloodbores."

13

Dr. Snowden grimaced as pain racked his body. Although his leg area was still tender, the poison had spread. The tingling sensation that rippled through him let him know the nanobots were still counteracting the poison. He hated being where he was, more so for Emily. With frayed nerves and an upset stomach, he was a wreck. He was trying to appear strong for Emily, but she seemed to be stronger than even he had realized. At least he was there for her. He could not imagine her having to go through this by herself.

The group walked along a small hallway and into the large room.

Evaran shielded the entrance they had used. He held his palm up to the krall, then flipped it around.

The krall walked a few steps forward and shook its head. A static sound rang out as a mostly transparent arced shield appeared in front of it.

It reminded Dr. Snowden of a bulldozer's front blade but reversed.

"Everyone stay here," said Evaran. "The two mercenaries are coming into this room from the opposite end in a few minutes, and I will deal with them. Make sure to stand behind the krall's defensive shield."

"We can help," said Emily.

Dr. Snowden was not sure how they could help, other than maybe being targets. He wished he had a weapon, although he was not sure he could use it, but it could be a deterrent.

"I can handle this," said Evaran. "If there is trouble, the krall will react. I will also drop the door shield behind you so you can run out. I have it up now in case something else comes up that hallway."

Dr. Snowden watched Evaran walk to the center of the large room. His casual stroll oozed confidence. Given the situation, it made Dr. Snowden think that Evaran had probably seen much worse. Dr. Snowden appreciated their tactical positioning. Their rear was protected, and with the krall in front of them, they were covered.

The room appeared to be full of dining tables and chairs, but the style was unusual. He squinted at the brightness in the room. It was like everything had been cleaned spotless and was shining. He sat down against the wall next to Emily and Jay.

The krall had made sure that it was in front of the group and was staring straight ahead.

Evaran scanned the door where the mercenaries were coming from with his ring.

A few minutes later, the two mercenaries strolled into the room. They immediately pulled out their weapons and trained them on Evaran.

Dr. Snowden could see the mercenaries in great detail. Maybe that was an aspect of his improved eyesight thanks to the nanobots. The two mercenaries looked like human men. The first man had on a trench coat or something like it, with what resembled a cowboy hat and high-tech sunglasses. This guy was straight out of a Western.

The second man had on a sleeveless shirt, baggy green pants, and a belt full of gadgets. A shiny machete-looking weapon hung off his belt, and markings covered his arm. He was bald, and his face screamed cockiness. It looked like the guy he saw in the video earlier who liked to sample the entertainment. The way they moved was telling. The first one seemed more secretive and reserved, the second one more cavalier.

The mercenaries moved cautiously toward Evaran.

"Well, well, whadda we got here?" said the second mercenary in a singsong voice.

Evaran bowed with his right arm across his chest. "My name is Evaran. I would advise you to not step in the slime near you. It is a vicious creature known as a Slivyn."

The second mercenary smirked and glanced at the first mercenary for a moment, then walked forward into the slime and stomped his boots. "Yeah, quite vicious." He exhaled sharply through his mouth and pointed at the first mercenary. "Galkett seems to know you already—said he recognized your profile from the video Simas and Rondall sent us. When they were found, they were nothing more than smear stains. You wouldn't happen to know anything about that, would ya?"

"They met their end courtesy of a Cepharus."

The second mercenary laughed. "A what?" He shook his head. "Galkett also claims you match the visual description of someone who has appeared in over a dozen civilizations across half a million years. Also busted Dolgus Kree and a few others." He shook a finger in the air. "The funny thing is he says you're a legend, but that sounds like a buncha crap to me. I ain't ever heard of ya. Anyways, you're talking to Hulldar now, and if the name doesn't scare ya, it should."

Galkett grimaced as he sidestepped the slime on the ground. "It *is* him. We should leave."

Hulldar glared at Galkett. "Leave? Enough with the legend crap."

"This isn't a fight we want to get involved with."

"Just watch my back. Damn. He's just a man."

Galkett backed away toward a table.

Hulldar faced Evaran. "That yer ship with the tough shield?"

"It is. You must be Bloodbore then."

Hulldar shot a defiant look at Evaran. "What if we are?"

"Then you have something I need."

Hulldar laughed. "And it looks like you might have something I need too." He gestured toward Emily and licked his lips. "Galkett, I claim first week with her."

"I'd like to see you try!" said Emily, jumping up with balled fists.

"Mmm, feisty. The best type. Nothing a few shackles can't handle," said Hulldar, shaking his torso vigorously.

Evaran turned halfway around with his hand down toward Emily. He then turned back to Hulldar and Galkett. "You have a data device of some type, as all mercenaries do. I would like to have it."

Dr. Snowden thought his eyes were playing tricks on him as he saw the slime begin to surround Hulldar's leg. It had crested Hulldar's boots and seemed to have leaked in to them. It was also approaching Galkett, who was backing away from it.

"I have a better plan. I'll take the girl as my personal assistant," said Hulldar, motioning at Emily, "and yer ship, and you and the others can be sold in the slave markets."

Evaran eyed Galkett. "Do you want to live? If so, climb onto that table."

Galkett trembled as he complied.

Hulldar bared his teeth as he snapped at Evaran. "Hey! Asshole! I'm talking to you!"

"Not for long," said Evaran, pursing his lips as he faced Hulldar. "You were dead ten seconds ago. I told you to avoid the Slivyn."

Hulldar snorted and tried to raise his leg. It didn't budge. He jerked around as he kept trying to lift his leg. "What the fuck is this? Galkett, help me out."

Evaran raised a hand toward Galkett. "Stay where you are. If you touch that slime, you will suffer the same fate as Hulldar. The Slivyn dissolves its prey very slowly. It injects a part of itself into the victim, which eventually leads to full paralysis. Once inside the bloodstream, it is over."

"Galkett! Not messing around, man. Get me out of this shit!" said Hulldar with a wavering voice. He fired at the ground around him.

The Slivyn had climbed to the top of Hulldar's knees. It dropped a tangent of slime to the ground. When it connected, it pulled Hulldar to his knees. The sharp sound of bones breaking ricocheted around the room.

Hulldar grunted twice, then screamed. He splayed out his arms to prevent going prone. His weapon slid out to the side into the Slivyn, which pulled it away. He tried to raise his arms, but the Slivyn held them down.

The Slivyn moved up his arms.

"Oh, shit! Galkett!" said Hulldar.

Sweat ran down Galkett's face. His nostrils flared as he looked at Evaran. "Help me, and I can help you!"

Hulldar screamed as the Slivyn climbed to his shoulders. "Galkett! Don't leave me here!"

Evaran pulled out his utility handle and formed a baton with a glowing orange end. He pointed it to the ground, in the direction of Galkett and then met Galkett's gaze. "I am going to clear a path to you. When it is clear, jump off the table and run along the cleared path. Any deception and I will stun you and leave you to the Slivyn. Are we clear?"

Galkett nodded his head violently.

Evaran fired an orange heat beam in a forty-five-degree arc at the ground. He swept it toward the table. Where it touched the Slivyn, the creature retracted.

Once a clear path was established, Galkett jumped off the table and ran toward Evaran.

The Slivyn attempted to intercept Galkett, but the beam beat it back.

Galkett cleared the path and stood by Evaran.

They turned toward Hulldar.

"Gaaalllkeeett," said Hulldar in a low, gurgling voice. The Slivyn had reached his lips and was pouring into his mouth.

Evaran faced Galkett. "He will be slowly digested over the next six hours, and he will be conscious for most of it."

Galkett's shoulders slumped as he let out a slow breath. His eyes turned down. He pulled out his weapon and glanced at Evaran, then at Hulldar. "I'm sorry, man," he said with a wavering voice. His hands trembled as he pointed his weapon at Hulldar. He fired a quick shot, which shredded Hulldar's head. Pieces of it fell back into the Slivyn.

Dr. Snowden recoiled when Galkett fired, and Emily gasped.

"God, that's fucked up," said Jay, standing with his hands on his hips.

Evaran sighed. "We need to leave this area." He extended his hand toward the hallway entrance where the others stood watching.

Galkett put his gun away and walked toward them with his head down.

Evaran followed Galkett, and when they neared the others, Evaran extended a hand out to the krall.

The krall shook its head, and its shield dissipated.

Evaran unshielded the hallway entrance door and then waved for the others to exit the room while holding a hand out, palm vertical at Galkett. Once the others were in, he indicated for Galkett to go in. Inside the small hallway, Evaran shielded the entrance. The door shields went up just as the Slivyn came within a few feet of the entrance. He motioned for everyone to go to the end of the hallway. Once they were there, he shielded the doorway, sealing them in the hallway. He gestured for Galkett to sit.

Galkett complied while breathing hard and eyeing the krall uneasily. "Are you gonna kill me?"

"I do not kill if it can be avoided. I am sorry for your loss, but I warned Hulldar."

Galkett drooped his head. "Yeah, I know. Hulldar doesn't listen to anyone. We were good friends." He licked his lips and pointed to the krall. "What is that thing?"

"That thing is a krall, but you prolly don't want to sample its entertainment value," said Jay.

Evaran extended a downward-facing hand at Jay and turned to Galkett. "You said you could help us. Elaborate."

Galkett sighed as he reached into his jacket.

Evaran extended his baton, which now had a luminous blue end, a few inches from Galkett's chest while the krall stepped forward. "What are you doing?"

Galkett raised his hands. "Whoa, whoa! You wanted a data device. I have one. I also have a location beacon. I was just getting them."

Evaran put a hand out to the krall, who stepped back. He retracted his baton and then gestured at Galkett.

Galkett pulled out a small cube with intricate designs on it and a small oval-shaped device. He held the cube up to Evaran. "I'm a member of the Zattari Cartel and former member of the Dalrun Spy Network. I infiltrated Jerzan's group several years ago. This cube has everything needed to incriminate him. I have tracked his activities since joining."

Evaran gestured at the oval device. "And that is the location beacon?"

"Yeah, and every Bloodbore has one. They allow us to see the direction and distance we are from one another. Hulldar's will most likely stop broadcasting soon, if it hasn't already, and Jerzan will come investigate."

Dr. Snowden shook his head. "Why're we listening to him?"

Galkett looked at Dr. Snowden. "I told them not to interfere with you. When Simas and Rondall transmitted the video of your group on one of the above walkways, I identified Evaran. He is well-known to the Zattari Cartel. Told them to avoid your group at all costs." He shook his head. "Jerzan didn't listen and ordered them to capture you. Apparently Simas and Rondall had other ideas, well, Simas probably did."

"Why should we believe you?" asked Dr. Snowden.

Galkett jerked his head back. "Betraying Evaran is foolish. Don't you know who you're traveling with?"

A chill fluttered across Dr. Snowden's body. He chewed on his bottom lip as he thought about what he really knew of Evaran, and it wasn't much. Apparently Galkett had a better idea of who Evaran was, and Galkett seemed fearful.

Galkett shifted uneasily and looked up at Evaran. "Whoever is on the opposite side of you doesn't end up well. I want no piece of that. Given your presence here, I suspect you will want Jerzan after what Simas and Rondall did, right?"

Evaran nodded at Galkett. "For that and a few other reasons."

"Like the Bilaxian most wanted list? I'm sure it was you who got Tolkus Gare, Jalt, and Dolgus Kree now."

"It was, and yes, the Bloodbores occupied the next slots after them."

Galkett took a measured breath and pointed at the shielded door. "Let me leave, and me and Hosk, a friend I can trust . . . I think, can take Jerzan's ship, which is actually a stolen Zattari ship. Hosk is there guarding it now. It would leave Jerzan stranded here for you to deal with. You could use the location beacon to determine how far away they are and in what direction. Since it won't be on me, Jerzan wouldn't know I was going to the ship."

"Or you could let Jerzan know where we are," said Dr. Snowden.

Galkett shook his head. "You're. Not. *Listening*. It's apparent you have no idea who Evaran is." He handed the location beacon to Evaran.

Evaran flipped the beacon around his hand and scanned it with his ring. "This will be useful. I can redirect pings from other location beacons to Hulldar's location beacon while still using it to get a rough idea of where they are. Jerzan will think you two are together in the room we were just in."

"So that's it?" asked Dr. Snowden. "We're just gonna take his word? We could at least use any weapons he has or something. Well . . . maybe not me, but Jay could use it."

Evaran glanced at Dr. Snowden as Galkett handed him the data cube. "Like the Krotovore weapons, these weapons are keyed to the owner. Mercenary weapons in this time and period are a little more dangerous. They blow up if someone else tries to use them. Besides, Galkett has enough information on me to know it is in his best interests not to lie to me. If he does, he knows I can track him down anywhere in space and time."

Dr. Snowden looked at Galkett, who was trembling. Evaran truly frightened Galkett. More than the loss of Hulldar even. Dr. Snowden wondered what the heck was in those stories.

Evaran scanned the cube with his ring and perused his ARI. "The data is good."

Galkett used the wall to slide up. "So we agreed?"

"Yes. Make sure that ship is gone by the time we get there. Any deception and you will be made priority."

Galkett nodded vigorously and raised his trembling hands. "No issues there, man."

Evaran unshielded the door opposite the one the Slivyn was behind. He gestured for Galkett to exit first.

Galkett stepped out into the main hallway. He squinted his eyes shut and took a deep breath while turning to face Evaran. After opening them, he said, "Thank you for sparing me. I have to ask, though. What're you doing here with a bunch of Dalruns?"

"They are not Dalruns. They are humans, from another galaxy, and are not supposed to be here at this point in space and time. I am taking them home."

Galkett swallowed hard with widened eyes. "And Jerzan messed that up." He shook his head. "He's fucked."

"His time is coming. Warden Borox has a cell for him and any other Bloodbores I capture. Consider yourself and Hosk lucky. Now go, and should you continue down the current path you are on, you may see me again. Take this opportunity as a chance to change."

Galkett gulped. He turned and ran down the hallway.

Dr. Snowden and the others assembled around Evaran.

Evaran faced them and tilted his head. "The ship is not too far away from here. Let us go."

Galkett hustled back to Jerzan's ship. Along the way, he saw mutilated corpses and blood of varying colors spattered around. There was no doubt in his mind that this ship was a death trap, and he had just escaped becoming a part of it. His lips drew down thinking of Hulldar. Although he was an asshole most of the time, he was also a close friend. Galkett knew though that Hulldar would kill on sight if Galkett's undercover status was blown. He had been given a second chance by Evaran. How rare that was, Galkett did not know, but from the historical records he had seen, not many second chances were given.

He reached the T junction outside docking bay three. To the left was Jerzan's ship, Hosk, and freedom. To the right were two small spiderlike creatures, who had paused and were staring at him. He fired a shot at one, killing it immediately, while the other ran off. They were no match for his weapons.

A chattering sound filled the air.

The thought that maybe those creatures were part of a swarm or something crossed his mind, similar to the ones he had seen earlier with Hulldar. Galkett sprinted to the left and entered the docking bay. Hosk sat on the ship's left wing with his weapon aimed forward. G-85 stood motionless in front of the ship with both weaponized arms pointing forward.

"Hosk, its Galkett!" shouted Galkett, raising his hands.

Hosk hopped down off the wing, and with a nod at G-85, he said, "Clear."

G-85 lowered its arms.

"Where's your beacon? I'm not getting a reading that it's on you. It says you're with Hulldar," said Hosk.

"Hulldar . . . is dead."

"What?"

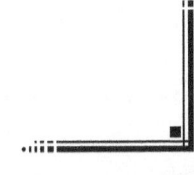

"We ran into Evaran, and Hulldar stepped into some slime that . . . just . . . ," said Galkett, grimacing, "digested him."

Hosk eyed Galkett. "Evaran spared you?"

Galkett licked his lips. "Yeah . . . on one condition. We leave with Jerzan's ship. He said any Bloodbores left behind have cells waiting for them in a prison run by a Warden Borox."

"I see. If you had fought Evaran, would you have won?"

"No . . . not even close. I would've been digested too, but . . . he gave me a second chance."

Hosk drew his head back a bit. "Why you and not Hulldar?"

"Probably because Hulldar ran his mouth, talking about what he would do to some girl under Evaran's protection. Evaran did warn him about that slime, but Hulldar . . . he had other ideas."

Hosk chuckled. "Ahh . . . that's so Hulldar. He went out true to form. Don't listen to nobody and talk shit."

Galkett looked around. It looked like a war zone, with dead creatures everywhere. He continued up to G-85, where Hosk was waiting. "What happened here?"

"These creatures tried to swarm in, some type of large insects. Never seen them before. Nothing we couldn't handle, but they did disable all my perimeter turrets I set up due to sheer numbers. G-85 mopped 'em up."

"I think I saw two outside in the hallway a bit away," said Galkett. "I shot one, and the other ran off."

"Yeah, probably to get more to hit us again."

Galkett sighed. "I know Hulldar was loyal to Jerzan, but I don't think you are. Am I correct in assuming this?"

"Jerzan gets the contracts, that is as far as it goes between me and him," said Hosk.

"Just to be clear . . . I'm actually with the Zattari Cartel. Is that a problem for you?"

"You're working with a member of the Zattari Cartel right now," said Hosk.

"What?"

"I was sent undercover after you."

Galkett wrinkled his eyebrows. "They didn't trust me."

Hosk shrugged. "They weren't sure you could do this. Jerzan has a way of sniffing things out. I was your backup."

"Then it seems there's no issue with leaving, which I'm thinking we need to do right now," said Galkett. "I never saw anything on your records indicating you were a member. You're good."

"Covering my tracks is essential in infiltration jobs, such as this one. Jerzan's massacre of the natives on Neoparene brought a lot of heat on the Zattari Cartel. Even though he is not a member, it was in our territory. It was a slap in our face," said Hosk.

"Yeah, I know. I stayed on the ship for that one, but . . . well, that's Jerzan for you."

Hosk nodded. "He's a bit too spontaneous. It's bad for business. I would have left earlier, but wanted to make sure you were embedded with no issues and also wanted to see if maybe Hulldar wanted to come with me. It was a slow process working on him. The Zattari Cartel agreed that whoever came with me would be cleared for membership, no questions asked."

"Let Jerzan rot with this ship," said Galkett. He eyed Hosk. "When is the last time Jerzan contacted you?"

"Just a bit before you came. We'll be long gone before he checks in," said Hosk. He walked over to a container and placed his location beacon, along with a small communication device. "This will let us stay in communication and respond if need be, but mainly to listen in. I'm . . . curious to see how this plays out."

Galkett smirked. "Funny how things work out."

Hosk and Galkett forearm shook, and then Hosk called G-85 over.

They started for the ship.

As Galkett walked up the ramp, he paused to take one last look around before boarding. It seemed even Hosk saw Hulldar's potential, probably as an enforcer, which would have been right up his alley. At least Galkett was alive, and with a crew of two, they would have ample food, a ship, and gear and not have to worry about the other Bloodbores hunting them down. He smiled thinking of when Jerzan found out just how screwed he was. It could not have happened to a nicer person. Galkett slapped the side of the ship and continued on as the ramp began to rise.

14

Jerzan looked around the room that he, Gaellus, Jahl, and the Rybox brothers were in. The room reminded him of cramped living quarters, except instead of beds, there were unusual-looking pods that were half open with dead aliens inside them.

Replacing Simas and Rondall would be time-consuming, and now having lost Henrital, they were down three. Tostik was not too far away, and Jerzan figured they could get to him in time. He raised a finger. "Checking on the others." He activated group comms. "Galkett? Hulldar? How're you two doing?"

Silence spread across the room as everyone listened in.

"Hey, shitheads, answer!"

After another moment of silence, Jerzan said, "Shit!" He closed his eyes for a moment and then sighed. "Hosk, have they contacted you?"

"Nope," said Hosk over comms.

Jerzan pulled up the rough map of the ship. "Looks like their beacons have them slightly away from where we need to go. Let's check it out."

"What about me?" asked Tostik over comms.

"Is that alien around you?"

"No . . . it's sorta quiet. I think maybe I shook it."

"Good. Stay hidden. This detour shouldn't be long," said Jerzan.

Tostik sighed. "All right. Hurry!"

Jerzan shut off group comms and switched to local comms. "Damn it. What the hell is going on here?" He waved forward. "Let's go."

The group hustled out of the room.

Twenty minutes later, they arrived at a massive hallway.

Jerzan pointed at one of the open doorways down a bit. "They're in there. Be prepared to fight."

Everyone pulled out their weapons and readied themselves.

When they got to the doorway, Jerzan peeked in. He gritted his teeth at the sight of a body missing the skin. The muscular structure of something Dalrun-sized lay on the ground, covered in slime.

Gaellus shook his head. "I think we know what happened to Galkett and Hulldar."

"I see only one body in there," said Jahl.

"Both location beacons are showing that they're on that body," said Jerzan.

The slime began to move toward them.

"What the hell?" asked Gaellus, stepping back.

Doran stepped forward and aimed at the ground. He flipped a switch on his side-mounted gun and shot out a flame.

The slime retreated.

Goran joined Doran, and together, they cleared a path to the body.

The others followed in behind them.

When they got to the body, Jerzan searched for the beacons. "This is Hulldar's beacon, but I don't see Galkett's."

Gaellus and Jahl rooted around the body while the Rybox brothers forced the slime to keep retreating.

Jerzan shook his head. "All right, out to the hallway. There's only one beacon here." He slapped his forearm device. "I'm not sure why this damn device thinks Galkett's beacon is here too."

The group hustled out of the room.

"Hosk," said Jerzan over group comms. "Where do you see everyone's beacons?"

"Except for Tostik, and Henrital's beacon where he died, everyone is where you're at," said Hosk.

Jerzan kicked the wall. "Damn it! Hulldar is . . . melted or something, and Galkett is nowhere in sight. Maybe that damn slime ate him already, but his beacon shoulda still been there, unless the slime ate that too. Then again . . . it woulda ate Hulldar's beacon too. Something's not right here."

Jahl tossed a hand out. "At least Tostik is still alive. I don't think we should split up, and after getting Tostik, we need to get off this tomb."

The Rybox brothers nodded.

"We agree on something," said Gaellus.

"Fine," said Jerzan. Over group comms, he said, "Hold tight, Tostik, we're coming."

"So . . . Hulldar . . . and Galkett . . . are dead too?" asked Tostik.

"Yeah," said Jerzan.

Tostik sighed. "I think I hear something . . ."

"We're on our way," said Jerzan.

The group charged down the hallway toward Tostik's location.

As they ran, Jerzan said, "Any creature in our way, waste 'em. I'm done playing games with these stupid things. It's time they learned who's on top of the damn food chain."

"I hear that," said Gaellus.

Jerzan's blood boiled. Losing five crew members that would be hard to replace was not only bad business, but he had personally recruited them. He knew that not everyone would get along, but they were all good at what they did. Hulldar and Galkett were part of what he always considered the core of the group. To think they were killed by a slime made Jerzan think there was something else at play. Maybe it was Evaran, but Jerzan did not hear Hulldar or Galkett call out that they had seen Evaran. At least they could get Tostik, then get off the ship. The price for sticking around was just too high.

───────────────────────

Dr. Snowden rubbed his legs. They were feeling much better, and after walking in silence for the last twenty minutes through various hallways and rooms, he thought he could almost hear his nanobots repairing them. There was still a bit of pain, but it was more localized instead of shooting all around. He wished he could say the same about his nose. The stench of rotting bodies filled the air as they came to a large corridor.

Evaran interacted with his ARI. "Down this corridor and off to the right is a storage room. It should provide us a shortcut."

"Why didn't we just follow Galkett?" asked Dr. Snowden.

"I do not fully trust him. If he were to be deceptive, it could lead to one of your deaths," said Evaran. He looked down for a moment. "I . . . was not willing to take that chance. Also, having him around may be distracting considering he is a Bloodbore."

Dr. Snowden nodded. "I can see that. I'm not sure I'd have anything kind to say to him."

"Yeah, probably best since it'd be hard for me to hold back from beating his ass," said Jay.

Evaran glanced at Jay. "I am aware of that and factored it in."

Jay nodded and then waved a hand in front of his face. "Damn, what is that smell?"

"We are near the Krotovore living quarters. The strength of the scent leads me to believe there are a lot of dead Krotovore there."

Despite Dr. Snowden's lingering hatred of the Krotovore, he felt bad for the ones caught in their living quarters. "Yeah, let's not check that out." He went over the interaction with Hulldar and Galkett as they continued down the corridor. Something about it troubled him. He wrinkled his eyebrows and looked at Evaran. "Could you have saved Hulldar back there? Like maybe by stopping him physically from going into the Slivyn?"

Evaran paused and turned to face him. "Yes. I could have grappled him to me, repulsed him back, or shot a heat beam at his feet."

Dr. Snowden swallowed hard as his fingers went cold. He remembered Galkett saying they did not really know Evaran. Maybe Galkett was right. Evaran had let someone die when he could have prevented it. "Umm . . . I had come to believe you respect all life."

"Most life. At the massacre of Neoparene, Hulldar and Gaellus killed over fifty women and children. They did not do it quickly. They tortured them for several months before killing every one of them. That is unacceptable," said Evaran.

"Oh . . . The people of Neoparene were friends of yours, I assume."

"They were," said Evaran as he turned around and continued walking.

"No wonder Galkett was scared shitless of you, man," said Jay.

Evaran half turned his head toward Jay. "He knew my view on those like Hulldar and Gaellus, so that would be an expected reaction. Galkett's concern was if I would find him guilty by association."

"Maybe, but he was *terrified*, and he didn't look like the type that scares easy. Like he was more scared of you than death. He had one thing right, though. We don't know much about you."

Evaran glanced at the ground for a moment, and then looked forward. "You know more about me than most, and that is a dangerous place to be. This situation has caused me to share more than I normally would."

"No worries there, man," said Jay, tossing a hand out. "I still have a hard time believing half this shit anyways, or even understanding it. I mean, hell, living slimes, headhunters, mercenaries, giant insects, and a big-ass high-tech dog." He extended out a hand toward the krall. "No offense."

The krall tilted its head at Jay.

"Not to mention you and your wild devices. All we need to round it out is some killer clowns. Damn, I could use a beer about now."

V flew near Jay. "Correction. Killer clowns are not on the ship specimen roster."

Jay shook his head. "I know that, Blue Ball. I'm just saying, we keep running into shit that I didn't think existed."

"Analysis. There are twelve known clowns with the killer attribute on Earth."

Emily glanced at Dr. Snowden, then at Evaran. "Is V being serious?"

"V is always serious," said Evaran, eying Emily.

A tingling sensation ran through Dr. Snowden. He really didn't like clowns. They creeped him out, and now he knew there were at least twelve known killer clowns on Earth. He exchanged a look of surprise with Jay.

They walked in silence for ten more minutes before approaching a large storage room.

The krall growled, and its skin turned a light shade of red.

Jay scrunched his nose. "Damn. Smells even worse here, like someone shit their pants. Man, not sure I'm liking this enhanced-smell thing."

Evaran put his finger up to his lips. "Listen." He motioned for V to enter the room.

The sound of a man gurgling in pain emanated from within.

V flew back out. "Analysis. One life-form detected. Life signs are diminishing. Death is imminent."

They entered the room and followed V.

The room had a wide path to the other side, leading to another entrance. On each side of the path were large high-tech shipping containers stacked in groups of three. The groups were laid out in a grid fashion.

They followed V down a row to the immediate right of the entrance and arrived at the last container stack in the row.

The krall paused and sniffed the air. It growled and walked menacingly toward the end of the row.

V flew forward and scanned around the corner.

Evaran rushed to where V was scanning and put his hand out to the krall.

Dr. Snowden and Jay gathered around Evaran and found a man covered in blood. The man was holding his neck and squinting hard as blood gushed out. His eyes dulled, and his motions slowed.

A catlike humanoid alien with blue-and-orange fur and white stripes jumped from the top of the container and landed behind Emily. It grabbed her and put its left arm around her body and a claw from its right hand against her neck.

The krall wheeled around and roared at it.

"Stand back!" said the alien.

Evaran motioned for the krall to stand down as they turned to face the alien. He tilted his head. "We mean you no harm. We did not know you were here, although I am not sure how that is possible."

The alien growled and nodded toward the now-dead man on the ground. "Your kind is not trustworthy, although . . . this one can understand your language."

Evaran narrowed his eyes and tilted his head. He pointed to the dead man. "This man. He tried to attack you?"

The alien hissed. "He hunted this one and killed my sister. Tried to put collars on us. This one killed him and his partner."

Evaran sighed. "Judging by the gear he is wearing, this man was part of another group on this ship. They are hunters. Like you. They call themselves the Bloodbores." He pointed to Jay and Dr. Snowden, then at Emily. "We are not hunters and just want to leave this ship."

The krall stepped forward.

The alien growled, stepped back, and nodded at the krall. "She means to kill."

Dr. Snowden furrowed his eyebrows. So the krall was female. It reminded him of how little he actually knew about the krall. He noticed she had bonded with Emily more so than with him or Jay. Maybe it was a maternal thing to protect the young, but he figured it was more likely he was anthropomorphizing her.

Evaran motioned for the krall to step back, and then interacted with his ARI. "You are a male Farethedan hunter, correct?"

The Farethedan tilted his head. "Yes. How do you know this?"

"I have access to information on those aboard this ship. My name is Evaran. To my left is Dr. Albert Snowden and to my right is Jay Beerman. The big female is a krall, as you already noticed. You are holding Emily Snowden, Dr. Snowden's niece. They were all captured like you and brought here, and I am taking them home. I can take you home as well. Do you have a name?"

The Farethedan squinted his eyes and scanned them for few moments. "Kazryn."

"Kazryn, okay. There is no need to hold Emily hostage."

"You wear the clothes of a hunter," said Kazryn, growling. "This is a trick! Drop my guard and then you will attack me with a weapon of light." He walked backward toward the main path in the center of the room.

Emily whimpered.

The group followed Kazryn cautiously.

Evaran put his hand out. "Wait! There is no need for this. We have lost one of our own already to these hunters."

They reached the path in the center of the room.

Kazryn walked out to the middle of the path with his back to the entrance they had come in from.

The group assembled across from Kazryn and Emily.

Emily trembled with closed eyes.

Dr. Snowden tapped Evaran's arm and stepped forward. With a raised hand facing Kazryn, Dr. Snowden said, "You lost your sister and are alone now, right?"

Kazryn growled and narrowed his eyes.

Dr. Snowden's breathing shortened. "You are holding the only family I have left. If you kill her, I will be alone, like you. You would have done to me what the hunters did to you." He grimaced and squinted hard as his eyes watered. His breathing went ragged. "I don't want to go on without her in my life. If you want to take someone as a hostage, take me. But let her live. Please."

Kazryn's eyes softened, and he scrutinized Dr. Snowden for a minute. After sniffing the air and uttering a low growl, Kazryn released Emily.

She ran to Dr. Snowden and wrapped her arms around him.

Kazryn adopted a defensive stance, as if expecting an attack. "This one gives you family."

Evaran stepped forward as Dr. Snowden, Emily, and Jay moved behind the krall. "Do you remember where you came from?"

"This one does not. This jungle is unusual, made of metal. This one and this one's sister woke up and explored it. Met two of your kind. They tossed slave restraints at us and tried to enslave us. This one's sister did not make it." Kazryn gave a deep, guttural growl. "This one killed one of them. Came here. Killed the other one. This one is now alone."

"The mercenaries you killed have location beacons. The others will come looking for them. You do not need to be alone. You should join us. We are on the way to my ship and can figure out where you came from and take you home."

Kazryn turned his head out to the hallway, then looked back. "You smell like a matter mage. This one does not trust matter mages."

"Matter mage," said Evaran, rubbing his chin. "I have not heard that term in a long time. I may share certain traits with them, but I assure you, I am not one of them. However, I do have an idea of where you might be from now."

V flew in behind Kazryn.

Dr. Snowden had not even realized V had been gone.

"Analysis. Multiple life-forms approaching. Visual profiles indicate ninety-six-percent match of dungol and five mercenaries, including Jerzan."

Kazryn roared and flashed his hands out with extended claws. He turned and bounded out of the room and down the hallway.

"Wait!" said Evaran. He put his hand on his forehead and sighed.

"What was that all about?" said Dr. Snowden.

Evaran sighed. "He did not trust me and now seeks vengeance for his sister. The Farethedan, based on the Krotovore logs, appear to be a hunter society. He is honor bound to avenge his sister."

Jay snorted and gestured toward Evaran. "This ain't the place to be doing that shit."

Weapons fire and a high-pitched roar rang out from the hallway.

Evaran tilted his head. "We need to move now. They are approaching fast according to the location beacons. I do not think Kazryn was successful."

Dr. Snowden shook his head. Evaran had tried to help Kazryn, but Kazryn didn't trust Evaran. At least Kazryn hadn't hurt Emily. Dr. Snowden remembered that it took him several hours to believe Evaran, so Kazryn not trusting Evaran in a matter of minutes was definitely possible. Still, Kazryn trusted Dr. Snowden enough to release Emily. He wished Kazryn would have joined them.

They moved toward the entrance opposite the one they came in from.

Loud grunting noises filled the air when they reached the other room entrance.

Dr. Snowden froze. It was the dungol, and it was barreling toward them. He remembered Evaran asking him what he would do if he were to face one. Running sounded good.

The krall shook her head and deployed her shield as she stepped in front of the group.

As the dungol crossed the midpoint of the room, five mercenaries entered from the other end.

Dr. Snowden recognized Jerzan immediately.

"There they are!" yelled one of the mercenaries.

"Get 'em!" said Jerzan.

The mercenaries took aim and fired at the group. Orange beams sliced the dungol that was in the way. It let out a final grunt as what was left of it slid into the krall's shield, pushing her back some.

Emily and Jay ran into the hallway and around a bend. Dr. Snowden joined them, but paused to peer back to see what Evaran was going to do.

Evaran slapped the back end of the krall.

She shook her head, which dissipated the shield, and turned and ran into the hallway.

Evaran stood for a moment with his shield raised as beams and projectiles bounced against it. Jerzan and Evaran locked eyes. He then ducked into the hallway.

Dr. Snowden heard Jerzan say to get Tostik. Maybe that was the name of the person who had died in the room. Dr. Snowden snapped back to reality as Evaran rushed by.

Evaran motioned at V. "There is a shortcut through the worm pit ahead. Take us there!"

"Acknowledged," said V. He took off ahead of the group.

Evaran pointed forward. "Everyone follow V!"

Dr. Snowden swallowed hard as he tried to focus on running. It was not something he did often, and his legs were letting him know about it. The Bloodbores were hot on their tail, and he suspected they were out for blood. They probably thought Evaran was responsible for all the deaths. A worm pit seemed like an odd place to go to, but if it provided a faster way to Evaran's ship, then that is what they would do. Dr. Snowden sighed as he concentrated on keeping up with the group.

15

Galkett eased back in the copilot chair of Jerzan's ship as he viewed the data-filled screen in front of him. It had readouts and advanced metrics showing that they were a bit away from the alien ship. Hosk's device was still active, but they were getting close to the range where they would not be able to relay any communication. Galkett was glad that Hosk had come along, and every minute away from the ship made Galkett feel better. He gestured at the screen. "We're almost out of range."

"Yep," said Hosk. He eyed Galkett. "You're enjoying this more than I thought you would."

"Getting out from under Jerzan is one thing, but getting a second chance from Evaran? I know he's offered that to others in the past, I'm just glad he offered it to me."

"What if we had refused him? You think he would have hunted us down if everyone escaped?"

Galkett nodded. "Without a doubt. It's like his ship can travel anywhere in space . . . and I'm beginning to think time too. I don't think he's so much long-lived as just able to move around time. There would be nowhere we could run. Think about that."

"Thankfully, I don't have to."

Galkett's console chirped at him. He peered at it for a moment, and then his eyes widened. "Oh, shit, it's a Bilaxian cruiser."

Hosk examined his console. "Yeah, and it's not alone." He glanced at Galkett. "Evaran or not, we woulda had to deal with that too."

"Yeah . . . and look at the speed of the alien ship. It'll hit the sun before the cruiser can get to it."

"Yeah, and if we're the only ship in range after it hits the sun, we'll be easy to detect. The Bilaxians probably already detected us, but they're far enough away we can outrun them and disappear."

"If we had detected them earlier, then we woulda never gone on board," said Galkett.

Hosk narrowed his eyes. "You think Evaran knew that and that's why he altered the ship's trajectory and speed?"

Galkett bobbed his head for a moment. "It's possible. If his ship is as advanced as I think it is, it probably could have detected much farther out than we could." He narrowed his eyes for a moment. "Come to think of it . . . once that alien ship goes into the sun . . . there'll be nothing left for anyone to scavenge." He shook a finger at Hosk. "*That* sounds like Evaran from what I read."

"I'm glad you're an expert."

"Less expert and more just aware. It's how I've survived this long. Evaran seemed intent on punishing Jerzan."

As if on cue, the communicator turned on.

"Hosk, you there? Hulldar and Galkett are down, and . . . Tostik is too. We found their beacons. Hulldar and Galkett were digested by a slime, and Tostik looks like he was mauled to death. We also found Evaran and his group and are currently pursuing them. After we capture them, we're going to the ship. Prep it for takeoff. We're getting the fuck out of here," said Jerzan over the ship comms.

Hosk grinned at Galkett for a moment and then pressed a button to his side. "Damn, the ship got Simas, Rondall, Tostik, Henrital, Hulldar, *and* Galkett? That's some crazy shit."

"Don't worry about that for now, and keep it together. The last thing we need is to lose you and G-85, or more importantly, the ship. We've lost too damn much already."

"All right. I'll prep the ship," said Hosk. He pressed the button on his side, closing communications.

Galkett laughed. "I guess that's our final communication with Jerzan. He's gonna be so surprised when he finds out we're gone."

"Let's hope Evaran deals with him, because if he doesn't, then you know Jerzan will come after us."

Galkett shrugged. "Maybe . . . but how's he gonna get off the ship? And even if he does, there'll be a Bilaxian cruiser group on them." He shook his head. "No . . . I think Evaran will deal with Jerzan and whoever is left."

Hosk narrowed his eyes for a moment. "I'm surprised Evaran didn't just follow you back if he wanted off the ship. He would've reached it about the same time you reached this ship."

"I thought about that too, but he had some injured person with them who probably wouldn't have kept up. He may have also considered me a threat to the others. After Simas and Rondall, I don't think he was taking that chance. Besides, I don't think he's leaving that ship without dealing with Jerzan."

Hosk pointed at the large central screen between them. "We're out of range in five . . . four . . . three . . . two . . . one. Done."

Galkett pumped his fist in the air for a moment. "All right, my reptilian Greer brother, where to?"

"You tell me, my pale-skinned Dalrun brother."

They shared a laugh.

Galkett's muscles relaxed. Although he wanted to stick around and find out what happened to Jerzan, risking Evaran's wrath when given a second chance was not worth it. Dealing with a Bilaxian cruiser group was not something Galkett wanted to mess with either. One of the first things they would need to do is replace Jerzan's ship with a new one. No need to leave any trace. They could hit up one of the black market shipyards scattered around.

Evaran was not quite what Galkett had expected. *Rational* and *fair* were words that came to mind when thinking of Evaran. *Merciful* and *compassionate* as well. He was helping those who would have surely died without his help. If the stories Galkett had read were true, then they left out some of those details. He suspected meeting Evaran was rare, but at least the second-chance part was now verified. Meeting him outside this event would have been interesting.

A sense of giddiness rushed through Galkett. He had escaped what should have been a death sentence, after everything he had seen. Being given a second chance was something that Galkett would make good of. A thought did run through his head that Evaran might do a checkup. It would not matter. This was a time for a change, not just in ship, but in lifestyle. Galkett would not do anything that might draw Evaran's attention. With Hosk at Galkett's side, he felt like a new beginning was before him, and he planned to take advantage of it.

Dr. Snowden concentrated on trying to keep up with V. How he was able to fly was a mystery, but Dr. Snowden figured he could ask about that later. For the moment, just sticking with the group was proving to be a challenge. Emily and Jay seemed to keep up without issue. Maybe their nanobots were kicking in. Dr. Snowden wondered if his would as well. In the distance, he could hear weapons fire. He did not know what was going on, but he was not going to pause to find out.

As the group ran through several hallways and rooms on their way to the Krotovore worm pit, Dr. Snowden noted the carcasses of various aliens and creatures that they passed. He gagged at the smell. Some were partially intact, exposing their insides to the world. It hit him that everywhere he had been on the ship outside the medical lab reeked of the smells of death. Tack on the mist and poor lighting, and there was a recipe for ominous. Sometimes there was no body, only clothing and different-colored liquids around them.

After ten minutes of navigating, they rounded a corner to a short hallway leading to the entrance of the Krotovore worm pit room.

Dr. Snowden peered back and noticed that Evaran was not with them. "Hold up."

The group paused.

Dr. Snowden glanced around. "Where's Evaran?"

Emily and Jay looked around the hallway.

The krall walked toward the corner they had turned.

After a moment, Evaran appeared, flying out of control and into the wall. He crumpled to the ground, then jumped up and dodged a blue blast. As he rolled toward the entrance, he said, *"Move!"*

They followed Evaran to the entrance.

Dr. Snowden surveyed what he could of the room. The entryway was large like the main bridge concourse. The floor was about twenty feet down, resembling a deep pit, with walkways above it, connecting the entrance they had used with three others, forming a crossway. The walkways all had guardrails and converged into a center platform that was a bit lower than the walkways. The platform had a circular structure with consoles ringing it. Small ramps sat at a slight angle between each walkway and the platform area. The pit below the walkways and center platform had a brown surface that spanned the whole room, and a musky smell with the strong scent of feces permeated the air.

Evaran motioned for them to enter the room. "The worms are below. Do not worry about them."

They scurried across the raised walkway to the center platform.

Evaran motioned for them to keep going straight.

They crossed over to the other walkway, which ended with a light-blue shielded door with a physical door behind it that was barely open.

"Wait here and see if you can get that door open," said Evaran. He motioned at the krall, which turned to face the direction they had come in from.

She shook her head and deployed her frontal shield.

"What is this worm pit exactly?" asked Dr. Snowden.

"A place to store worms that are used as a nonreplicated food source. According to the Krotovore logs, the worms used to prey on the Krotovore, now they use the worms as a delicacy and backup sustenance."

Emily grimaced. "That's so gross."

Evaran nodded and then walked back to the central platform and placed his UIC on one of the consoles.

The UIC emitted a stable light after a few moments.

Jerzan and his mercenaries burst into the room.

Evaran interacted with his ARI, and the angled ramps between the platform and walkways receded into the walkways, leaving a roughly ten-foot gap between each walkway and the central platform.

Dr. Snowden, Jay, and Emily went to work trying to open the physical door after the light-blue shield disappeared.

Evaran jumped back onto the walkway and turned to face Jerzan, who had walked to the edge of the receded walkway on the other side.

"So . . . the great Evaran," said Jerzan. He glanced back at his mercenaries while pointing at Evaran. "This is what Galkett was scared of."

The mercenaries laughed.

"You're quite the pain in the ass," said Jerzan. He pointed at Evaran. "I saw your handiwork with Simas and Rondall."

"That was not me. That was a Cepharus," said Evaran.

Jerzan laughed. "Right . . . and I suppose Hulldar and Galkett were killed by that slime thing we found."

"Hulldar was killed by it. Galkett left with Hosk on your ship," said Evaran.

Jerzan's smile wound down. He tapped at a device on his forearm. "Hosk? Report."

After a few moments of silence passed, Jerzan tried again, but no response. He turned to one of the mercenaries and waved for him to move. "Jahl, go."

Jahl took off out of the room.

Jerzan pivoted back to Evaran. "Now why'd he do that?"

"We made a deal," said Evaran.

Jerzan exhaled sharply through his nose. "Enough of this! You're outgunned here, and you know it. Why don't you reattach these walkways and come quietly. Otherwise we'll just shoot and stun everyone."

"Why don't we just shoot this asshole already?" said one of the mercenaries.

Jerzan turned his head to the side and raised a hand. "Shut up!"

"You can try. However, you will not be able to get over here, much less carry anyone across the gaps," said Evaran.

Jerzan faced Evaran. "It seems like we have a Bilaxian standoff. We noticed the ship changed course, guessing more of your handiwork. We can wait here as long as it takes. You can end this now."

"As can you. I would normally suggest you leave on your ship. Since it is gone, I would ask you to stay close to mine so I can deal with you after getting my friends to it."

"Damn, you're a cocky son of a bitch," said one of the mercenaries.

"Not cocky. Experienced," said Evaran.

"I don't get your bravado," said Jerzan. He crooked his thumb at two of the mercenaries behind him. "While I could take you down, I'm standing in front of you with Goran and Doran, the toughest Bilaxian enforcers around. They could take you down by themselves. You're acting like you have a chance of getting out of this. We have you pinned, and there's *nothing* you can do about it."

Dr. Snowden paused from trying to open the door to look at the mercenaries. Goran and Doran had blue skin and towered over Jerzan. Their bald heads and the black patterns on half their faces made them look fierce. Doran had a big weapon on his back that looked like it was attached to a metal belt on his hip. These guys looked like they were serious damage dealers. Dr. Snowden shuddered thinking about what they would do if they captured him.

"I am familiar with the Rybox brothers," said Evaran.

Jerzan crooked his thumb at the other mercenary who had been talking earlier. "If that's not enough, I have—"

"Gaellus," said Evaran. "Master marksman and butcher of Neoparene."

Gaellus laughed. "Ha! I guess my reputation does precede me."

Evaran's eyes narrowed. "You and Hulldar killed over fifty women and children there. You are beyond my mercy."

"So you know of Neoparene," said Jerzan.

"Yes, they were my friends. More importantly, you caused a timeline change. I will try to correct it when this is done."

"Shit . . . this is some of that crap Galkett was talking about," said Gaellus.

"You should have listened to Galkett," said Evaran. He wagged a finger at Jerzan. "You have issues in your own house to deal with anyway."

"What the hell you talking about?" said Jerzan.

Evaran half grinned. "Capture, not kill, correct? Seems Simas and Rondall did not listen to you. Perhaps because they did not respect you enough as a leader."

"They paid the price, now didn't they?" said Jerzan.

Evaran narrowed his eyes. "They killed someone under my protection. That is a dangerous place to be." He raised a finger. "Nonetheless, you failed to see that you had an under-cover Zattari Cartel member in your crew. Galkett informed you of my presence, but you failed again by not assessing the threat correctly. You should have sent out four-man teams instead of two-man teams."

"You're hardly a four-man threat."

"Maybe, but this ship would say otherwise. You have lost some of your crew to it already, while others took your ship. A four-man team would have had a higher chance of survival, and maybe you would still have your ship."

Jerzan threw his hands into the air and snorted. "Anything else you wish to critique?"

"No. We are done here," said Evaran as he turned to walk back to the krall and the others.

Jerzan pointed at Evaran. "I'm not done talking to you, asshole! Get back here!"

"Why are we still talking to this shit bag!" said Gaellus. He stepped to the side and fired an orange beam at Evaran.

Zzzt!

Evaran turned and raised his left forearm shield, which deflected the beam. He stumbled back.

Gaellus fired again.

Zzzt!

Evaran deflected the shot again.

Jay was trying to push the door open when the deflected shot went just over the krall's shield and hit his arm, cleanly separating it from him. He screamed as he fell to the ground and then passed out.

The krall moved in front of Jay lying on the ground.

Dr. Snowden and Emily rushed over to him to try to stop the bleeding.

"Evaran!" said Emily as her head whipped around.

Evaran tossed a device to Dr. Snowden. "Use this on the wound, *now*!"

Dr. Snowden caught the device. It looked like something you slid your fingers into, like a four-finger ring. He slipped his fingers into it and used his thumb to press the button on the side. A beam shot up out of it. He realized he had it on backward, then pulled it off and put it back on the right way.

Emily grimaced as she cradled Jay's head in her lap, holding up what was left of his shoulder.

Dr. Snowden bent down and applied the beam to the wound. A skin-like film began to appear over the bloody stump. He realized it was similar to what Evaran had done to his wounds, but this was a lot more severe. Maybe that is why a different device was being used and not Evaran's ring. Dr. Snowden looked at Evaran and the mercenaries.

Evaran turned back toward the mercenaries and ran to the center platform. After jumping up on it while extending his utility handle into a baton with a white glowing end, he pressed a button and aimed it at the mercenaries.

Boom!

The baton bellowed as white concentric circles emanated from it.

Jerzan, Goran, and Doran sprawled backward.

Gaellus held on to the guardrail and only caught the periphery of the blast.

Evaran jumped onto the walkway with the mercenaries. He rushed over and knocked the weapon out of Gaellus's hands and over the railing.

Gaellus grunted as he tried to stabilize himself.

Evaran then turned his baton toward Jerzan, Doran, and Goran, who were struggling to get back up.

Boom!

Jerzan and the Rybox brothers went tumbling out of the room.

Evaran interacted with his ARI.

The door Jerzan, Doran, and Goran were pushed out of was now shielded, and the walkways reconnected to the center platform.

Evaran clenched his jaw as Gaellus jumped up and rushed forward with a knife that had an orange glow to it.

Gaellus thrust forward with his knife.

Evaran sidestepped the thrust and kicked Galkett in the chest.

Gaellus rag-dolled to the other side of the walkway while his knife went spilling to the side.

Evaran walked over and stared at Gaellus on the ground. With a shake of his head, Evaran said, "To the people of Neoparene, I give justice." He raised his hand at a ninety-degree angle. His palm faced Jerzan, Doran, and Goran, who had gotten back up and were now staring in through the shielded door. Evaran balled his hand into a fist and shook it, then turned and walked back toward where Jay was being attended to.

Gaellus caught his breath and then hustled over to his knife on the ground. His eyes widened as the krall rounded the center platform and bore down on him.

She knocked him to the ground, sending his knife flying away again, and then roared.

Dr. Snowden jumped up at the roar. Evaran was rushing over to them, and the krall stood over Gaellus, with her monstrous teeth on display just a few inches away from his face. Dr. Snowden flinched as she popped Gaellus's head in one quick motion, like bursting a balloon.

The krall roared and then snapped at Jerzan and the other mercenaries behind the shielded door, causing them to jump away. She then strutted back over to Evaran.

Dr. Snowden returned the healing device to Evaran.

Evaran put it on his belt and scanned the wound with his ring. "The wound is now stable short-term, but we need some medical supplies. There is a research lab nearby that should have a gel that will cover it." He ripped off several strips of Jay's shirt and wrapped the wound.

The blood had stopped spilling everywhere, but the smell made Dr. Snowden's stomach churn.

Evaran stood and walked to the busted door, where he placed his now-retracted utility handle between the door and the wall. With a press of a button, the utility handle began to extend into a staff, which pushed the door back. With the door open wide enough for them to go through, he bent over and dragged Jay to the opening. "We need to move. Jerzan and crew will head to docking bay three since they know we must go through there. They will probably also want to verify if Jahl found the ship gone, assuming Galkett and Hosk did get away." He pulled Jay out, with Dr. Snowden, Emily, and the krall in tow. "Let us go."

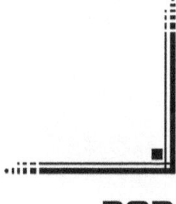

16

Jerzan watched through a semitransparent shielded door as Evaran and his group left. Gaellus dying was unexpected, but it seemed Evaran's group had some power. Retrieving Gaellus's body was not even an option at this point. Jerzan went through the brief skirmish in his mind. Evaran had just tossed everyone around like so much trash. Maybe Galkett was right about Evaran after all. Jerzan gritted his teeth. He kicked the wall several times and then walked around in a circle. "Damn it! Hosk and Galkett betray us, and now Gaellus is dead."

Goran looked at Doran for a moment and then at Jerzan. "We'll hunt them down and kill them."

Jerzan slapped their chests several times. "Damn right. It's no surprise the only crew left standing is me, Jahl, and you two. We're survivors and we *will* survive this. Then it's payback time."

The Rybox brothers nodded.

"All right, not much we can do for Gaellus. I'm gonna miss his trouble-causing ass," said Jerzan. He sighed. Losing crew members was getting old. Gaellus in particular hurt since they had been close. Jerzan's throat constricted. He knew he had to appear indifferent to losing Gaellus in front of the Rybox brothers, but Gaellus's loss stung, just like the deaths of Rondall and Hulldar. Jerzan would make sure that this was the last crew member death. He gnashed his teeth. "Let's head to the docking bay. If Jahl finds our ship gone . . . then we'll need to take another one." He grinned big. "And I think I know whose ship we can take."

The Rybox brothers laughed.

Jerzan motioned forward. "Let's move!"

After ten minutes of hustling through various corridors and rooms, the group paused as Jahl talked over group comms. "Damn. Those assholes did take the ship."

Jerzan sighed. "This day just keeps getting worse and worse. Is Evaran's ship still in the other bay?"

"Yeah."

"Good. We're gonna set up a trap since they need to come through where our ship was."

"Got it," said Jahl. After a moment, he said, "One thing. There were some insect-looking aliens near the T junction right before the docking bay. I counted maybe about five small ones and two medium-sized ones. I wasted some of them, and the others scattered off. I'm not sure if they're going to come back . . . so just a heads-up when you approach the docking bay."

"We'll handle the bugs," said Doran.

"All right. I'll check out the rest of the docking bay and see what we can set up. Out," said Jahl.

Jerzan glanced at the Rybox brothers. "Hosk and Galkett will wish they were never born when we get a hold of them. I want them to suffer."

"We can do that," said Goran, tapping at a large knife on his side.

Jerzan knew the Bilaxians could be downright vile with their torture, and the Rybox brothers were no exception. He recalled hearing that they had skinned a Dalrun but kept him alive and then chipped away parts of him over an extended period of time, making sure he was still conscious through it all. It was an art form to them. Hosk and Galkett would learn all about that in time. Jerzan nodded forward. "Let's go."

After another twenty minutes, they reached the T junction before the docking bay.

Jerzan looked off to the right and saw eight small alien creatures and four medium-sized ones. "Damn, those must be the aliens Jahl was talking about." He narrowed his eyes. "There seems to be a bit more, though."

Doran smiled as he faced the aliens and pointed his side-mounted gun at them. "Not anymore." He unloaded a barrage of projectiles that shredded most of the aliens.

The aliens who were not immediately killed ran off.

Goran harrumphed. "They're weak."

Jerzan rubbed his chin. "Yet . . . they came back, even after Jahl shot them. Let's hope there aren't too many more of those damn things coming back."

The Rybox brothers nodded.

The group went left and then into the docking bay, where they met Jahl.

"The place is defensible. We can use the containers as cover and set up a kill zone," said Jahl.

Jerzan looked around. "We need Evaran alive. Oh . . . and the girl too. At least we won't have to share her as much with just us four, right? That's at least one positive. We can waste the others."

"Works for me," said Jahl, grinning. "I guess since I'm second in command, I get seconds."

"You know it," said Jerzan.

Jerzan pointed at the southwest area of the room. "Jahl, you take that spot." He pointed to the northwest area. "Doran, that's you. I'll take the other side, and, Goran, you take the other side from Jahl. Jahl, set up some proximity mines on the hallway that goes to the other docking bay since you're over there. If they get that far . . . then maybe we deserve to die, so make absolutely sure that when you're firing, you don't aim in that direction. We clear?"

Everyone acknowledged Jerzan.

"All right. Get set up, and then we wait," said Jerzan. He watched as the others spread out. His mind was still on fire about being betrayed, and losing some of his most loyal crew ate at him. Evaran would pay, and so would Hosk and Galkett. Revenge would be served.

Dr. Snowden limped along behind Evaran, who was carrying Jay. Emily and the krall seemed to have no issues keeping up, and several times Emily had to drop back a bit to help Dr. Snowden. How Evaran was able to effortlessly carry Jay was a mystery. Dr. Snowden realized Evaran was strong, but there was no sign of exertion.

Jay's wound seemed to be stable, and Dr. Snowden was not fully sure he understood how that was possible. Half the things he saw Evaran do seemed impossible. In the back of Dr. Snowden's mind, he knew it was probably advanced technology that he was unaware of.

After twenty minutes, the group came upon the main research hub entrance.

Dr. Snowden took a moment to catch his breath. He was surprised he was able to do as much physical activity as he had. If he were back on Earth, he would be laid out, but between a perpetual state of fear and adrenaline and nano-bots coursing through him, he was able to keep up. A long nap was due after all this, assuming he lived.

Evaran dipped his head toward the hall inside the entrance. "This is one of their main research hubs. There is a lab I wanted to check out, so we can do that and get medical supplies. V, scout mode."

"Acknowledged. Scout mode engaged," said V. He shimmered out of view as he flew away.

"Is Jay going to be okay?" asked Dr. Snowden.

"He will be fine. The nanobots are repairing the severed area now, but it is a stopgap measure. According to the Krotovore data, they have a gel and some device that allows for regeneration of lost body parts. This research lab should have quite a bit of it."

"Do the Krotovore have a problem with lost limbs or something?"

"This *is* a research area."

Dr. Snowden's mouth went dry. He wondered how many specimens went under the knife in the name of research. "At least he's alive."

Evaran nodded. "Jerzan and crew will get back to docking bay three before we do, as they have a shorter path and do not need to stop. We will need to devise a plan after Jay is patched up, but we should be secure for now. There is still plenty of time to get to my ship."

Dr. Snowden acknowledged Evaran and then glanced at the krall walking alongside them. Evaran had allowed her to kill Gaellus, and his bloodstains stuck out against her silver fur. Apparently Hulldar and Gaellus learned the hard way what happens when they cross Evaran's line.

V returned and projected a holographic display several feet off the ground of a high-level research labs map. One of the labs had a red glow to it. "Analysis. Twenty-four labs. One inaccessible. No life-forms detected. Unknown energy source detected at inaccessible lab."

Evaran stepped into the hallway entrance and motioned for Dr. Snowden and Emily to step in. After they were inside the hallway, Evaran shielded the door. "This is the only way in here, so we should not have any surprises. Now, on to that inaccessible lab."

Over the next ten minutes as they walked to the lab, Dr. Snowden peered into the open rooms as they passed them. The mist was faint in these areas, and the lighting was better. Some of the rooms had dead creatures on slabs similar to the ones Emily and he had lain on. These creatures were not wearing specimen robes. He shuddered at the thought that maybe there were no robes because they would have gotten in the way of being sliced up. Other rooms had tables with unusual objects on them. He did not know what they were, but they must have some value to have garnered the attention of the Krotovore.

When they reached the inaccessible lab, a physical door sat behind a light-blue shielding similar to the one at the worm pit.

The krall growled at the door.

Evaran glanced at the krall and then perused his ARI. "She senses what I am sensing. Be alert."

Evaran laid Jay down and then walked up to the door console and placed his UIC on it. His UIC emitted a blue light after a few moments.

Dr. Snowden noted that the UIC sometimes connected very quickly, like it did on regular doors, and sometimes slowly, like on the bridge and at the worm pit. Maybe it was due to the complexity of the system it was interfacing with.

Evaran unshielded the door, which also slid up into the wall. He stepped back and stretched out his right arm with a horizontal flat hand toward Emily.

The krall gazed at Evaran for a moment, then walked to Emily's side while focusing intently at the door.

"Both of you, get behind me," said Evaran as he pulled out his utility handle. He extended it into a staff and adopted a defensive stance, "V, scout mode."

"Acknowledged. Scout mode engaged," said V. He shimmered out of view as he flew into the lab. After a few moments, he faded back into view next to Evaran. "Analysis. No life signs detected. One inactive life-form detected. Power is minimal. Illumination required."

Evaran relaxed and then used his thumb on the utility handle, causing the two poles to retract, before placing it back on his belt. He then took two orbs off the right side of his belt and pulled each one apart a bit, twisted them until a soft beeping sound played, then pressed them back together, causing a snapping sound.

Dr. Snowden squinted as the orbs glowed, illuminating the surrounding area.

Evaran tossed the orbs into the room. He picked up Jay and entered, with everyone else in tow.

The glowing orbs hovered above at opposite ends of the room, lighting up the inside of the research lab.

There were several slabs, but the one in the middle of the room was the first thing Dr. Snowden saw. On it was a decayed Krotovore with wires injected all over its body. The strange black mist surrounding the body obscured it somewhat, but he was still able to get a good look at it. The eyes appeared to be sewn shut, and it had restraints on its legs and one over its body. The dead Krotovore was missing two of its arms.

"Gross," said Emily.

Dr. Snowden wrinkled his nose at the strong ammonia scent coming off the Krotovore. "Yeah . . . what she said. What the heck . . . ?"

Evaran laid Jay down on an adjoining slab and then walked over to the decayed Krotovore in silence. As he moved around, he placed the UIC on one of the side consoles. When he reached the base of the slab with the Krotovore, he swept his hand in an arc over it. A yellow beam emanated from his ring onto the slab, cutting through the black mist and revealing the Krotovore underneath it in more detail.

Dr. Snowden glanced at Emily and the krall, who were both staring intently at the dead body. The krall's skin had turned a slight tinge of red. She really seemed to dislike the dead Krotovore. Emily's face was one of dread, something he had only seen a few times.

"Very interesting. I know what it is now. It is a Daedrould. Although I could sense it, I wanted to verify," said Evaran. He interacted with his ARI and looked at Dr. Snowden. "To clarify, because I know you will ask, they are beings that have a specific energy signature. They also commonly have unique abilities. This one could see and find other unique energy signatures, including rifts. I refer to beings of this subtype as seekers, and I have never seen one so powerful, though, that can do it over the distances this one could. The Krotovore outfitted this Daedrould with a biomechanical interface to translate the rifts it found into coordinates."

"What do you mean by a specific energy signature? Like an aura?" asked Emily.

Evaran raised a finger. "Yes. Everything in the universe gives off an aura of sorts. I can read them via a scan, which separates out the energy, similar to when a spectroscope separates light into a spectrum."

"Oh," said Dr. Snowden. He gestured at the Krotovore. "It looks like a Krotovore, though. I don't see any aura or anything."

"You would not, as you do not have the ability or technology. However, it is a Krotovore with a Daedrould energy signature. Imagine if the Krotovore had a pure-green aura, but it also had blue streaks in it. If the blue streaks represented the presence of Daedrould energy, you would know it is a Daedrould. I have come to learn that specific signatures correlate to specific abilities. There are humans with Daedrould signatures," said Evaran as he walked over to the console. Once there, he interacted with his ARI.

The room's power came back on, and the consoles lit up.

"How would, say, Emily and I ever know if a human was a Daedrould if we can't see their energy signature?" asked Dr. Snowden.

"Since you have nanobots inside you now, you will be able to tell nonhumans from humans by the way they move and smell. Without knowing their energy signature, you would not be able to distinguish what type of nonhuman they are," said Evaran.

Dr. Snowden shook his head. He wanted to believe and thought Evaran was probably being honest, but this sounded too fantastic.

Evaran walked over to a panel on the wall opposite Jay's slab and opened it. After scanning inside with his ring, he said, "Here it is. The gel in this container should work on Jay." He grabbed a round medium-sized container the width of a dinner plate. A cord ran out the top and ended in a large, square, cloth-like material at the end. The edges of the cloth appeared to have some type of metallic lining. Evaran set the container beside Jay.

Dr. Snowden and Emily joined Evaran at the slab.

Evaran pointed at Jay's wound. "I need to put the cloth-like material around the wound and then secure it. Once secured, the container will pump the gel to the wounded area. As the body uses up the gel for regeneration, it will pull more. The piece connected to the limb will then slide down as the limb grows."

"That's some powerful gel," said Emily.

"It is. Can you hold up Jay's stump?"

Emily gripped her hands in front of her and looked at Dr. Snowden with wide eyes.

Dr. Snowden smiled. "I'll do it." He walked up to Jay's shoulder area and lifted the arm stump.

Evaran wrapped the cloth ending around the stump and then twisted a circular device that connected it to the cord.

The cloth ending molded itself over the stump like wax sealing a bottle.

"That should do it," said Evaran. "It will take a long time to regenerate fully, but at least it will regenerate. I am going to take some of this gel for my own research." He walked over to a large screen on the side of the room opposite the entrance. "Since we are here, there is some information about your abduction I would like to learn more about. Relax for the moment."

Dr. Snowden sighed. Relaxing was the furthest thing from his mind. Looking at Jay on the slab was disheartening, but at least he was getting healed up. Losing an arm is not something Dr. Snowden could even fathom happening to himself. He was sure Jay would feel the same way when he became conscious.

Emily had sat next to the krall, who looked like it was enjoying stretching out. Evaran was busy interacting with his

ARI, and Dr. Snowden wondered what was being shown. At least for now, he could take a break. A nap would be better, but his body was still on full alert. His muscles loosened up some as he sat against the slab Jay was on.

17

Emily slumped down next to Dr. Snowden. Seeing Jay lose his arm not only made her skin crawl, but it intensified her general uneasiness. This ship was death, and without Evaran, she and Dr. Snowden would either be dead from creatures or from the ship crashing into the planet. Although she felt alive when fighting the Grynge, that was pure adrenaline. It was wearing off, and her body was telling her that not everything was all right.

"You okay?" asked Dr. Snowden.

She grimaced and laid her head on his shoulder. He was the only family she had left, and with the way things were going, nothing was certain. She wrapped her arm around his and sighed. "I'm trying. This ship doesn't want us here."

"I don't think it banked on Evaran stopping in."

"Yeah," she said.

"And we have the krall with us now too."

Emily looked over at the krall, who gazed Emily's way.

The krall sauntered over and lay down in front of them, facing the door.

"I think she's much smarter than I initially thought, hand signals or otherwise," said Dr. Snowden.

"I'm getting that feeling too," she said. She licked her lips. "She took out that Gaellus guy without much effort."

"To be fair, he didn't have a weapon," he said. "But yeah, she's pretty tough. I'm just glad she's on our side."

Emily cleared her throat. "It's going to be weird going back to Earth, assuming we can, and having these . . . virtual memories."

"Hopefully they won't mess with us too much," said Dr. Snowden. He lightly squeezed her shoulder. "Whatever happens, we'll be there for each other."

She clenched her jaw. "Yeah. I guess we can have one of your famous dinners of cheeseburgers and fries. That'll let us know if everything is real."

He eyed her.

She forced a grin. It felt weird to have any emotion other than dread, but Dr. Snowden seemed to lighten things. It could also be that they had a lull. Running around from one crazy incident to another was mentally taxing. Her mind switched to Jerzan. The expression on his face as they left the worm pit was one of pure anger. "I'm not looking forward to running into Jerzan and crew again. Why can't they just leave us alone?"

Dr. Snowden nodded. "I think after losing most of his crew, either to the ship or betrayal, then Evaran getting the best of them in the worm pit, Jerzan is pretty pissed about now. I suspect we're the focus of his anger."

"He deserves a swift kick in the butt."

He eyed her again.

"Sorry. I don't feel like my usual self."

"It's okay. I don't either. I haven't had anything to eat, and oddly enough, I don't have the urge to relieve myself," he said. He tossed a hand out. "There's been plenty of situations where that could have happened involuntarily."

She squeezed his arm. "Yeah."

Dr. Snowden rubbed his legs. "It feels good to take a break from all this walking. I think I got my ten thousand steps in for the day."

Emily studied his leg. "Are you still feeling pain?"

"A little. It's not really on the wounds, it's just . . . all over. I don't think we would have survived that without these nanobots."

"I'm sure they helped. I'm surprised you didn't lose your temper, as short as it can be sometimes."

"I was too busy trying to stay alive for that," he said with a grin.

It did her good to see that he was trying to keep it light. That was one thing she loved about being around him growing up, at least before he moved away. Regardless of how dire a situation was, he could always lighten it. He had the effect of disarming people, although she also knew he had another side. When angered, his temper would surge, and it did not take much to trigger it sometimes. Thankfully it was not all the time, although she had seen it when the draug attacked them. Maybe the nanobots could help some in that regard.

V hovered in front of them. "Query. Do you require food? I possess multiple Earth food patterns I can replicate for you on the Krotovore replicator."

Emily raised an eyebrow. V was an enigma to her. From what she understood, he was a flying computer that was self-aware. She had seen movies on that premise, and they usually never ended well. "I'm okay. Thank you for asking."

"Of course," said V. "If you need either food or drink, please do not hesitate to ask me to get you some."

Dr. Snowden nodded. "It's appreciated." He tilted his head. "What do you make of this situation?"

"You are with Evaran, so you will be okay."

"You're pretty confident. Is this something normal for him?"

"Yes, although this one is less dangerous."

Emily and Dr. Snowden shared a look.

"V, there is no need to scare them," said Evaran, looking over.

"Analysis. I ran a query on all situations and weighted them using a difficulty factor."

Evaran shook his head. "Perhaps so. I have learned that with humans, sometimes ignorance is desirable to maintain confidence." He raised a finger. "Nonetheless, I have completed my analysis of their abduction." He glanced at Dr. Snowden and Emily. "Do you wish to know about it?"

Dr. Snowden stood. "Yeah, I'd rather not be ignorant about that."

"I'd like to know too," said Emily, joining Dr. Snowden.

Evaran motioned for them to come over. "Excellent. Then let me inform you."

Dr. Snowden and Emily walked around the slab to the large screen next to Evaran. The interface was different from the others Dr. Snowden had seen previously. While the others had a busy interface, this one was relatively calm. It had a simple circular menu wheel on the bottom left, with the rest of the screen displaying submenus on the bottom and the main content above it.

The krall walked slowly around the slab as well, never taking her eyes off the Daedrould. She looked at Emily while proceeding to the corner of the room near the screen. The krall lay down and closed her eyes after getting there.

Dr. Snowden scrutinized the large screen.

"This screen shows a list of their rift jumps," said Evaran, gesturing at the screen. "They cataloged all of them. Unfortunately, this room has a damaged holographic interface like the rest of the ship. I was hoping since this room was disconnected, it might have been spared. At least we have the backup interface in the screen."

"That would've been cool to see," said Emily.

Dr. Snowden agreed with Emily. He really wanted to see the holographic interface and wondered what it would look like and how it would act. He turned his attention back to the screen.

Evaran pointed to the rift jumps on the screen. "You can see there were eighteen rifts based on this list."

"The last one should be Earth, right?" asked Emily.

"Not quite. The last one was the one they took to get out here. Emily, press on the seventeenth rift in that list."

Emily complied, causing a muted click sound.

The main content area switched to a detailed three-dimensional galactic map. A semitransparent gold line connected some of the planets. Each planet the gold line intersected had a number next to it.

Emily glanced at Evaran. "Which one do I pick now? Hard to tell which one is Earth."

"Down here," said Evaran, pointing to a planet near the end of the gold line. "They called your planet 17-31. The seventeenth rift jump and thirty-first planet they encountered. They did not bother with names. Even though this lab was disconnected, there is still some missing data. I am guessing some security system was trying to wipe it before it got shut down."

Emily pressed on Earth.

A green outline appeared around Earth, and then the screen zoomed in, showing Earth at the top of the screen. The bottom of the screen had several large round orange menu options.

After several moments of scanning the options, Emily pressed the specimens one.

The specimens option lit up, and the other options disappeared. A horizontal list of square images of several humans appeared.

Emily squinted as she studied the images, then looked at Evaran. "Hey, there's me and Uncle Albert!" She tilted her head. "There's Sanjay and Jay, but I don't know who those other two are."

"Yes, apparently you are specimen number three, and Dr. Snowden is specimen number four," said Evaran. "Sanjay was specimen number five, and Jay was the sixth. Touch the first specimen."

Emily glanced at Dr. Snowden and then touched the first specimen image.

A pale, slender human appeared on the left side of the screen. To the right were details and statistics. A comprehensive notes section spanned the screen under the image and details.

Dr. Snowden peered at the notes. They seemed to touch on various aspects of humanity that seemed familiar to him. It was the note on blood consumption that caught his eye. He reread the note, then touched the screen, causing the area under his touch to highlight. He faced Evaran. "It says here that this guy drank blood? Like a vampire or something?"

"A good observation. Most vampire types are Daedrould. However, that is but one type of Daedrould. The Krotovore missed many other types living on your planet," said Evaran.

Dr. Snowden harrumphed. "You're serious? Vampires are real?"

"A few hours ago, you learned aliens are real."

Dr. Snowden paused as if in thought. "Point taken, but this is on Earth. I'm sure if they existed, we would've known about it."

"There are a lot of aliens on your planet as well, but you do not know about them either."

Dr. Snowden paused to ponder Evaran's words. It seemed that Earth was a lot more than it appeared to be. Aliens and Daedrould. He wondered what else was living there and how they could have remained undetected for so long. Although Evaran was probably telling the truth again, it was still difficult for Dr. Snowden to accept it. It was a matter of putting aside what he thought he knew and opening up to the new reality unfolding before him.

Emily pointed at a paragraph halfway down in the detailed notes. "Look here. It says they tried to pull this one, but the crew was killed. The retrieval ship crashed, but not before the data transmitted. I'm guessing the vampire had something to do with that?"

"Most likely. Krotovore are not physically strong, so a vampire of the magnitude they picked up would have easily broken any restraints and disposed of them. However, being in an unfamiliar alien ship with nothing flying it would lead to a crashed ship," said Evaran.

"Wonder if it survived," said Dr. Snowden. "Let's see what's behind door number two. It better not be a killer clown or something." He pressed the second specimen image.

A burly man with muscles bulging through his flannel shirt replaced the vampire. The man had a thick beard, bushy eyebrows, and a look that indicated anger.

Dr. Snowden peered at the notes and noticed that like with the vampire, the crew died and the ship was destroyed, but not before the data transmitted. It appeared this man turned into an animal when beamed up. "I guess this is a werewolf or something?"

"Close," said Evaran, raising a finger. "They did not have a word to describe what animal it was, other than it was big, furry, and strong. It is a bear shifter and comes from another realm. They are not Daedrould and are instead known as Outsiders. They too have specific energy signatures. The Krotovore most likely abducted him in his human form due to his unusual readings."

"Another realm?" asked Dr. Snowden.

"That is a bit complicated to explain. Suffice it to say, there are areas that exist outside the timelines but are still part of your universe. This bear shifter is from one of them. You may be more familiar with traditional Outsiders, like the Greek and Egyptian gods," said Evaran.

Dr. Snowden exhaled sharply. "You're saying all the gods in history were Outsiders?"

"The ones I have met are. The last one I met was the Greek god Hermes. He has some issues to work out."

"So vampires, werebears, and now gods. How have they remained undetected for so long?"

Evaran looked off to the side for a moment, then back at Dr. Snowden and Emily. "Humans have a bad tendency to attack what is different. Daedroulds and Outsiders have been on your planet as long as humans, some even longer. They have integrated into human society, with the Outsiders doing so much more successfully than the Daedrould and others. They have their own governing bodies, politics, religions, and the like. The one thing they have in common is being able to remain undetected. However, as humanity advances technologically, this is becoming harder for them. Humanity purges them if detected, well, except for one class of Outsiders. This also applies to aliens and others."

"I can't believe these things are walking around," said Emily, gesturing toward the screen.

Evaran walked over to another console on the side of the room. "You will notice them when we get back. They have emotions and goals in life just like you do. I am going to get some more data. Feel free to look around. When I am done, we will need to figure out something for docking bay three."

Dr. Snowden spent the next several minutes going over the interface a bit more, checking out some of the other stops and specimens that were picked up. There were a lot. He was surprised at how many humanoids they picked up from planets around Earth. Some were reptilian, some avian, but almost all were more or less derivations of a humanoid form. The oddest one was around the first planet. The alien looked like a meatball with two legs, four arms, and an extended neck. He wished he had more time to look through the system thoroughly.

He sighed as he now understood the scope of what the Krotovore had done. Picking up all these creatures was dangerous in its own right, and now that their containment was down, it was a zoo of wild beings. Although dread still had sway over him, perusing the Krotovore interface had piqued his curiosity. He could at least understand the interface now, and playing around with it for a bit was just the thing to get his mind off the situation.

18

Fifteen minutes passed as Dr. Snowden read about some of the Krotovore encounters with various civilizations. It seemed not all allowed the Krotovore to come within their space borders. The fact that there were so many civilizations, solar system configurations, and stellar phenomena was amazing. Compared to what he had studied and taught, the Krotovore information was on another level. A part of him wondered if he was supposed to know any of this information, but Evaran had not interfered with the data browsing.

Dr. Snowden could hear Emily walking around the room. He did not think she was bored, but he knew walking was her way of staying busy. She was at the room entrance and had peeked her head out.

The krall opened her eyes and looked around the room. She leaped to her feet and growled.

Evaran paused and tilted his head. "Emily! Get away from the door!"

Dr. Snowden's heartbeat shot up.

A slight scuffling noise in the hallway echoed out, and then two thick, veiny green tentacles grabbed Emily by the ankles and pulled her hard enough to knock her down.

She screamed as she disappeared from view.

Dr. Snowden lurched forward toward the door but was mowed down by the krall as it barreled out of the room, growling.

"Dr. Snowden, stay here!" said Evaran. He had pulled his utility handle out and extended it into a staff by the time he was at the door.

Dr. Snowden got back up and followed Evaran out of the room. No way in hell was he going to sit still with Emily in danger. Adrenaline stormed through him when he got into the hallway. He recognized the large walnut-shaped shell with random holes in it as the Cepharus. It was about the size of a medium car. Much bigger than V's projection had led him to believe, like the krall. Out of the holes popped massive green tentacles.

Evaran rushed toward the Cepharus's left side while scanning it with his ring.

The krall charged toward the Cepharus's right side, where Emily was being pulled to the shell. With two massive bites, the krall cut through the tentacles that had grabbed Emily.

The Cepharus emitted a high-pitched shriek.

Emily slumped to the ground.

Dr. Snowden moved to the wall nearest Emily and crept along it toward her.

The Cepharus had lost interest in her and focused on the krall, who was busy snapping at the Cepharus's tentacles.

Evaran hit the tentacles with his staff. Every time his staff touched a tentacle, sparks shot out.

Dr. Snowden figured Evaran did not want to use the repulsion blast with the krall so close. The fact that the Cepharus could fight both Evaran and the krall at the same time was both amazing and terrifying. No wonder it ripped those two mercs apart with ease. After an excruciating minute, Dr. Snowden reached Emily. He grabbed her by her armpits and pulled her back along the wall. Putting two fingers on her neck verified she had a pulse. He continued to drag her toward the research lab doorway. A loud shriek from the krall turned his attention back to the fight.

Severed tentacles lay around the Cepharus. It had pulled the krall toward its shell at a great cost, and wrapped her up in a way that her head was not in range of any other tentacles. The tentacles then constricted her.

Evaran switched sides and began hitting the tentacles wrapped around the krall.

Dr. Snowden had reached the research lab door with Emily. He looked in on the fight and was not sure if he was having residual blurriness from his adrenaline or if Evaran was just moving that fast.

Evaran hit the tentacles with such speed and precision that the Cepharus dropped the krall to counter his attack. He kicked the shell out a bit and pointed his staff at it.

Boom!

White concentric circles bathed the Cepharus as it went tumbling down the hallway. Several of its tentacles got crushed on the way. It righted itself and began to come back.

Boom!

The Cepharus went tumbling again.

Crack!

Its shell had small fractures in it when it came to a stop farther down the hallway. The Cepharus shrieked and fled.

Evaran chased the Cepharus until it was out of sight. When he came back to the doorway leading to the other research labs, he activated the door's shields. Once they were up, he walked back over to where the krall was. Looking over at Dr. Snowden, Evaran said, "How is Emily?"

Dr. Snowden grimaced and palmed the back of his head. "She's alive, but not sure other than that. She isn't conscious. Is the krall . . ."

Evaran scanned the krall with his ring. "She is barely alive. I shielded the door, so we should have no more surprises while we are here, and yes, I know I said that earlier. The Cepharus must have come in through another way we were unaware of after V's scan."

Dr. Snowden had thought it, but did not say anything. "What'd it do to the krall and Emily?"

"The tentacles have small barbs that inject a paralyzing toxin. Once it gets prey close to its shell, it constricts," said Evaran. He scanned Emily with his ring. "Emily is just bruised, and her nanobots will heal her. Five more seconds and she would have been crushed against the Cepharus's shell."

Dr. Snowden's chest tightened as he realized how close he had come to losing Emily again. It happened so fast. If they did not have Evaran, there is no way they would have survived an encounter with the Cepharus.

Evaran raised a finger. "As for the krall, the Cepharus paralyzed her, but her natural regeneration is already healing her. She also has a broken front leg that will take several days to heal. That is a problem, as we do not have a way to move her effectively. I can only carry Jay or her, and I cannot leave Jay here."

Dr. Snowden's muscles tightened up, and his face turned red at Evaran's implication to leave the krall. No way was Dr. Snowden going to leave without her, not after she had saved both Emily's and his life. He could see why the Grimlyn used them. Their hearts were as big as their physical size. He gritted his teeth and bore a gaze through Evaran. "We aren't leaving her here to die! That's not an option!"

Evaran put his hand on his chin and studied Dr. Snowden. After a minute, Evaran extended a hand out, palm down. "Relax. We will wait until Emily is back up and able to move. I will check the lab to see if there is anything that might help the situation."

Dr. Snowden let out a deep breath as his muscles loosened up. He wondered if Evaran was testing him. Dr. Snowden picked up Emily and carried her over to the krall. He sat down next to her and cradled Emily. It seemed no place was safe on the ship, not even in areas deemed secured. With a sigh, he brushed a lock of Emily's hair out of her face and then scratched the krall behind the ears. Hopefully Emily had no lasting damage, and the krall would get better. He swallowed hard as he tried to keep it together.

Over the next hour, Dr. Snowden watched over Emily and the krall. Emily had regained consciousness and was stirring. The krall had also begun to revive, but only the laborious thumping of her tail gave any indication she was alive. At least they were not dead.

The Cepharus would live in his mind as a nightmare. It must have been brutal on the world it came from. The power of an anaconda with the armor of a walnut shell. It took the force of Evaran and the krall to take it down. He wondered if it had encountered any draug. Evaran had been in and out of various research labs during that time and had also studied the krall's collar. Dr. Snowden wondered what health monitoring information was on the collar.

"What . . . what happened?" asked Emily as she sat up and rubbed her temples.

"You were attacked by a Cepharus. It paralyzed you, which knocked you out. The krall bit the tentacles wrapped around your ankles before—" Dr. Snowden removed his glasses with his right hand and rubbed his eyes with his left forearm, then cleared his throat. "Evaran and the krall fought it off, but she is barely alive with a broken leg."

"No, no, no, no, no," said Emily as she crawled over to the krall. Tears streamed down her cheeks as she stroked the krall's face.

The krall rolled her eyes to look at Emily.

Emily looked up at Evaran and wiped the tears from her cheeks. "Is there anything we can do?"

Evaran glanced at Dr. Snowden. "She is coming with us. Fortunately for her, she had not used her emergency regeneration stimulant. Every krall in service to the Grimlyn Empire has one. I activated it, but she will not be able to walk for a while. My ship can fully heal her when we get there. Are you able to walk?"

"Yeah, I just . . . need to orientate myself, and I feel like crap," said Emily. She hugged the krall and then motioned for Dr. Snowden to come over. With his assistance, she was able to stand up.

"A side effect," said Evaran. "It will pass. As for the krall, I found a hover slab in one of the rooms. The Krotovore used it to move specimens around. We may be able to use it for Jay and her." He knelt in front of the krall and clasped both hands in front of him while shaking them.

The krall moved her head to look at Evaran but laid it back down.

Emily sat again and stroked the krall's neck.

"She knows that the stimulant has been activated, and . . . she is appreciative of our efforts to aid her. We still need to figure out what to do in docking bay three. For now, everyone relax. I will get some water from the replicator in the lab and then see about that hover slab," said Evaran.

Dr. Snowden sat back against the wall with a thump. The situation was bad, and he wanted off the ship. Everything on it seemed out to get them. He watched as Emily stroked the krall's head and talked softly to her. At least they were okay, until the next monster or mercenary group showed up to murder them. He sighed as he hung his head.

Evaran came back after a few moments with two cups and a bowl filled with water. He handed the cups to Dr. Snowden and Emily and placed the bowl by the krall's head.

Emily took a sip out of her cup while the krall lapped from the bowl.

Dr. Snowden sniffed the water. It had a strong chlorine smell to it. He scrunched his face and took a sip. It had no taste.

"The hover slab is bigger than I expected," said Evaran. "It appears it was made to move two specimens at a time. I will be back with it shortly." He pivoted and left.

After a few moments, Dr. Snowden stood up and walked over to the lab to see if Evaran needed any help. When Dr. Snowden got to the door, he noticed Evaran had the hover slab out. It reminded Dr. Snowden of a metallic rectangular box that hovered off the ground and was about chest high. A single indented line went around the box about halfway between the top and bottom. The bottom of the slab was different from the top, and a light-red glow emanated from underneath it.

Evaran looked up when Dr. Snowden entered the room. "This is it. I only found one, as it seems the others are missing. It is weight rated well past the krall's and Jay's weight combined, so it should work. We will need to push it, though. Care to give it a try?"

"Sure, why not," said Dr. Snowden as he walked to the short end of the hover slab that Evaran was near.

Small bars ran across the edges on the top of the hover slab. Each bar connected to posts at the corners, and there was a small console on the end with several options such as lock, unlock, raise, and lower. There were also directional arrows on the right side of the console. A green glowing hollow tube wrapped around the hover slab just below the top of it.

Dr. Snowden put his hands on the end of the slab and pushed.

The slab glided forward with little resistance.

"Not bad at all," said Dr. Snowden.

"We can put Jay on the bottom slab," said Evaran. He tapped at the lower panel on the hover slab.

The panel slid out with a whooshing sound.

Evaran walked over to Jay. "Dr. Snowden, please grab the gel container and hold it nearby while I carry him."

Dr. Snowden complied.

Evaran lifted Jay, and together they got him onto the hover slab's lower panel.

Dr. Snowden put the container by the arm stump.

Evaran tapped at the panel, and it slid back into the hover slab. "It will auto adjust the environment for him. Let us head back to Emily and the krall." He extended a hand toward the ceiling, and the glowing orbs descended. When they were within reach, he grabbed and deactivated them and then put them back on his belt.

Dr. Snowden pushed the hover slab out of the room. He was able to turn it by applying more pressure on one side. Like the holographic ring, he noted that this would be revolutionary back on Earth. Evaran probably would not let technology like this get back to Earth, based on his decision to not let this ship and its technology stick around in this time period. Dr. Snowden pushed the hover slab over to where the krall was lying. "So . . . how do we get her up there?"

"Leave that to me," said Evaran. "Align the hover slab parallel to the krall, on the side where her legs are."

Dr. Snowden pushed the hover slab so it was parallel with the krall's body and closest to her legs. Evaran lifting her seemed absurd, given her size. Then again, the absurd seemed to be abundant of late.

Evaran knelt in front of the krall and moved an open hand back and forth in front of her face.

The krall's eyes blinked slowly as Evaran stood up.

Evaran walked around her so he was facing her back. "When I lift her, move the hover slab under her. Emily, I will need you to hold her head."

Dr. Snowden went to the longer side of the hover slab opposite the krall and put his hands on the edge bars. He had to see this. Evaran was strong, and Dr. Snowden was curious if Evaran would strain or not.

Evaran placed one arm under the krall's haunch and the other under her chest and then lifted her straight up without any strain while Emily kept the head stable.

Dr. Snowden pushed the hover slab toward Evaran until it was just touching his belt.

Evaran lowered the krall onto the hover slab.

Emily stroked the krall's neck as the slab dipped a bit, then reset itself back to its original height.

"You're a lot stronger than I thought," said Dr. Snowden. "Carrying Jay, and now this."

"Relative to a human, perhaps. Now, who wants to push the krall?" asked Evaran, closing the top slab.

"I will," said Emily with a defiant face while glancing at Dr. Snowden. She positioned herself on the end with console as Dr. Snowden stepped back from the long side of the hover slab with raised hands. With a tap at the bar, the hover slab moved forward a foot or so. "I got this."

Evaran nodded at Emily. "Follow me."

They followed Evaran to the main research hub entrance they had initially come in through.

Evaran unshielded the door and then motioned at V.

V shimmered out of view as he flew through the entrance.

Evaran reshielded the door. "V is going to docking bay three so we can see what we are dealing with." He pulled his UIC off the door console and walked over to the hover slab, where he placed it on the slab's console. After perusing his ARI, he said, "Intriguing. This hover slab has a shielding mechanism. The interface to turn it on is not on the slab. It has to be done remotely. However, I can access it. The edges will be outside the shield, though, so it can still be pushed."

Dr. Snowden glanced at Emily, then at Evaran. "So this hover slab can act like a moving shield then."

"A good tactical observation. If there was another, you and Emily could have gotten in it, and I could have used both of them as moving shields. Nonetheless, the design intent of the shielding mechanism was not to keep things from getting in, but to keep things from getting out."

Emily swallowed hard. "They must've been scared while in there."

"As I mentioned earlier, this *is* a research area."

Dr. Snowden rubbed his left inner palm with his right-hand thumb. He wondered how many specimens were tortured in these research labs. No wonder that when the specimens were given the chance to roam free, the Krotovore died quickly. The Krotovore would probably have brought him and Emily here at some point. He could not imagine waking up out of the virtual simulation to be stuck on a hover slab like this and then taken to a room to be researched. Jay would have been the poster boy for needing shields like that.

Evaran pulled out an orb and tossed it in front of him.

A projection shot up showing a top view of docking bay three.

Evaran interacted with his ARI, and four red dots appeared in the view, one in each corner, nestled among the shipping containers. He pointed to the clearing in the center of the room. "The red dots are Jerzan's crew, lit up courtesy of their location beacons. It seems they have set up a kill zone." He pointed to the bottom entrance. "This is where we would come in from." He pointed to another entrance centered on the left side of the room. "That is where we need to go. The path to it is either through the kill zone or along the bottom left wall immediate the entrance to the corner, then up along the side wall to the other entrance. They have both paths covered."

Dr. Snowden sighed and pushed up his glasses. "That's just great. I really hate that guy and these . . . Bloodbores."

Evaran rubbed his chin for a few moments before speaking. "We can take the path to the immediate left behind the containers as soon as we enter the room. I will rush the mercenary in that corner and take him out, and then we will continue to the corner and up to the entrance. It should be a straight run to my ship then."

"What if they come out and begin shooting into the area?" asked Emily.

Evaran pointed to the containers in the bottom left of the map. "The containers will provide some cover. By the time they get there, we should be close to the other entrance. We can also use the hover slab to provide some defense."

"Sounds risky, but I don't see another way. Jerzan doesn't seem like the type to give up or be reasoned with," said Dr. Snowden.

"I would concur," said Evaran. He shut off the projection and then grabbed the orb and placed it back on his belt. "I have sent V ahead to my ship in docking bay four. He is going to prep it for when we get there. Are you two ready for this?"

Dr. Snowden glanced at Emily, and then they acknowledged him.

"Okay then, off we go," said Evaran. He unshielded the door, and they left to go to docking bay three.

19

Jerzan surveyed the corner of the docking bay that he had set up. He stood on top of a container that had another container in front of him. It provided cover and was also the perfect position for checking out the center of the bay without being seen. His weapon lay to the side, and for a brief moment, everything was still. At least the environment was. His mind was somewhere else.

It had been twenty minutes since he and the rest of the Bloodbores had come to the docking bay, and now everyone was in position. Gaellus's death had hit him harder than he thought it would. Jerzan's mind switched from grief to anger, and it was a struggle to comprehend just how quickly it had all happened. It took some focus, but he was able to suppress the rage that was inside him. He tapped at his forearm device and, over group comms, said, "Meet up in the center."

Everyone assembled in the designated spot.

Jerzan gestured at Jahl. "How's the proximity mines?"

"Ready to be remotely activated," said Jahl.

"All right . . . and I shouldn't have to say this again, but I will. You assholes better not shoot at it until I turn it off."

The group laughed.

"Now, to bigger things. We know we're dealing with Evaran, a girl, an old man, another person without an arm, and some alien creature. Evaran and the alien creature are the main threats. I've gone over the situation from our previous fight. That creature should be weak on the sides, so target those areas."

Goran nodded. "I'll shoot up that damn thing."

Jerzan slapped Goran's chest. "I'm counting on it. As for Evaran, he's quick, and he has some type of forearm shield that can repulse our weapons fire." He raised a finger while smiling. "But I doubt he can deflect fire from more than two positions at once. He's the main target, but aim for the legs. We need him able to function."

"No problem," said Doran. He slapped his chest. "If that fails, I'll slap him unconscious."

Jerzan nodded. "Let's hope we don't fail. This damn place has already taken more than it should."

A skittering sound echoed out from the hallway leading up to the docking bay.

Jerzan motioned forward. "Check it out."

"I got this," said Doran, grinning. He moved to just outside the docking bay. Over group comms, he said, "Looks like more of those alien bugs we saw earlier."

Jahl narrowed his eyes. "It's almost like they're testing us. Seeing how far they can get and what our response is."

"Smart bugs? C'mon, man . . . ," said Jerzan.

"That's what it looks like to me."

"Let's see how they like this response," said Doran as he opened fire with his hip-mounted weapon. When it wound down, he laughed. "Guess there'll be no response this time." He went back to the group.

"Good. The last thing we need is to deal with more creatures, smart or not, while facing Evaran and his group," said Jerzan. He looked around. "All right. Everyone get to their positions and check in every five minutes. If this goes as planned, we'll have a ship, entertainment, and slaves to sell, assuming the old man and the armless one survive. As for the creature, just kill it." He waved a finger in the air. "We're fucking Bloodbores. We don't go down without a fight."

Everyone shared a look and acknowledged Jerzan, then went to their respective positions.

Jerzan exhaled from his nose as he moved around the containers. As simple as he thought the fight would be, everything so far had been anything but. He had to believe that between the four of them, they could take Evaran and his group. There were simply too much firepower and too many angles for Evaran to compensate for. Jerzan sighed as he pulled himself onto the container. He grabbed his weapon and verified it was ready to go. Looking out beyond the container made him breathe harder. There could only be one winner from this fight, and he would do everything to make sure it was the Bloodbores.

Dr. Snowden reflected on the upcoming situation. The goal was to get to Evaran's ship in one piece. It sounded simple, except for Jerzan's trap in docking bay three. Everything would be much easier if Jerzan would just leave them alone. Still, Dr. Snowden trusted Evaran to get them through this. Even getting this far had some casualties, but at least they were finally nearing a conclusion. Whether or not it would be good remained to be seen.

They walked for ten minutes to just outside the entrance of docking bay three.

The entrance was large, and part of the interior was obscured by the massive stacked shipping containers just inside the door. He was not sure why he looked down the hallway in the opposite direction, but he could see dead draug. "Uhh . . . that looks recent."

Evaran studied the area where Dr. Snowden was looking. "That means the draug will respond in greater numbers. I suspect we have not seen the last of them."

"Great," said Dr. Snowden, shaking his head.

Evaran pointed into the docking bay. "We will go immediately to the left in about four minutes. Jerzan is having them check in every five minutes, according to V. After their next check-in, we will have the full five minutes to knock out Jahl in the corner and get to the other hallway entrance."

Dr. Snowden looked at the hover slab. "How should we position this when we go in?"

Evaran pointed toward the upper right of the room. "You will initially want it to face Jerzan's location, until we hit the first container. Once we are behind it, you will turn it to face the lower right of the room. Once we are past Jahl and moving toward the other hallway entrance, you will face it to the upper left. Make sure whatever direction it is facing, you are behind it."

"Sounds simple enough," said Emily, nodding.

"Also note, we will move when V has determined that they do not have line of sight on the entrance."

Dr. Snowden and Emily acknowledged Evaran.

After four minutes, Evaran motioned for them to move.

They used the shipping containers that obscured a part of the entrance to slip down the first row to their left.

Evaran motioned down toward the corner. He ran up ahead, then ducked into one of the pathways created by the containers.

Dr. Snowden helped Emily turn the hover slab to face the lower right of the room and then pull it toward the corner.

After another minute, a zapping sound broke the silence as they neared the pathway where Evaran had gone.

They froze.

Evaran popped out of the pathway, making them jump. "Jahl is down, and I have his communication device. We need to move."

"Wow, that was quick," said Emily.

"To be fair to him, he was urinating in a corner and had just finished checking in with Jerzan," said Evaran.

Dr. Snowden exhaled sharply. "We just gonna leave him?"

"For now. We need to get to my ship first. Then I will deal with him afterward," said Evaran.

They hit the corner and turned the hover slab to face the upper left of the room. After pushing it for a minute while staying in the pathway between the wall and the containers, they approached the left entrance that led to docking bay 4.

Evaran raised his hand for them to stop. "Hold on." He scanned two devices near the other hallway entrance. With a sigh, he motioned for them to head back to the corner.

"What's going on?" asked Dr. Snowden.

"Proximity mines. We go near them, and it will take out the power grid for this area. That means the whole docking bay decompresses if the main shield is shut down. The Krotovore really should have used physical doors for this bay."

A chill ran through Dr. Snowden. Although he had always studied space, he did not want to see it this way. "Can you disable them remotely?"

"Unfortunately not. My UIC would trigger it if it went—" Evaran tilted his head and raised a finger.

Emily's face turned white. "Draug."

Dr. Snowden's skin went cold. He could hear the faint shrieking and chattering noises of the draug brood now. It was not something so easily forgotten. It seemed the draug were not happy with their last encounter. "You've gotta be kidding me. They're getting closer and gonna come in here, aren't they?"

Evaran narrowed his eyes. "They would even if we were not here. Jerzan and his crew have a strong odor, and they have antagonized the brood."

They reached the corner and turned the hover slab to face the entrance they had come in from.

Dr. Snowden sighed. If they went to the hallway entrance leading to Evaran's ship, they would get flushed out to space. If they tried to go back the way they came, they would run into the draug.

Evaran held up the communication device he grabbed off Jahl and pressed a button on it. "Jerzan . . ."

"Evaran? Where's Jahl?" asked Jerzan.

"He is sleeping at the moment. There is an issue bigger than you or me now. A draug brood is approaching this room and will arrive in less than two minutes. You need to disable your mines so we can all get out of here," said Evaran.

Jerzan chuckled. "I don't know what a draug brood is, but I'm pretty sure we can handle it. If you're referring to those damn alien bugs, they're not a threat. As for the mines, they go down when you surrender."

"We do not have time for your foolishness. The draug brood is in the hundreds, judging by the sound. Your last encounter has riled them up. You stand no chance with them. However, you do stand a chance of living if you listen to me."

Jerzan laughed. "Ahh . . . resorting to begging now, huh? Must hurt. I have a stun grenade aimed at your general area. It will knock out anything in a ten-foot radius. You put Jahl to sleep, I can put your friends to sleep. You can make this easy. Just walk out and surrender."

"I will not do that. Do you not wish to live?" asked Evaran.

Jerzan snorted. "You messed with the wrong mercenary this time. You were right earlier. I should've listened to Galkett. I now know we're not physically a match for someone of your ability, but that's not your weakness. Your weakness is trying to protect those who can't stand up for themselves. That's why you'll surrender. You already lost one, and another is maimed. You refuse, and you will lose the other three."

"You have thirty seconds before the draug arrive. You should consider doing as I say."

"Don't tell me what to do! You know what? *You* have thirty seconds. If you're not out here by then, your group goes down."

"Another poor decision," said Evaran. He pressed a button on the communication device and faced Dr. Snowden and Emily. "We can speak freely now."

"We aren't really going to surrender, are we?" said Dr. Snowden.

"No, of course not. I have another idea. I hope you are not claustrophobic," said Evaran. He pulled out his utility handle and extended it into a staff while angling it in the air toward the center of the room.

A small device flew over the containers toward them. *Boom!*

Evaran's repulsion blast sent the small device flying back.

A few moments later, a zapping sound rang out.

Evaran rushed up to one of the large shipping containers and placed his UIC on the container's console. He interacted with his ARI, and the end of the container extended out and then slid up with a whooshing sound. His head turned back to where the first device had come from, and he angled his staff again.

Boom!

The stun grenade went flying back.

Evaran pointed to the inner cargo boxes in the shipping container. "Jerzan is persistent and impatient. Get those boxes out!"

They began pulling out the boxes that were stacked in a two-by-two configuration.

Dr. Snowden reached in and pulled out one of the top ones. He was surprised he could move them. They must have been empty.

Evaran motioned for Dr. Snowden to place it so it would block the path to the entrance the draug would use.

Dr. Snowden complied and went back for another.

Emily had stacked one as well, and between the two of them, it only took a minute to clear out the first section while Evaran continued to deflect the stun grenades.

Dr. Snowden saw that only the draug scouts had begun to trickle into the room. His stomach tightened, as he knew the larger portion of the brood would be close behind.

The draug had drawn the attention of Jerzan and his mercenaries. Instead of tossing more grenades, they were firing on the draug.

A shot hit the containers being stacked, knocking them down.

Evaran ran to the containers and raised his forearm shield. "Get the next four out and then get the hover slab and yourselves into the container!"

"Why're we going in there?" said Emily.

Evaran half turned his head. "To keep you safe if this docking bay decompresses and flushes everything out into space. These shipping containers are essentially automated space-worthy ships. They are built to carry both cargo and animals. The cargo can fly itself from ship to ship or ship to port. I have programmed it to take you out to a safe distance if it gets flushed out. It may be a rough ride initially, though."

Dr. Snowden raised his eyebrows. "What?"

Another shot rang out, hitting Evaran's shield. He stumbled back a bit. "Just trust me on this. Go!"

"This is nuts," said Dr. Snowden.

They pulled out the next four cargo boxes over the next few minutes as Evaran repulsed incoming draug. Once the container's inner area was clear, they pushed the hover slab in on the right side.

Emily moved in on the left side.

Dr. Snowden took a last look down the pathway to the entrance. He saw Goran shooting at the draug.

A large claw broke through the wall and grabbed Goran, who screamed out in surprise. It shook him, then pulled him through the hole in the wall.

The draug swarmed in through the hole.

Dr. Snowden's stomach tumbled. "Oh, crap! It's that big thing!" Apparently the draug were done messing around.

Evaran rushed to the shipping container. "Get in!"

Dr. Snowden jumped in and knelt next to Emily.

Evaran grabbed an illumination orb and activated it, then tossed it into the shipping container between Dr. Snowden and Emily. After tossing in another orb, Evaran said, "The illumination orb will give you some light, more than the container will provide, and the other is a remote viewing orb, which you are familiar with. It is tied to my chest piece, so you will see what I do. This is so you are not in the dark."

Dr. Snowden removed his glasses and wiped them with his shirt. He swallowed hard. "You sure about this?"

"Absolutely. It is about to get chaotic. You will be safe here, and that is my main concern."

Emily jostled past Dr. Snowden, stepped out, and bear-hugged Evaran. "Good luck." She then hopped back into the shipping container.

Dr. Snowden could see that despite the wild situation, Emily saw Evaran as their savior. As scared as Dr. Snowden knew Emily would be, Evaran was a calming presence, even with alien bugs swarming a room with mercenaries.

Evaran nodded at them and interacted with his ARI.

The shipping container door closed.

Dr. Snowden scrutinized the projection from the remote viewing orb. The illumination orb lit up the enclosed space just enough so that the projection was clear. It showed the shipping container door closed and then Evaran grabbing his UIC off the console.

Evaran ran over to Jahl and tossed him over his shoulder.

Dr. Snowden's left eye wrinkled. Evaran was still trying to help, even if it was a mercenary. He could have left Jahl, but did not. Thankfully for him, he had not crossed Evaran's line. Unfortunately, Jahl was also half-covered in his own urine.

Evaran jumped on top of the shipping container to get a better view.

The draug were pouring into the room. The lower right was swarmed, and the remains of Goran were nowhere to be seen. A massive barrage of weapons fire from the upper left of the room shot out as Evaran turned to see Doran advancing toward the lower right. His hip-mounted weapon was shredding the draug in its path. When he got to the entrance, he let out a primal scream and charged into the hallway with his machete raised.

Dr. Snowden jumped as the projection showed the same claw that had grabbed Goran reach out and grab Doran.

The massive creature came fully into view as it proceeded to rip Doran in half.

Emily began to breathe harder.

The large creature shook Doran's halves like salt shakers, sprinkling his entrails onto the floor, where the smaller draug competed for it.

Emily turned away and dry heaved.

Dr. Snowden winced as he thought about how that could have been them. What a horrible way to go.

Evaran aimed his staff at the ceiling in the center of the room. A yellow beam shot up and flattened out when it came in contact with the ceiling. He tapped on his utility handle and was pulled upward at an angle. With the press of another button, he stopped halfway to the ceiling and used the momentum to swing to the far upper right corner of the room. When he landed, he ran along the back upper right wall to a hatchway. He opened it and tossed Jahl in. Evaran then turned up the pathway to where Jerzan was. After a brief moment, Evaran had closed the distance to Jerzan and jumped up behind him on the container.

Jerzan turned around with wide eyes. "You!" He turned his weapon toward Evaran.

Evaran used his staff to knock the weapon out of Jerzan's hand.

Jerzan stumbled to the side.

Evaran kicked Jerzan's legs from underneath him and then grabbed his vest.

"Damn you!" said Jerzan, grunting.

Evaran tossed Jerzan off the container toward the hatchway. With a quick hop, Evaran landed next to Jerzan.

Jerzan coughed up blood and squinted hard at Evaran. In effort to move away, Jerzan clawed at the ground.

Evaran grabbed Jerzan by the vest and dragged him to the end of the pathway.

"Get off me, you son of a bitch!" said Jerzan as he struggled to release Evaran's grip.

When Evaran was close to the wall, two draug soldiers appeared.

One had climbed on top of the container, and one was on the ground.

Evaran slung Jerzan toward the wall and repulsed the first draug soldier on the ground.

The one on the container jumped at Evaran.

Evaran stepped to the side, dodging the downward swipe of its claw. When it landed, he side kicked it in the chest, sending it flying down the pathway he had just come down. He then turned back to Jerzan.

Jerzan lay sprawled out and was breathing hard. He laughed and held up a device. After licking the blood from his lips, he said, "Looks like you're a bit late. If I go, you're going too. I'll see you in the nether realms, asshole." He pressed on the device.

Boom!

The lights dimmed, and the docking bay's outer shield began flickering as the proximity mines detonated.

Evaran shook his head as he rushed to the wall where Jerzan lay. Once there, Evaran planted his right foot against it, then grabbed Jerzan by his vest. Using his left hand, Evaran swung Jerzan in a 180-degree arc, launching him into the hatchway. Evaran looked in at a startled Jerzan. "I am not allowed in the nether realms anymore. Enjoy your stay in a Bilaxian prison." Evaran interacted with his ARI, and the hatchway door closed.

There was a whooshing sound as the life pod launched away.

Dr. Snowden squinted as the projection showed the room, and then the wall, in a cyclical pattern as Evaran tumbled toward the now-open docking bay door. If Evaran was exposed to open space, he would be dead. Dr. Snowden gulped. That meant that he and Emily were now alone, unless V could find them somehow.

After a few moments, the projection showed space, and the Krotovore ship moving away, leaving a trail of cargo.

Dr. Snowden slipped backward as the shipping container was flushed out of the docking bay and into space.

Emily tumbled into him.

Dr. Snowden heard the clanking of other objects hitting their shipping container.

After a few moments, there was silence.

"Are we in space?" asked Emily, righting herself.

Dr. Snowden straightened himself and pushed up his glasses. "I believe we are. I would've thought we'd be floating, unless these shipping containers have some type of artificial gravity. I would guess they do if they're space-worthy."

Emily gasped as the projection blinked out. "What happened?"

"I'm not sure. Evaran's projection showed him getting flushed out too. Maybe it's a distance thing. I don't know if that was part of the plan or not, though. If it was, how the heck can he survive out here?" A tingling sensation ran through him as he rubbed the goose bumps on his arm. "We may be alone. Maybe since he's different, he can survive and find us." He stretched out an arm to Emily.

She crawled over to him and put her head on his chest.

Dr. Snowden had no idea how to contact V, or even where the ship was. Nothing could ever go as planned or be easy. All that was left to do was wait.

20

The silence made the hairs on Dr. Snowden's neck rise. He was not sure how long it had been since they had lost the projection or how long they had been out in space. It felt like an eternity. A disturbing thought that this was how he would die crept into his mind. Emily trembled as she rested on him. Hopefully he could keep it together at least for her. The last thing she needed was for him to lose it.

After a while, a loud clanking sound echoed throughout the shipping container.

Dr. Snowden looked around with wide eyes. They should have been far enough away that nothing was hitting the container.

The container door extended out and then up with a whooshing sound. A robot with fibrous mesh arms and legs covered partially by semitransparent silver armor stood in front of them.

Dr. Snowden leaned forward with his left arm shielding him and Emily. "Who are you?"

The robot tilted its head at Dr. Snowden. "I am V. This is my full-body mode."

"V!" said Dr. Snowden as he exhaled and relaxed his muscles. He glanced at Emily, who was staring intently at V.

"Evaran is waiting for you on the bridge," said V.

V grabbed the hover slab and began to pull it outside. "It is good to see you both are safe."

"Yeah, I'm just glad for that," said Dr. Snowden, motioning for Emily to exit the shipping container. He was aware V had system modes, but not physical modes. Dr. Snowden stepped out of the shipping container behind Emily and onto a light-blue walkway leading up to Evaran's ship. It stood out in contrast to the dark space around it. He exhaled from his mouth. "How can we breathe out here?"

"There is shielding around the ship that has a breathable atmosphere within," said V.

Dr. Snowden wanted to ask more about it, but V had already turned to go back to the ship. With a deep breath, Dr. Snowden took a look around. He steadied himself as he turned, gazing out into deep space. Maybe this was how astronauts felt. It was beautiful, yet he knew how menacing it truly was. Emily was gone. She must have already walked ahead with V through the light-blue doorway at the end of the ramp.

The ship reminded him of a hockey puck sitting on an upside-down cymbal. He figured it was probably about fifteen feet tall and thirty feet wide. The white, slightly angled bottom was reflective, causing him to shield his eyes. As he walked up the light-blue ramp that seemed to be made of light, he noticed the fine black fiberglass-like mesh that wrapped around the middle section of the ship.

He faced the door and paused. It was semitransparent, with a hex pattern covering it. He pushed his finger through it and then yanked it back out. With a final look around, he shook his head and stepped through the shield. It was an amazing-looking ship, if a bit small. He wondered how it was going to get them home.

He surveyed the interior. The flooring was dark blue, and the walls were a mix of dark gray, silver, and white. Looking to his left, he saw three doors along the curved wall. A ramp past the doors led up to a walkway that ran along the wall to another walkway. To his right were three more doors along the curved wall, as well as a ramp farther up that led to the same walkway as the left ramp.

He moved toward a table with replicator pads. Resting his hands on the cool metallic table, he studied what looked like an elevator entrance behind the table. He ran his hands along its sleek surface. Where it went he had no idea. Looking up, he saw a white ceiling that went as far as the central walkway. Past that on the ceiling, it looked like glass with several support beams on the outside.

V had pushed the hover slab into the room behind the first door on the right and was interacting with the console. Given the dimensions of the ship, the room should be impossible. It was large, with side rooms branching off every side. The center of the room had several slabs of various sizes. To the right of the slabs was a console station, and there was a table with replicator pads on it to the left. Behind the slabs was a series of sleek stainless-steel-looking cabinets with several large matching containers to the side of it. This was definitely a medical bay of some sort.

He continued up the right side, ascending the ramp to a walkway separating the entrance area from the rest of the ship. Three people or so could walk comfortably next to each other on it. What appeared to be a command area extended beyond it. Evaran sat on a large chair just inside the space, with two ramps on either side, allowing access, while Emily was to his right, looking around. Dr. Snowden grinned thinking that her Snowden curiosity streak was at play.

To the sides of the ramps were guardrails that extended out. The area stood out from the rest of the ship, as the ceiling over it and the curved walls surrounding it had a glass-like surface. It had various support beams running across it on the top that stretched down to the front of the ship.

Dr. Snowden realized this gave a good view of what was outside.

The large chair had arms packed with various consoles and gadgets. Along the front of the ship was a large console that stood out several feet from the front glass-like wall. It was a large U-shaped fiberglass-like desk with two legs. A large screen outline was on the front wall.

Dr. Snowden did not see anything on the screen, which allowed him to see through it to the outside of the ship. He was impressed that he could see so much out there. To the left and right of the ramps were U-shaped seating areas, with a table similar to the one in the front of the ship. This was unlike anything he had ever seen.

Emily ran up to him when he walked over to where Evaran sat.

Evaran turned toward them. "Ahh, there you are. Welcome to my ship, the Torvatta. Please, come and sit." He motioned to them to sit in the U-shaped area to the right of his chair.

They complied.

Evaran interacted with his ARI and then pointed to the screen.

The screen showed V in the medical room, buzzing around the krall and Jay, who were on slabs. Several robot arms attached to the slabs were moving around them, attaching tubes and scanning. Digital readouts hung off to the side of them in the air.

"V, krall status," said Evaran.

V stopped and turned toward the screen. "Analysis. The krall is in good condition. The front leg is being mended, and all traces of the paralyzing toxin are being purged. Several bruises on the ribs have been healed, and the collar has been removed. Recovery time is fifteen minutes and forty-two seconds."

Evaran nodded. "Jay status."

"Analysis. His body has been stabilized, and regeneration has been accelerated. Full recovery is one month."

Evaran narrowed his eyes. "Interesting. Come to the front when the krall is healed completely."

"Acknowledged."

The screen went back to showing outer space.

Dr. Snowden tilted his head. "Umm . . . how is that room possible? I saw the size of your ship, and there's no way that room could extend out like that."

"Dimensional mechanics. You will just need to take my word on that," said Evaran.

Dr. Snowden wanted to know more about dimensional mechanics, but it seemed Evaran did not want to discuss it. The effect was obvious, though. Having six doors that can lead to other rooms on a small ship, yet not affect the overall exterior size of the ship would be a huge advantage.

Evaran half smiled at Dr. Snowden. "We have about fifteen minutes before the krall will be ready to move. Then we can take her home. This would be a good time to go over some things. Now, you both have seen a lot. Others must never know about it. Dr. Snowden, you publish papers. You cannot describe any of this in those papers. Emily, you play sports.

If you get hurt, you will need to avoid any type of medical interaction. That goes for both of you in that regard."

"I doubt anyone would believe us anyway," said Dr. Snowden.

"That is not the issue. You will be investigated if anyone of power finds out you have this type of information. While the knowledge is in itself not critical and can be explained away, the presence of your nanobots cannot be. If your nanobots are found, they will be extracted."

"How would anyone know how to take them out?" asked Emily.

"Whether you are alive or not as they are extracted would most likely be of little concern to those who would extract them."

Emily gulped and looked at Dr. Snowden. "What groups should we be looking out for?"

"If you keep this information to yourselves, you will not need to worry about it. There are too many groups to mention. I cannot stress this enough."

Dr. Snowden glanced at Emily, then at Evaran. "Is this what you do? Travel around, help people, and serve justice? If you hadn't shown up, we would've been toast."

Evaran eased back into his chair and put his hand on his chin. "Even with my presence, we still lost Sanjay. Nonetheless, I travel and observe wherever I land. The Torvatta can detect rifts, and I usually investigate them. I only involve myself in an event if I feel there is a severe injustice or something needing fixed. If other issues arise from my interference, then I deal with those as they come. In your case, I felt it would not be right for your lives to end in the way they would have. There was also a timeline component to it, so I interfered."

"We appreciate it. I'm sure Jay and the krall feel the same way," said Emily.

Evaran nodded.

"Where will you go next?" asked Dr. Snowden.

"Back to Earth to study it across time. After that, I am not sure. I like to visit ruins and then go back in time to visit the culture that built them. I also find it fascinating to live in cities across the timescape for a short while, absorb their culture, and interact with the natives," said Evaran.

Dr. Snowden sighed. "I wish I had the opportunity to do that."

"Me too!" said Emily.

Dr. Snowden was glad to see that Emily was in a better mood. He bet her mind was on fire learning these things. "You mentioned you have been studying us for a while. Was that just out of curiosity then?"

Evaran paused before speaking. "Not quite. Regarding those groups I spoke of, there are many of them, more than should be on your planet. The Daedrould, for example. Typically there are several hundred, maybe several thousand in a galaxy. On your planet, there are hundreds of thousands. That is an anomaly. I am unclear as to why that is. It is . . . intriguing, so I am investigating. Also . . . I discovered Earth when helping another human and have been there ever since."

"Huh," said Emily. She rubbed her arms. "It's still hard to believe there are vampires and who knows what else on Earth."

"Fortunately both of you can detect them, as I mentioned earlier. My suggestion is to avoid them. They may be able to detect you, but will not know you have nanobots. Most groups anyways."

"We'll be careful," said Emily. She cocked her head. "Don't you get lonely traveling by yourself?"

Evaran half smiled at Emily. "Due to the nature of my abilities, it comes with the territory. I made V not only as an assistant, but also as a companion. I will say that I have enjoyed your company, more so than I expected, even if we did have to go through a ship full of deadly creatures and mercenaries. Traveling with humans is refreshing."

They shared a chuckle.

Dr. Snowden wished he could spend a few more days on this ship. There was so much he could learn. A hurricane of ideas swirled around in his mind, and he knew that would not go away easily. He cleared his throat. "What'll happen to Jay?"

"He will stay here for a month. When he is fully healed, I will drop him off a bit after I drop you two off."

"And Sanjay?" asked Emily.

Evaran pursed his lips. "I am not sure what to do there yet. For now, we wait until the krall is fully healed, and then we will take her home."

Dr. Snowden looked down. Poor Sanjay. Dr. Snowden figured Sanjay would show up as a missing person after they got back. Just another statistic. Dr. Snowden planned to watch for it when he returned. Thankfully the krall would be arriving home healthy. He eased back into his chair. For the first time in a long while, he truly felt he could relax.

···⋮⋮▪ ▬▬▬▬▬▬▬▬▬▬▬▬▬▬▬▬▬▬▬▬▬ ▪⋮⋮··

Dr. Snowden walked around for the next fourteen minutes while waiting on V to bring the krall up. The console near the front of the ship had caught Dr. Snowden's attention. There was a set of layered interfaces at a thirty-degree angle a few inches off the console. Although he could see what the interfaces were showing, he was not sure what half of it meant. The fact that the interface was holographic was not lost on him. He moved a hand through the interfaces, but they did not react.

"Do not worry about doing anything with the interfaces," said Evaran. "They are only responsive to V and me."

"Oh. I was just curious."

"Yes . . . yes, you were," said Evaran, eying Dr. Snowden.

Dr. Snowden chuckled. Evaran's mannerisms were strange, but it seemed like he got a kick out of just observing.

Emily joined Dr. Snowden at the console. "This is cool."

"At least it's not hot," said Dr. Snowden, bumping her.

She shook her head.

V walked up to the bridge with the krall in tow.

The krall walked over to Dr. Snowden and Emily, who ran to hug the krall while Dr. Snowden scratched the krall behind the ears. The krall blinked slowly.

"The krall is at one hundred percent operating capacity," said V.

Evaran nodded as he interacted with the chair arm's console. "Good. V, take us to these coordinates I found on her collar."

"Acknowledged." V walked to the front console and interacted with it.

The front screen split in two, with a view outside on the left and, on the right, a galactic map.

V pressed another control, which zoomed in to a section of the map showing a solar system view.

A green outline appeared around a planet.

Dr. Snowden heard a winding-down sound. He watched as the outside shimmered to pure darkness.

The sound reversed, and the outside faded back into view.

"What the heck was that?" asked Dr. Snowden.

"We just went back one hundred ninety-four thousand years. Now we go to the planet," said Evaran.

Dr. Snowden's eyes popped open as he watched the screen fade and a gold beam shoot out from the front of the ship. A circular portal opened up with a thin silver border. The interior was light blue with a rippling pattern. It reminded him of a lake with a light wind blowing across the surface.

The Torvatta moved forward toward the portal and then flew through it. The tunnel they were in had semitransparent walls.

Dr. Snowden could see what he thought were stars appearing, then disappearing.

The Torvatta exited the tunnel above a planet with a reddish tint.

Dr. Snowden rubbed his eyes.

"We just traveled three hundred twenty light-years," said Evaran.

"Was . . . that a rift you created?" asked Dr. Snowden as he walked up to the front guardrail and looked out the window.

"Not quite. The Torvatta is capable of creating these portals and is unique in that regard," said Evaran.

"I suppose that's something that requires more time to understand," said Dr. Snowden, sighing.

Evaran half smiled. "You are an inquisitive being. I am glad to see this event has not dampened that."

The Torvatta broke cloud cover on the planet and descended toward the outline of a forest. After a moment, it landed on a patch of orange-colored grass. The soft impact caused the krall to walk over to the window. Her skin turned light orange as her eyes narrowed.

Dr. Snowden looked out. The ship was sitting at the edge of a forest of unusual-looking trees. He shook his head. "I'm honestly not surprised that we time traveled and jumped all those light-years, given everything I've seen so far." He exhaled sharply. "My first alien planet."

Emily walked beside him and grabbed his arm.

"In this time period, the Grimlyn Empire has already fallen. This planet was one of the few that still had kralls on it. She will be able to live out her life without fear of being captured for service," said Evaran. He stood and then walked over to the ramp leading to the back of the ship. With a clap of his hands, the krall walked over to him.

Dr. Snowden and Emily followed Evaran and the krall to the Torvatta exit.

Evaran walked down the angled entrance ramp leading outside and paused after exiting the Torvatta's shielding.

The krall walked down the ramp toward Evaran, but paused to look back.

Dr. Snowden wondered if she was thinking why they were not coming.

The krall looked forward and grouped up with Evaran outside.

Dr. Snowden and Emily walked to the edge of the shielding.

Emily began to breathe heavier as she grabbed his arm again.

When Dr. Snowden looked at her, he saw her eyes were misting. She was as attached to the krall as he was.

The krall's eyes softened as she looked back directly at Emily. After the krall glanced at Evaran, who nodded, she turned around and walked up to Emily.

Emily sniffled as she wrapped her arms around the krall's neck. Tears flowed freely on Emily's face, dropping onto the krall's big paws.

The krall reacted by nuzzling the side of Emily's head.

After a few moments of Emily crying into the krall's neck, Emily stood back and smiled, wiping the tears from her eyes.

The krall turned and walked over to Dr. Snowden. She looked at him as if expecting a hug as well.

The look stirred something in Dr. Snowden. She had saved his life, and his pent-up emotions burst forth. He leaned forward and hugged her.

She nuzzled the side of his head as tears flowed down his face.

Dr. Snowden did not like crying, but he'd done it more in the last day than he had all his life. He was losing a good friend. She had survived, as he did, against all odds. After a few moments, he stood back and adjusted his glasses while rubbing his eyes.

The krall looked at them both, then turned and walked back toward Evaran.

Dr. Snowden sighed as he watched them walk out of sight.

After Evaran and the krall had left, Dr. Snowden and Emily rushed back to the command area.

Dr. Snowden noted that although Evaran and the krall moved fast, the screen showed them up close. Evaran put his fist on his chest and then moved his arm out, pointing forward. He then opened his hand as the krall fixed her gaze on it.

The krall pointed her head down.

Evaran put a hand on each side of her head and placed his forehead in contact with hers.

"What's he doing?" asked Emily.

"Saying goodbye," said Dr. Snowden in a cracked voice.

The krall raised her head and looked at the ship as if able to see Dr. Snowden and Emily through the window, then turned and ran off into the nearby forest.

Evaran turned to look at the front of the ship before he walked back. After a few moments, he walked up the ramp and into the command area.

"She said to say goodbye and good travels and hoped you get better," said Evaran.

"Get better?" said Dr. Snowden, looking at his hands and arms.

"She could smell the nanobots in you. They produce a certain smell via your sweat," said Evaran. He tapped at his ARI. "V, take us to these coordinates."

"Acknowledged."

Dr. Snowden raised his eyebrows at Emily. Hopefully that would not be an issue when they got back to Earth. The last thing they needed was to be hunted again.

They took their seats as Evaran took his.

V's hands flew around the interface.

The Torvatta began to ascend, and after a few moments, they were back in space.

V pulled up the galactic map and swiped at the controls, causing a new galactic map to appear. He pressed on a region.

The screen zoomed in to a solar system.

Dr. Snowden recognized it as home. The Torvatta's outside dissipated and then faded back in. How the Torvatta could go through time was a mystery he would love to understand.

The Torvatta flew through a similar portal as before.

His eyes were intent on trying to see the lights that appeared and disappeared on the walls inside the tunnel. Due to the speed at which the Torvatta traveled through the portal and exited, he did not see much. What he did recognize was the planet they were orbiting. It was Earth.

Evaran glanced off to the side and tapped at his ARI. "V, stealth mode."

"Acknowledged. Torvatta stealth mode engaged," said V.

A smaller screen off to the right of the large screen showed the Torvatta go from a textured view to a wire outline. Underneath it were some statistics.

Dr. Snowden scrutinized the display as the Torvatta descended. The Torvatta was powerful in that it could go through space and time and cloak, and it had dimensional rooms. It was clear that Evaran with the Torvatta and V possessed immense power, yet Dr. Snowden did not believe Evaran was corrupt. That could just be a projection of the notion that power caused corruption. Maybe that was a human behavior and not a universal one.

The Torvatta descended to a dark patch of highway I-70.

Dr. Snowden could make out the outline of a car on the side of the road. There were no other cars around, and it was quiet. He remembered hearing about abductions occurring on dark and lonely roads at night and had dismissed them out of hand. That would not be the case anymore. One thing he planned to do was scour the Internet and see if he could find out more about alleged abductions. Maybe there was some truth to them.

The Torvatta landed off to the side of the car.

"We are now on Earth by your car, one hour after your abduction. It is time to go," said Evaran.

"As a point of inquiry . . . is there an earlier version of us flying to the Krotovore ship in our solar system?" asked Dr. Snowden.

"There is," said Evaran as he half smiled. "However, we know how that turns out."

Dr. Snowden was not sure how there could be two versions at the same point in time. He was just glad to be back.

They followed Evaran outside.

Dr. Snowden recognized his car sitting silently on the side of the road. He checked to make sure his car keys were still in his front pocket and then unlocked the passenger's front door. "That's my car all right."

Evaran walked around the car. When he was on the other side, he bent over.

Dr. Snowden heard a clinking sound, but when Evaran stood up, Dr. Snowden saw nothing out of the ordinary.

Evaran walked back around the car. "Your life is now free to continue as it was. I will stop by, let us say, in three months, on May 5, 2012, at 6:00 p.m. I want to make sure you both are doing okay, and I should have enough information to extract the nanobots should you so desire."

Dr. Snowden nodded. "We'll definitely be looking forward to seeing you again."

"Remember what I said about keeping this to yourselves," said Evaran as he extended his hand to Dr. Snowden.

Dr. Snowden shook Evaran's hand and then pulled him into a hug.

Emily hugged both of them.

Dr. Snowden was going to miss Evaran. The abduction was one of the roughest experiences in Dr. Snowden's life, and Evaran had been there to help. He had been fair to them, more than was required, and he was one of those people who just stuck out, not because of what they wore or what they said, but what they did. Dr. Snowden stepped back, wiping his drenched eyes.

Emily grabbed Dr. Snowden's right arm and wiped her eyes.

Dr. Snowden's perspective on life, and reality in general, had changed in his time with Evaran. Situations could be complicated, and Dr. Snowden learned that he shouldn't dismiss them based on misunderstanding. He also learned that Emily was not a little girl wanting airplane rides anymore; she was a strong young woman. First impressions were not always absolute, like with Jay and Sanjay. Perhaps the biggest change was Dr. Snowden's realization that it was okay to show emotions like he had with Kazryn and the krall.

"Oh, you may want this. I will need it back when I return," said Evaran as he handed a disk to Dr. Snowden.

"What is it?" asked Dr. Snowden.

"The logs the Krotovore kept on you. It does not contain any technical or engineering details, just their observations and a bit of their history. I replicated a disk that your computer will understand and transferred the information over to it. It will read like a set of log entries, and if anyone read it, they would think it is a work of fiction," said Evaran.

Dr. Snowden's eyes lit up.

"I am still unclear as to why they selected you four, but I will sift through the data on my ship later and see what I can find. If I find something, then I will let you know. You two will be fine. When I come back, dinner is on you," said Evaran with a half smile.

"You got it," said Dr. Snowden with a cracked voice.

"We'll be watching for you," said Emily.

V flew out of the Torvatta in orb mode. "Please stay safe."

"Right back at you, buddy," said Dr. Snowden with a grin.

Emily smiled at V.

V's lights glowed a bit brighter.

"Everything is as it should be," said Evaran. He bowed slightly and returned to the Torvatta. When he reached the shielding, he paused to look back.

Dr. Snowden saw Evaran wave, turn around, and walk up the ramp while looking at something in his hand. Now the time to get back to normal life was upon them, and as Evaran had said, everything was as it should be. At least Dr. Snowden hoped so.

The End

EPILOGUE

Jay's eyes burst open as he sat up on a slab. His breathing went ragged as he slid his legs off the side. A pain shot up his regenerating arm. He ran his hands over the bag covering what was left of his arm. It all came roaring back to him how he lost it. Where he was and what the bag was doing were not immediately obvious. He swiveled his head as a robot entered the room.

"You are awake. How are you feeling?" said the robot.

Jay jumped off the slab. "Who the fuck are you, and where the hell am I?" The thought that maybe he was in a virtual simulation of a virtual simulation crossed his mind.

The robot tilted its head at Jay. "I am V, or Blue Ball as you have designated me, in full-body mode."

"Blue Ball! Damn, glad to see you, man," said Jay, relaxing a bit. He looked around. "What's going on?"

"Analysis. You passed out after you lost your arm. Evaran found a Krotovore gel that is regenerating your arm. In a month, it will be fully restored."

Jay wiggled his arm stump around. "It doesn't hurt too bad." He looked up at V. "So it looks like we got off the ship. What happened with the others?"

V walked over to one of the replicators on the side of the room and picked up a container of water. He took the container over to Jay and handed it to him. "Dr. Snowden and Emily are back on Earth, and Evaran saved Jerzan and one of his mercenaries. They are in a Bilaxian prison, which is where we are now. Evaran wanted to talk to you before heading in to see Jerzan."

Jay nodded and then took a sip of water.

After a few moments, Evaran walked into the room. "Jay, you look well."

Jay exhaled. "Yeah. Doing all right, I guess. Heard you got Doc and Emily back safely and saved some of those merc assholes."

"I did. Dr. Snowden and Emily will be glad to see you when you get back to Earth. As for Jerzan, I am about to visit him and Jahl. However, I wanted to show you something before I go. Also, if you have any questions, feel free to ask them." He walked toward the medical lab entrance, with Jay in tow.

Jay scratched his head. "What's the date?"

Evaran half turned his head as they exited the medical room. "March 16, 2013, two weeks past the events of the Krotovore ship. I made several stops while you were unconscious and then traveled to this point in space and time. From my perspective, it has only been a day since the Krotovore ship."

Jay sighed. "More of that time-travel crap. Not sure I fully understand all that."

"You do not need to. Come," said Evaran. He stopped outside a door that was two doors to the left of the entrance ramp.

Jay looked around. "So this is your ship."

"It is. V will be your guide for the month you are here, and he can give you a tour of it. Step into this room, and I will show you something I believe you may enjoy."

Jay followed Evaran and V. Looking around made Jay squint. The room was large and had a white floor and walls. "What the hell is this?"

Evaran gestured to the back of the room. "It is my holo room. You can recreate anything you can imagine in here, within reason."

"Anything? Not following."

Evaran interacted with his ARI. "I've turned on voice activation, although you can use a holo menu, but we do not need to get that technical for now." He looked up at an angle. "Computer, run program Jay Home One."

The white walls shimmered as the room changed into a replica of the street Jay's house was on.

Jay stumbled back. "What the fuck!"

"We are still in the room. These are just solid holograms."

Jay reached down to touch the street. His eyes widened.

"V will help you learn how to use it. He is interested in learning more about Earth culture, so this will be good. Any other questions before I head out?"

Jay smirked. "Can it create living things?"

"It creates an approximation."

Jay's smile widened as he pointed at Evaran. "Ahh, man, you know what I'm talking about."

Evaran half smiled. "I do. V, make sure the room's busy signal is set appropriately. I will be back soon, and we can have dinner, or if you wish to discuss more things, we can."

Jay slapped V on the back. "I think me and Blue Ball will be okay. When you see Jerzan, slap the shit out of him for me."

Evaran nodded and walked out of the room.

Evaran exited the Torvatta, where two Bilaxian guards awaited him alongside Warden Borox.

"It's been a while," said Borox.

"It has," said Evaran, forearm shaking with Borox.

"I didn't think you were going to come back, but I see you sent Jerzan and . . . I guess what's left of the Bloodbores here."

Evaran nodded.

"Funny thing . . . the life pod they were found in didn't match anything we've ever seen before. There was a broadcast though that said to send them here. I suspect . . . that was all you."

"It was. I am sure you heard of the alien ship that flew into the sun."

Borox nodded.

"Jerzan and the Bloodbores were trying to salvage parts of it, but then decided to come after me and the group I was helping."

Borox laughed. "It didn't work out for them apparently."

"It did not," said Evaran. "I let Hosk and Galkett go and believe they may change their ways now that they know I was involved. Also, the life pod had no technological advancements that would further disrupt things."

"Makes sense. Jerzan and Jahl are in their cell. They've made friends with that Greecho character you brought before. Still . . . they're Dalruns, in a Bilaxian prison. They've had a few rough days since they've been in here."

"I appreciate you letting me visit."

Borox eyed Evaran. "After all you've done? You're always welcome here. All right. Before you leave the prison, I'd like to chat with you if you have time."

"I will stop in."

"Good. I almost forgot . . . is V around?"

Evaran half smiled. "Yes, and I am sure he would like to talk with you since you knew his previous incarnation as U4."

"We can do that," said Borox. He nodded at the guards.

The guards acknowledged Borox and Evaran and then escorted Evaran into a large building built inside an asteroid. After twenty minutes of various checkpoints, they arrived at a dimly lit hallway with metallic doors on each side. They walked to the second door on the left where one of the guards pressed a button on the wall console outside the door.

"Hey! Assholes! You have a visitor," said the guard.

"What?" said Jerzan.

"A visitor."

"Who is it?"

"Evaran."

The sound of thumping and dropped metal rang out.

The guard pressed another button, and the door slid open. He faced Evaran. "You have twenty minutes. Do I need to get a body bag?"

Evaran wrinkled his eyebrows. "No, I am not here to harm them. Just to talk."

The guards laughed. "They ain't gonna survive here for long. If it ain't you, it'll be someone else."

"Noted." Evaran walked into the room.

Jerzan and Jahl pressed their backs against the other side of the room.

"You come to finish the job?" asked Jerzan.

The door slid closed.

Evaran raised a hand toward them. "I am not here to harm you. I just have a few things to say. Please sit." He gestured toward the tattered beds on each side of the room.

Jahl looked at Jerzan, then sat on his bed.

"So what the fuck you want?" asked Jerzan, exhaling sharply as he sat on his bed.

Evaran walked to the center of the room. "First, the people of Neoparene have forgiven you."

Jerzan laughed. "What? We kick their ass, and they forgive us? Their weakness is irritating."

"They were initially planning on giving you Teelah Crotoris. I talked them out of it."

Jahl scrunched up his face. "What's that?"

"A disease. It forms an exoskeleton and takes forty years or so to develop. The remaining years after that are excruciatingly painful from what they said."

Jerzan and Jahl grimaced.

"My second topic deals with the impact of what you did. Your massacre on the planet has caused the Bilaxian Empire to elevate Neoparene to a member planet due to knowledge pollution. They went from a simple society to one with access to advanced tech. That usually does not turn out well. I disagree with the Bilaxians on this," said Evaran.

"Good for them, I guess. Sounds like we helped them. What does that have to do with us?" asked Jerzan.

Evaran looked down at the ground for a moment, then glanced back up at them. "I have traveled up and down the timeline in this area for a while now. My first visit two thousand years or so in the future was some time ago. The Neoparene and Dalrun were the dominant powers in this region. They had a rivalry but got along for the most part. The Bilaxian Empire had fallen, and the Neoparene, with their advanced intellect, took their place."

Jerzan shook his head. "Time travel. I swear. Galkett actually believes you can."

"That is because he does his research. Now, I went back to the future to check if the Bilaxian embrace of Neoparene had any impact. My second visit showed only one dominant power, and it was the Neoparene. The Dalrun Empire was broken and scattered. Apparently the Neoparene advanced much faster technologically, which gave them an edge. They were also aware of what was out there and built technology to prevent what you did from ever happening to them again."

Jahl harrumphed. "So you think we're guilty."

"Partially. I am guilty as well. I showed the Neoparene better farming techniques. This led to them being detected by your crew. If I had not helped them, you would not have detected them, as they would have hidden from you instead of thinking you were another person from the stars out to help them. I did not know you were going to pass over the planet and . . . do what you did, but it is done," said Evaran.

"What do you want us to do about it?" asked Jerzan.

"Nothing. I wanted you to know what the consequences of your actions were. That is all I have to say," said Evaran. He turned and walked back to the cell door.

Jerzan licked his lips and stood up. "Wait! If you can time travel, maybe you could take us back to our younger selves and we could change all that."

"That is not how it works," said Evaran, shaking his head. "It is already woven into my past, and I am a part of events now." He walked over to the cell door and pressed a button on the wall console.

The door slid open.

Evaran half turned his head back around. "I took the liberty of visiting this prison twenty years in the future to check on your status." He walked out and turned to face them. "There was nothing to get a status on."

The door slid shut.

NOTE FROM
THE AUTHOR

I hope you enjoyed the second edition of book 1 in the Evaran Chronicles! Although I loved the first edition since it was my first book ever published, my writing style has changed since then. This second edition is a more accurate reflection of the other books in the series.

For those who have read the first edition, the second edition has many new scenes, and the existing ones were overhauled. The other books also help inform this one, and the transition from the prequel to book 1 is much smoother.

If you liked the book, and have the time and inclination, a review would go a long way in helping out this indie author. If you do submit a review, I'll put in a word to Evaran should you find yourself captured by aliens! Want to be notified about new book releases? If so, you can sign up below.

www.AdairHart.com/MailingList.aspx

I will only send you email about new book releases, major updates, and the occasional newsletter, usually once a month. I dislike getting spammed too, so I will use this sparingly to keep you in the loop.

ABOUT
THE AUTHOR

I have been dreaming about fictional worlds since I was a kid. I devoured anything related to fantasy and science fiction. I developed a setting over the last twenty years and struggled to find a medium I could express it in. Several years ago I discovered I enjoyed writing. It is a passion of mine now, and exploring my setting with it has been an awesome journey.

I work in the information technology field and have my bachelor's and master's degrees in it. It has helped me to shape some of the concepts I write about. I also enjoy keeping up on futurology and science in general.

I live in central Ohio and enjoy walking, reading, gaming, learning, listening to music, and trying to keep up on my never-ending list of TV shows and movies to watch. If you want to contact me, you can do so on my website at:

www.AdairHart.com

YOU CAN ALSO REACH ME ON

Facebook............................fb.com/AdairHart
Goodreads.....www.goodreads.com/AdairHart
Email..............Adair.Hart.Author@gmail.com

DEDICATION

*To my grandparents, who continue to inspire me.
They may be gone now, but their life lessons and
legacies live on with me.*

ACKNOWLEDGMENTS

This was a great journey for me, but I wouldn't be here without the help of others. I would like to thank, in no particular order,

My amazing editor, Laura Petrella. She has been with me through this series and has helped me shape it. I simply cannot imagine doing the series without her eagle eyes. She has been a good mentor, and I appreciate everything she has done!

My cover artist, Tom Edwards (tomedwardsconcepts@gmail.com), for another fantastic cover. I opted for a character display on this one relative to the others, which usually have the Torvatta and an environment.

My family and friends who helped encourage me along the way.

My proofreader, Alexa, for doing a great job in making that final pass to make sure everything looked good.

My formatter and interior designer, Colleen Sheehan (www.ampersandbookinteriors.com/), for helping make my interior shine!

BOOKS

··:::::===================::::··

You can see all books in the Evaran Chronicles series at

www.AdairHart.com/Books/Books.aspx

··:::::===================::::··

THE CURRENT LIST OF BOOKS
IN THE SERIES AS OF THIS
PUBLICATION ARE:

PREQUEL - *The Arrival*
Evaran rescues Jake Melkins and Kathy from a Seceltor slaver named Greecho. It is Evaran's first adventure in the Milky Way galaxy and introduces him to Earth.

FIRST SERIES ARC

BOOK 1 - *The Awakening*, second edition (The one you just read!)

BOOK 2 - *The Fredorian Destiny*

Dr. Snowden and Emily travel with Evaran and V to help Fredoria, a planet of human ex-slaves, become a full trade partner with the Kreagan Star Empire, the local galactic superpower in Earth's region of the galaxy. Hampered by Seeros and bounty hunters, they must secure the Arkaron for the Fredorians to give to the Kreagan emperor.

BOOK 3 - *The Purification*

They fight the timeline invaders known as the Purifiers, a human-supremacist group led by the overlord, that tries to change Earth's history.

BOOK 4 - *The Time Refugee*

They tangle with Billozein, a rogue time traveler, while helping Jane Trellis, a time refugee who is pulled out of her timeline.

BOOK 5 - *The Evaran Origin*

They discover Evaran's origin and meet Levaran, another one of Evaran's plane forms, while fighting the Time Wardens, a timeline-void race that hunts rift travelers.

SECOND SERIES ARC

BOOK 6 - *The Shadow Connection*

They group up with Jake Melkins and the nonhuman community to defend Earth from the ambitions of Caltorus, a dimensional being that rules over a vast empire encompassing worlds in many dimensions.

BOOK 7 - *The Human Factor*

They head to AD 10105 and deal with a ruthless AI known as Salazar, in addition to fixing the timeline.

BOOK 8 - *The Cosmic Parallel*

They jump through parallel Earths in an effort to get back to the Torvatta after being trapped by a rogue group, one they must deal with.